FORTITUDE

MARCOS F. EGUIA

RIVER CITY SIREN PRESS

Chapter One

THE CODE OF VIRTUES

Continental Map
Nations below the Edgen Walls

Thyra

Year 475 After the Division, in a Jattarian town far from the Fifth Wall

Daddy and I dream of peace and fixing broken things; Mommy dreams of war. I am only five, but she prepares me anyway.

"Are you ready for bed, young girl?" She pokes my tummy, checks the wounds from today's lessons, then tucks me under the blankets. Mommy closes the curtains on my window to keep light and cold away. The fluffy covers are up to my cheeks, tickling. Her blue eyes are almost black, her hair is short and dark, and she is the best warrior in history. My older brother Nefri looks a lot like her, and practices in the bedroom next to mine. He wishes to attend Solitude's prestigious School of War and be a decorated soldier in the Jattarian Army like Mom, but that takes dedication. I hear him smacking the dummy with his wooden sword. The thin walls barely soften the sounds.

Clack, whack, chuck!

Mom runs her fingers through my hair, which is yellow like the sun and shiny like water. "How will you fight the Edgens with hair this long?" she asks.

"Ja, Mutti." I use the old tongue so she likes me more. "I will cut it as short as yours." I make scissors with my fingers and pretend to chop. She grins a tiny bit. I love my long hair, but cutting it will make her happy.

She puts the heavy Code of Virtues on her lap. *Thump!* She flips through a million crackly pages until she finds the correct section. I smell the scent of those old pages and the oil she used to treat the leather covers. "You remember all the Virtues?" said Mommy.

"Fortitude, Solitude, Certitude, Magnitude, Rectitude, Servitude, and Gratitude," I say, waiting for some reward. Sometimes, she brings us candy from the big city.

"Well done!" says Mom. "Fortitude, the first of all Virtues, aligns body and spirit with purpose, helping us reach our goals."

I mouth the words along with her but stay quiet. First-Star-ranked officer Lagas Ener hates interruptions. A high officer of the Army like her demands respect. Her dry, callused finger scratches against the book's thin paper. I spy her forearm, completely covered in tattoos showing her ranks, missions, and accomplishments. No one in town has this many tattoos on their arms. Not the veterans nor the Korps officers.

Whack! Whack, whack! Nefri increases the force with which he hits Woody, the practice dummy.

Mom ignores the noise. "You will need Fortitude's strength at the *Edgeslag*, for the war against the Edge. Edgens might be a weaker, smaller race, but they are devious, and their weapons are powerful." She rests her hand on my chest. I like the soft pressure. "The Virtues can unlock this power left in us by our ancestors, the Colossi. Imagine having the strength of a twelve-foot-tall warrior! Their speed! Their ways of war!" She looks at the ceiling, smiling.

I nod, dreaming of one day serving Jattaria and the Highest, our glorious leader. "Hopefully, I can be an engineer like Daddy; then, I will not have to fight and kill little Edgens."

She frowns. "War comes for us all." Mom leans closer and puts a hand by her lips, ready to tell me a secret. "I have unlocked some of those Virtues, *wissen sie?* I am mastering those ancient ways of war the Colossi developed." She grins and raises her eyebrows a little bit.

"Is that why you are so strong?" My eyes get wider and wider. Mom never talks to me like this.

She leans closer still; her voice becomes even softer. "I have been teaching the Virtues to you. One day, you'll be stronger, faster, and larger than me or any other Giant in Jattaria."

"Even larger than Nefri?" I look at the wall. Past it, my big brother keeps working on his style. He always insists on learning the graceful ways of Servitude, but Mom won't budge: Fortitude first.

Thuck! Whack!

"Nefri can be great; you could be greater still." She pulls away and puts a finger to her lips. *Shhh.* "For now, we must keep training. Harder than before."

"I will be ready, Mommy," I say, touching her hand. "Can you tell me a bedtime story before you leave?" I squeeze her finger and reach for Berlin, my stuffed bear.

"Sure. What should it be? Taking out Edgen vehicles? Storming strongholds?" She looks up, considering.

"What about 'Hanz and the Sleeping Dragon'?"

Thap!

Mom snaps the Code of Virtues closed. "There is no time for *those* stories. Sleep well, Thyra." She walks to the door and puts out the oil lamp. My little room gets very dark. The air smells of burnt oil and wick. "I will see you in a few months. Train with tutors, but remember to never practice with your friends or brother, *ja?* Not even playing. Only with your masters. I'll test your progress when I return."

"I love you, Mommy."

She is about to reply, then doesn't. Mommy closes the door and goes to Nefri's room. "Wrong stance. Angle your feet properly," I hear her say through the thin wall. "Fortitude's style is about withstanding attacks until the right time to strike, not about looking fancy. You are nine, old enough to know better."

"Sorry, Mom," answers Nefri, panting. I can picture him frowning, focusing on the right way to hit Woody.

Dad opens my door and sneaks in. His blonde hair is in messy, thick braids. His puffy beard is long, too, with bits of wood and metal from the shop hiding inside it. Sometimes, he also has food in his beard. "Hey, *rakas*. I will tell you that story," he says softly.

"Thanks, Daddy," I say and slide under the blanket to be close to him. He is so heavy the mattress rolls me toward him. He takes the book from my bedside table and starts the story, which we know by heart. Hanz must defeat many dragons hiding in castles to free the kingdom of which he is unknowingly the heir. I am half-asleep before he makes it to the easiest dragon to defeat. "Heart, heart, heart," I say just before passing out.

He kisses my cheek. "Heart, heart, heart," he replies, then quietly leaves my room.

Chapter Two

THE EDGE

Continental Races Biometrics

Agnor

Eight years later, in a trench close to the Fifth Wall

The tattoo on my arm is fresh: a black circle to show my rank and to mark me as a weapon for Jattaria, the great nation of

Giants. I won't be a lowly First Circle long, I feel it. Soon, I will be serving this country as a high officer.

The warm summer breeze brings the scent of prey, stirring the beast within me. The smell of the forest behind me is intense, overwhelming, but the sweat of a thousand anxious Giants cuts through it. I peek over the trench and tremble as I squint into the fog and the growing darkness. Across this muddy field stands the Edge's Fifth Wall, made of stone and concrete, almost a hundred feet tall and running from sea to sea, splitting the whole continent. Every century, they build a new wall, pushing us further into the Cold, the land of glaciers and Titans. In a few years, they'll build the Sixth and take the last of our land. Where will Jattarians go? To freeze in hell, I guess.

We must stop them. It's time *I* die so *we* can rise.

"Hey, Agnor," says Emma, sliding closer until our shoulders touch. Her cute, little face swims up at me from the depths of her oversized green coat. Silvery locks of hair curl under the lower edges of her helmet. "There's more to life than killing, *wissen sie?*" she says, knowing my thoughts.

"To you, maybe. To a brute like me? *Nein...* killing is all I have." I look away, determined not to let her distract me.

But she gets closer still, easily sabotaging my efforts. "Don't worry. The Edgens may have gas muskets, but our crossbows hurt plenty. They'll get the job done." She caresses her repeating crossbows' wood frame and flicks the fierce arrowhead peeking out. *Ping!* Emma just graduated from School of War too, but she has the relaxed, confident air of an experienced soldier. Even in the orphanage where we grew up, she was this confident.

"No need to be scared," she purrs into my ear, making me shiver. "I'll protect you."

"*Bitte!*" I scoff, trying to sound at ease. "Why would I be scared? There are a thousand of us, and we have that big tank hidden in the forest. The Edgens are tiny, even smaller than you." I smirk and poke her side.

She squints and pretends to be serious. "Everyone is small compared to you, mister Titan."

I pull back, panicking. "Shush! Emma!" I look around, wondering if anyone heard her. "You can't joke like that," I say, desperate. I have always been ostracized for having enemies' blood in me.

"Relax, Agnor," she says, rolling her eyes. "You are eight feet tall. A glance at you, and they know you are part Titan. You are not the first or the last half-Titan to be in Jattaria. It's one of the things I love about you, *du vet?* A slice of a world beyond ours. If only you had their strange accent too..." she says, dreamily.

I swallow hard and convince myself she is right. Never mind the dozens of fights I was in because of my size, if the Army took me in, then I must be good enough. I breathe slowly, then pick up from where we left off. "I am not scared. Their weapons won't matter," I say, avoiding her playful eyes so I don't get lost in them.

"The Edgens have been killing us and building walls for five hundred years. We should be wary, but we must bite down our fear." Her eyes get distant. "I wonder what's beyond the Fifth Wall," she whispers. "A whole continent with lakes, rivers, mountains, and deserts? A sun that always shines? Cities as beautiful as Solitude?" A little smile plays on her lips. She wasn't meant to be a soldier, but war comes for us all. "I die, we rise," she says sharply, shaking her head. "Fortitude is with us. Tomorrow will find us covered in honor." She eyes me in that naughty way that has gotten me in trouble endless times. "Maybe then we can finally get married," she says softly, her voice like marmalade. She kisses my lips. "For good luck, my future husband."

Someone taps my shoulder. "Agnor, right?" It's Nefri, another Circle-ranked soldier I have seen around. "Any letters for your loved ones? Last chance."

I shake my head no. I am an orphan, after all. I have no one but Emma. "She is the only one I love," I say. "I'm not dying tonight, anyway."

After hours of waiting, the fog grows dense enough to hide our night skirmish. A First Diamond officer walks into my trench, stinking of tobacco. "Intruder Squad, you'll be the first wave," he says, addressing my unit. "You know what we are up against. Edgens are a much inferior race." He spits. "Crush 'em! It's wet work, but you need the bath, you filthy animals!"

Some soldiers laugh. I can't. I am too tense. It's my first mission, the first time I will face Jattaria's enemies. I blow my lungs empty, trying to exhale anxiety along with my breath. Emma notices and squeezes my hand. "Easy, boy," she whispers.

I look at the two-hundred-yard-wide strip of land before the wall. Grass grows strong here, watered by the blood of hundreds of Giants who tried to breach this wall before us. An army of bones rests beneath our feet, waiting for the day we avenge them.

The officer continues. "Neutralize personnel and cannons along that section of the wall before the main attack. Do this and I'll sloppy kiss each of you," he says, winking.

"I'll do it if you promise not to," grunts Dolphen, a wiry Second Circle who looks bored. The squad chuckles; this time, I join them.

A pair of hands falls on my back. "Gear check," grunts the soldier, Tiv. "Freezing death!" he curses. "Dolphen! Look! This kid is like eight feet tall!"

Seven-ten, actually.

Dolphen shrugs. "I've seen bigger."

"Where? In Antares?" scoffs Tiv, shaking his head. "Alright, kid, put more mud on to camouflage, and you're good to go." He slaps my shoulder.

I do as he says, then grab my newly issued repeating crossbow. I finger its grooves and mechanisms while I wait for the order to -

"Go," says the officer in charge, leaning against a thick tree. A newly lit cigarette dances on his lips. His face turns orange when he draws, the ember glowing fiercely.

We crawl out of the trench, getting wet as promised. Grass softly scratches along my cloak and pants. My boots' toes sink into the soft ground as I push forward. The wall's base materializes out of the fog after thirty minutes of careful crawling.

"Climb," whispers someone. I obey without knowing who issues the order; they all outrank me, anyway. I go through the motions drilled into me during training, feeling like a witness to what my body is doing. I throw the grapple, pull, and barely dodge the hook as it falls back down.

"Give me that, you silly pup," says Emma, smiling. Her grin vanishes when she sees me. "I am scared too, Agnor," she whispers, coming closer. "We do horrible things, so we make it to tomorrow, *ja?*" She touches my cheek.

"*Ja.*" Electricity buzzes through me, but it dissipates with her touch. I breathe easier.

She tosses my grapple, hooks it, and hands me the rope. She throws hers and climbs up effortlessly. I follow, pulling almost four hundred pounds of weight up the thirty yards to the top before rolling onto the walkway atop the wall. I stop by two dead Edgens on the concrete. A dark pool of blood grows bigger around the tiny corpses. While I struggled climbing, my squad were busy killing.

"About time," says the Diamond in charge, looking at me. The rest of the unit glares as I get ready, their pale blue eyes gleam with reflected moonlight.

Up here, the smell of the fort's kitchen is strong. Bread and pork and rare spices, I think. The stench of the sewage and waste is stronger still.

The squad removes their boots for stealth. I do the same. The concrete floor is rough and cold on my bare feet as we descend the stairs towards our target.

"Agnor," says the Diamond. "Take care of the cannons," he grunts, tossing a heavy sack full of jam spikes and demon's oil at me. The contents clack when I catch the bag. He jerks his head, and the unit moves, walking like death, swallowing the lives of a dozen soldiers as we approach the stronghold. They leap from cover to cover, from target to target, burying deadly daggers into the small Edgens' bodies, killing them instantly.

We move forward swiftly, getting near the fortified castle. I jam spikes and pour demon's oil into the mouth of each gas cannon to neutralize them.

The Diamond motions me to join him behind one of the huge batteries. He leans in. "We are almost done here. Take those two," he whispers, pointing at two distracted Edgens ahead. We are about a hundred steps from the first towers of the castle, miraculously unnoticed. The Aftergods' favor is with us!

My targets are in conversation. Not even six feet tall, the two of them, maybe a hundred and sixty pounds of weight with gear on. Their uniforms are as strange as their accent: rounded helmets, long white socks, a dress-like garment with square patterns, and a wool cape over their armor.

One of them throws pebbles or seeds down the wall. "I ken't see one bit in this dreich night. Bloody mist mesk me blind!"

"*Dinnae ken me mind*, aye? The fog brings brutes, they say." He chuckles heartily. This one is unarmed, clearly unworried about a possible attack. "The beasts keep tryin' to take the wall." His laughter is louder still. "Bunch of bums."

The other one nods. He has his deadly gas musket across his back, hanging from a leather sling. Fools. Fragile and brittle like dry twigs. How did this little race of people take so much from us? How are they standing so casually here, feet away from Jattaria? How are *they* keeping us from taking it all back? They are nothing!

I pull two knives from sheaths on my back, spring forward, and stab them in their necks. The blades easily cut through fabric, skin, flesh, and bone. They twitch as I drag them back to the shadows, leaving trails of blood.

Shivering, I ponder their deaths. Why was this so easy? Two lives just ended. My first kills.

Some of the night's darkness drips inside me as I pull the knives out with shaky hands, trembling when the metal scrapes bones.

Clang! Clang Clang!

Bells go off in the nearest tower. Dozens of cries rise from the stone walls.

"Giants! Giants! We are under attack!" The fortress awakens like a wasps' nest.

"Find cover!" yells the Diamond, veins bulging in his neck. His head bursts into bits of bone and flesh; the crack of a gunshot splitting the air a half second later. His body collapses and slides off the wall. I break into a frantic run toward the hidden unit, toward Emma. My bare feet slap the concrete as I hurdle corpses and dash to safety. Bits of stone and metal rain on me as shots burst against the floor.

I dive behind a field cannon, finding relative safety next to Emma. Projectiles zoom by. Most shots hit the cannon's steel and its concrete emplacement, slowly making it disintegrate. I pat my armor desperately. "No blood. Thank you, Aftergods. Thank you for your protection!"

Around me, my unit gets mowed down. Dolphen, one of the few still alive, bolts to escape the carnage. "This is death! This is freezing death!" he yells as the Edgens' fire tears him to pieces. His broken body falls lifeless to the stone floor, but the bullets don't stop shredding him.

"Give us a break, you animals!" I scream, my voice cracking. I touch my chest, where I keep Mother's old letters, and feel the paper crackle softly. "I am dying after all! Oh, Mother, it was all for nothing!" I cry.

Emma grabs my hand and squeezes. "Stay with me, love!"

Niv peeks out from behind a battlement. "Retreat to -" He is destroyed before he finishes the sentence. All that is left is a red mist and a few bits of gore spread on the stone floor.

Death is closing in. Our cover is coming undone under the unrelenting rage of their guns. The air tastes of salt and chemicals, of dust and blood. *Despair, despair.* My mind begins to shut down. Then, a roar grows from the forest. The battle cries from our brothers and sisters charging!

"Now we'll crush them!" I say, holding on to hope. "It's a thousand Giants against these miserable Edgens!"

Emma pulls my arm. "Jump!" she says, diving into the darkness while the Edgens' focus is elsewhere. I follow her and pray I hit something soft.

I wake up after a momentary death. I had landed horribly. If pain is for the living, then I am very much alive.

Emma shakes me viciously. "Come on, Agnor! Run or the Jattarian fire will get us killed!"

I get to my feet and follow her as best I can. My pace is wobbly, and my breathing is difficult. "Go," I urge, pushing her forward.

"Not without you," she says, pulling me.

The fury of the two armies explodes like a thunderstorm all around us. Bullets and bolts fly over our heads as we run along the wall, away from the point where the two forces will clash. I look over my shoulder to follow the battle's progress and watch the stone wall shrug off everything my fellow Jattarians throw. The muddy field the attacking Giants run across erupts with each bullet the Edgens shoot. Some Edgen cannons explode due to the spikes and oil I jammed them with, but it doesn't seem to make a difference. Their firepower is too overwhelming, their position too strong.

Our assault is a glimpse of glorious bravery snuffed a moment later. Size and strength perish before their unbeatable weaponry. The Edgens' gas guns vomit punishment on us, obliterating them before we reach the wall.

We die by the dozens, by the hundreds.

The fight ends with the echoes of the cannon fire still hanging in the air. The breeze lifts fog and smoke, revealing the massacre. A defiant song rises from the theater of war. The few Giants who are still alive sing our anthem. I join them on the last lines.

This land is mine; they'll hear our cry.

I gladly die, so we can rise.

"We didn't have a chance," says Emma. Doubt clouds her gaze. "Fortitude isn't with us. We weren't strong enough to last a day! The sun will find us covered in our own blood." She is trembling, so close to me that I feel her heart beating wildly.

"They sent us to die here," I grunt. "Months of preparation, hundreds of men and women. The largest attack in decades and for what?" Pride becomes desperation.

"We must go," says Emma, tugging my sleeve. I rub mud on her silvery hair, which shines like a beacon. We lost our helmets at some point. She lost her jacket too. I give her mine and get moving once more.

Searchlights sweep the slaughter. The fortress gates open to release teams of Edgens. They take prisoners or kill those beyond help. Jattarians cry in anguish, begging for help or a quick death. Some still sing the anthem, but the voices die one by one. We crawl toward our trenches in the woods through broken bodies and severed limbs with a new sense of urgency. Warriors reach out to us, but Emma steers away. "They'll drag you down to hell with them."

We swim through this dark sea of horror, trying not to drown in it. "We are almost there," I whisper.

A strand of hair the color of the moon escapes her braid and sticks to her forehead. A little smile changes her expression when our eyes meet. "I thought I lost you," she says.

"We always find each other," I reply, quoting what she always says to me.

Vroooom!

The woods tremble. Trees crack and fall.

VROOM!

The war engine advances. The last-ditch weapon the high officers kept hidden in the woods, just in case things went badly.

ROAARR!!!

A metallic monster on wheels breaks free from the forest in an explosion of leaves and branches. The siege engine speeds toward the wall; its exhaust pipes cough smoke and flames, and its titanic steel and rubber tires roll and eat the distance to the wall, digging into the soft dirt and throwing it up as they spin.

I open my eyes wide and stop breathing. "We might still win, Emma," I whisper. She grips my arm tightly and curls against me in the mud.

The Edgens' bullets ricochet off the steel hull as it rampages through the field, trampling enemies and fallen Giants alike. It crashes into the stronghold gates with the sound of a falling mountain.

Then, a flash of light turns the night into day and my hope into dread. A thunderous explosion engulfs the castle and the hundreds of soldiers around it. I shield my face against the heat and my eyes against the blinding light. The skin of my hands seems to sizzle. The night is dark again, but the blaze stays imprinted in the back of my eyes.

"Forbidden fire," grunts Emma, grimacing. "They broke the Aftergods' First Directive." She shakes her head no, looking to the sky. "They will send the demons to kill us all."

The battlefield quiets. The dying hold their breath, surely wishing for a swift passing before the winged reapers arrive. Death in battle is Valhalla; death by reaper is freezing hell. The forbidden fire reaches out to the skies like crying tongues calling for a reckoning

The winged reapers are coming to deliver god-sent punishment. Emma slips into my arms, weeping, trembling. I embrace her and wait for death together.

An eternity passes, it seems, and then, finally, we hear it.

"Is that them?" asks Emma.

Another roar splits the silence. From above, we hear a mighty flapping of wings. Something flies overhead at incredible speed, and then the forest bursts into white flames. The fire's light draws a terrifying silhouette against the night sky: snake-like head, leathery wings, shiny scales, and powerful claws streak overhead before vanishing into a cloud.

Emma gets up suddenly. "Let's run!" She helps me up.

"Run where? We can't escape the gods' fury."

"Run anywhere. Come on!" She insists, pulling me up to my feet.

I stand up, ignoring my tortured limbs, and look down into her scared, muddy face. Her blue eyes are wide and shaky.

"Of course, Emma," I say, melting.

I would follow her anywhere. Warm liquid spatters my mouth and nose. I blink instinctively and wipe the stuff with my sleeve. A distant crack registers in my hearing: the delayed sound of a rifle. She looks down at her chest, no longer scared but confused: her life pours away from a new wound. Emma brings her wet, shiny hands to her face, studying them with a thousand questions in her eyes. The ring I made for her weeks ago is covered in red.

She coughs blood. "Go," she says with effort, choking

"No... not without you, Emma." I silence the cry that climbs up my throat and kneel with her in my arms. I bring her close to my chest and search for the shooter.

A lone figure holds a long gas musket at the wall with steam billowing from its muzzle. A white scarf on the sharpshooter's neck flutters playfully with the breeze, bright in the darkness. Still holding Emma, I pick a crossbow from one of the many dead soldiers around me and shoot at the sniper on the wall. The bolt flies up, up, then gravity sucks it to the ground. The confident sniper stands there, safe outside our weapons' range.

"Run, Agnor," she coughs. Her hand rests on my chest, and the reaper makes another pass. A wall of fire explodes in its wake.

"I can't leave you," I say. "I would be nothing..."

She shivers. "You must. Live. See it all and tell me about it later. Bring me stories to Valhalla. We'll find each other after. Promise me you will." Her voice is but a whisper.

"I can't," I cry.

"Promise!" She says, almost screaming. Her little fist hits my chest - then falls to her side.

"I can't," I say, but she is not listening. She is not here anymore.

Hell rains around me, and I am ready to burn. The reaper circles us, coming in and out of clouds of smoke.

Hands as hard as steel peel me off Emma's body. "Let go, man!" says someone as he drags me into the blazing forest. It's Nefri, the Circle who was collecting messages earlier. "Saxon! Come help!" he calls, and another soldier comes.

The two of them try to force me to let go of Emma.

"No!" I scream, but another shot finds me. A bullet hits me in the leg, making me let go. Nefri and Saxon drag me into the treeline as I kick and thrash. "No!" I scream. My throat gives; my voice cracks. "Emma!"

"She's gone, man!" screams Saxon, panting after all the effort.

"Leave me..." I beg softly.

Nefri throws me against a tree and slaps me hard across the face. "Is that what she wanted?" He screams, shaking me by the collar, pointing in Emma's direction.

"Was that your girlfriend? Your wife?" Saxon asks gently.

"She was going to be my wife," I reply, surrendering.

"Then you know she would have wanted you to live," he says. "Stay with us, now."

Out of strength, without any will left, I nod

The reaper still soars above us, out of sight past the treetops.

Saxon looks up. "How do we escape that?"

Nefri runs a hand through his dirty black hair. "Antares."

"That's treason," I mumble, remembering the oath I made during graduation a few weeks ago.

Nefri shakes his head and punches the tree trunk. "*We* are the betrayed!" he growls, stabbing a finger against his chest. "Forbidden fire? *They* are the traitors!" He takes a few breaths and wipes his bleeding mouth. "There is nowhere else to go but Antares. We would have to go Cold, across Jattaria, and then across Sargena."

Saxon takes a deep breath, shaking his head. "We will probably die on the way there, and the Antarian Titans will never take us if we make it."

"Maybe the Jattaravkalt will," says Nefri.

"The Jattaravkalt are all criminals, traitors," I argue, but I know it's pointless.

"They are Giants like us." He shakes his head. "But if we stay here, death is certain. Whatever we do, we must go far from here. Far from that," he finishes, tilting his head up. The reaper's fire is setting it all ablaze. The flames are closing in, the smoke making us choke.

Saxon's expression is vacant, hopeless. He knows as well as I do that Nefri is right. There is no future in Jattaria after today.

I would crawl back to Emma and die in the fire, but she asked me to live. "Goodbye, love," I whisper, looking back. Then, without conviction, "I die, we rise."

TENDER

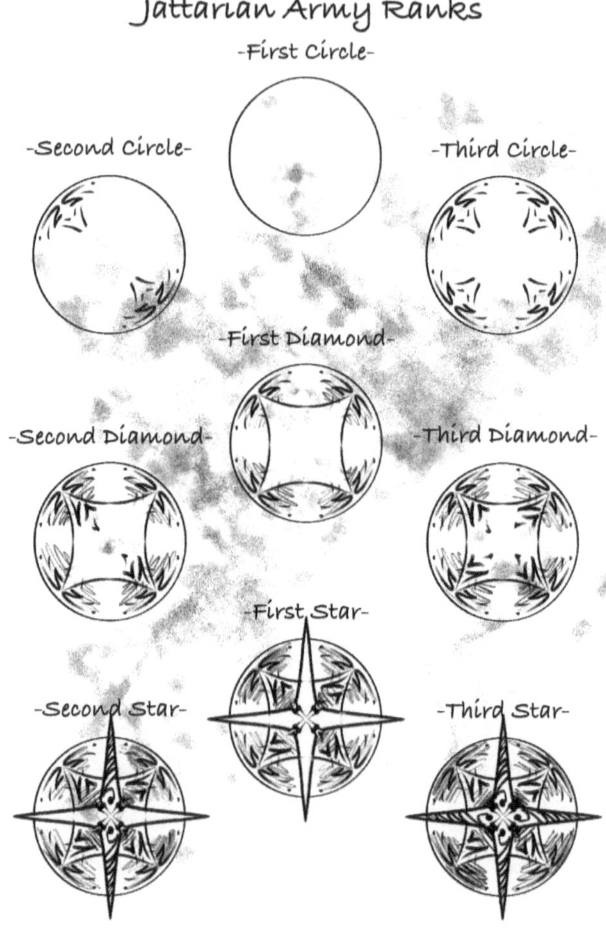

Thyra

A few days later, in Thyra's home, far from the Fifth Wall

War did not come to me: another thing in a long list of things Mother was wrong about. I am thirteen years old now, and I am still home, with Dad, and doing what I love.

My heart belongs in this old shop behind our house, where we fix things while Mother and Nefri kill Edgens up Warm. They can have the Edgeslag; I'll have pleasant days with my father.

The heat from the forge comes steadily, melting me inside the leather apron. Metal crashes into metal, and the handle jerks in my gloved hand. The impact rings sharp and loud, but I am used to it. The little anguish in my ears is almost a source of joy.

My swings are not meant to destroy my target but transform it. I squeeze the hammer and heft it over my head once more. Gravity and every fiber in my body brings the tool in a downstroke and finishes the work with a loud bang. I remove the goggles and take a close look at the plate. This cover will fit some machine in the factory yards where Dad gets his contracts.

"Nice work, Thyra." He tousles my blonde hair, already dirty from working all day. "Make sure it's clean before we deliver it."

"Daddy, this isn't my first time." I squint at him and stick my tongue out.

I shouldn't have.

He grabs my tongue with two gloved fingers, and I taste all the sawdust and oil he has collected in years of work before he lets me go. "Ugh!"

"Give me that thing, you!" He snatches the plate from my hands and inspects it. Solid, practical, austere. It will do the job in the most economical way possible, just as the Jattarian demand. "The guys at the factory can't believe a kid is making these plates." Dad takes his detailing tools and decorates the polished face with his signature stamp. Totally unnecessary, but it is his style, and Jattaria doesn't seem to mind.

He puts it on the pile of finished work, opens a drawer, and takes a small bowl out. My mouth waters. "I stopped by the shops today," he whispers with a mysterious voice. He puts the little bowl out of my reach to tease me. "The Sweet Spot has a broken oven, and we might get paid in candy. *Frau* Gwendolyn gave us these in advance." He takes one of the pieces and puts it in his mouth. "Go on. We can get back to work after a short break."

I take one and unwrap it: red with green stripes. It tastes like sweet bliss on my tongue. I let it dance and slide, clicking softly against my teeth. "Mint and cherry," I whisper. Dad slips two more into my pocket—typical of him, but Jattaria doesn't seem to mind this slight excess either.

The life of engineers like him is full of tiny allowances. Most Jattarians go to war and serve their ten years. Some stay longer, some retire and struggle to find something to do, and most die in battle. That's not for me. I want the calm life Dad has.

"Amberson Ener." Cold, loud, to the point. The unfamiliar voice makes us jump and turn around. "Message for you."

A young Giant in military uniform stands at our shop's entrance. He is half a foot shorter than Dad, with short brown hair and clean-shaven. His green cap under his arm and severe frown mean nothing good. He hands Dad a letter with the Jattarian Army shield stamped on it.

"My condolences." He looks down at me. "*Fraulein*. Sorry for your loss." He exits as quietly as he came. Hundreds of similar notices must be getting delivered at this moment around Jattaria. The death of loved ones is an everyday thing in our country.

The day isn't over despite the news. We Jattarians must remain productive. I drop the hammer. I try to catch my breath. My heart doesn't want to slow down. I picture that pump in my chest as a miniature machine of wounded flesh. Each beat pushes a crippling ache through my veins.

"Well done, Thyra." Dad's face is red; his eyes are red too. His low voice reminds me I am part of this world, even if it's cold and shattered. The shop is real again, not just a blurry background. The sad news comes back as well. I spit the candy, crushing it under my heel.

Nefri, my dear brother, is dead.

I wipe the tears before they fall. The rough fabric of my gloves scratches my skin, already irritated from all the crying. My anger turns to sadness, then to anger again. The piece I just finished looks nothing like the ones I made earlier. This one is dented and bent.

"Maybe we call it a day," says Dad, his voice cracking. He relaxes his fist holding the letter. We read it an hour or so ago, and the words still linger like a heavy presence. Beating metal to break through the emotions didn't work. "We'll clean up tomorrow."

"*Ja*, Dad."

He tries to be cheerful for my sake, but he has also been crying. "Will you try for the School of Knowledge next year?" The timing of this question is hardly a coincidence: he doesn't want me to end up like Nefri.

I look up at him: seven feet tall, with broad shoulders and a gentle face. His blonde hair and white beard hang in long, messy braids, which he ties with cords. He smiles despite it all. Maybe one day I will be strong and big like him, able to bring peace to the ones around me.

"Why did he have to die, Dad?"

"The Edgeslag is a hungry beast that feeds on the lives of our loved ones." He offers his hand, calloused and riddled with small burn scars. I have seen those thick fingers bend steel, but with me, they are so gentle. I curl my fingers into his, mine so small in comparison, and let him lead me to the house. We walk across our small yard. The day's last sunbeams make long shadows all around us and reflect off the windows of the homes along our street.

Nefri, so fun and loving, left for Solitude's School of War three years ago. He aced Selection, every class, and even Trials. "Mother's training and his hard work paid off," he said once.

He had just graduated this season and is now gone at seventeen. The Edgeslag took him forever. According to the letter, his entire battalion was destroyed days ago. The Edgeslag didn't even leave a body for us to bury. Did he meet a girl and fall in love? Did he marry her in secret, like the heroes in my stories? Did he die bravely?

He wrote often, but the letters got more distant the longer he was in training. Father said Solitude's School of War is a hard place and Nefri had to become tough, too. The last time we saw him, he seemed distracted and bored with us, with me. His friends were around, and he couldn't be seen showing affection.

"I hate them. I hate our gods. I hate the Edgens. They took my big brother. They take and take. Why, Daddy?" But I know. The words I repeat every week in First School echo in my head. They didn't mean anything before, but now I see they are true: Jattaria's enemies will not stop until they take everything from us.

Or until we kill them.

I shiver. My mind's voice speaks such violence. I look down at my tiny fist. I cannot destroy a nation. How could this single arm do enough damage?

For the first time ever, I wish I could crush lives at will.

If Mother were here, she'd continue my training to make me a killing thing, but she is up Warm fighting the same war that killed my brother. She would know how to turn me, this soft piece of flesh, into a deadly weapon. She would know how to beat me into shape, the way I forge formless metal into useful tools.

My knuckles crack inside my tight fists.

Oh, dear brother! You shouldn't have died!

It's late. My cuddly blankets rustle, and now I am awake. I shiver in the cool night breeze. The curtains flap like lazy wings. The scent of pine trees crawls up my nose, and a slice of moonlight hits me in the eyes. My spike-back gator, Kora-Elena, runs inside her cage and thrashes against its walls.

"Wake up, Thyra," says a smooth voice. I see him. Hair as black as Mom's, eyes so blue they hurt: my brother.

"Nefri!" I curl up and hug him tight. "I dreamed you were dead!"

"No, baby Thyra. I am alive. I am here with you."

I let go of his neck and look at him. He is wearing light battle armor. Bloody. Dirty. He stinks of smoke and sweat. His face is worried and hurt.

"It wasn't a dream," I say slowly. "Daddy got the letter. It said you died with your entire battalion."

His expression transforms into a sadness so sharp it stabs my chest. "I came to say goodbye, little sister. I am leaving Jattaria."

"You can't leave, Nefri! Only traitors leave!"

"I know."

"Where will you go? Sargena? The Titans will kill you there."

He shakes his head. "Farther than Sargena. Antares. To the Jattaravkalt."

"What about your oath? This is not what the Code of Virtues taught us. And Mother?"

"Don't tell anyone I came. Let them think I died." He squeezes my cheeks softly and kisses my forehead.

I hold his wrists with both hands and try to bring him close to my chest, but he slips out of my grip, leaving a small bundle in my hand.

"This hurts more than anything, sister. My heart was always in the wrong place." He touches the right side of his chest. "Take care of Dad, *ja?*"

I reach for my bedside table, take the two candies Dad gave me, and hand them to Nefri. He puts them in his pocket and smiles the saddest smile. "Heart, heart, heart."

Like a breeze, he slides out through the window and closes it. He kisses his fingers and presses them against the glass. Steam forms around the skin, and by the time the fog dissipates from the window, my brother is gone.

There's a dirty piece of fabric in my hand: his name and rank tag. "First Circle Nefri Ener," I read. I pull the blankets to my chin and turn myself into a ball. I will miss my brother, but how will I keep this a secret? How will I protect my family from what Nefri just did? It could be the end of me, the end of my family, the end of Dad.

Oh, dear brother! You should have died.

Chapter Four

LEGACY

Jattarian Outfits

Agnor

A day later, in a farm a few miles from Thyra's town

I'd die this very moment, but Emma wouldn't forgive me.

Promise, she said. How? I only made it this far because of her.

She wanted to see it all; I wanted glory and honor. I wanted a great military career, to climb through the ranks, and, gods willing, have a chance to challenge the Highest and take his post as leader of Jattaria.

What an imbecile. My dreams become nightmares.

This pain will make sense someday. It's like she still speaks to me, giving me courage. Until then, I must survive this festering wound on my leg or my collection of stories for Emma will be embarrassingly short. The flesh is hot, discolored, and smells like decomposing meat. The bullet went deep into my flesh before exiting, tearing muscle and skin on its path.

"Keep cleaning. It's getting better," says Uma, but her wrinkled nose disagrees. We came across several survivors on our way out of the woods, and this dark-haired woman is the only medic in the group that formed. Uma puts more hay under my knee and gives me a friendly pat before leaving to join the other deserters working on whatever task was assigned to them. The poor family that owns this property is tied and gagged in a corner. The mother, father, a daughter, and two sons shiver as they look at us.

Yana, a blonde Third Diamond of about twenty, supervises it all with calculating hazel eyes. "Walver! Pack that wagon with all the food you can find. Who knows how long it will take to find the Jattaravkalt. As soon as the other survivors join us, we get out of here, so be ready."

"*Ja*, Boss," says Walver, an athletic man near forty with eyes like ash. "You two, come with me," he barks at a pair in the middle of a game of knights. They get moving after rolling their eyes, leaving the cards on a crate. As they leave, Walver throws a nasty sneer at the five prisoners tied in the corner and kicks a baby goat out of his way. The little animal scurries off, crying. Walver killed its mama this morning and left her spine and head hanging at the barn's entrance. "Behave or you'll end up like her," he warns the family, patting the severed goat head. Flies disperse.

"Are you going to be able to walk when we leave?"

I turn to the voice. It's Yana, grilling me with her greenish gaze.

"Yes," I reply, panicking. "Medic says it's getting better."

"Good," hisses Yana. "You'd pass for a Titan. We'll need that in Antares and Sargena. Get better or we'll have to leave you behind. Do you know what the Regler Korps do to traitors?"

I shake my head.

"They torture them for hours, then hang them and their families in public." She pulls an invisible rope up, cranes her neck. She even sticks her tongue out to play dead.

"I have no family," I say dryly, trying to hide my panic. Without the right medicine to stop the infection, I am damned. "I won't slow you down."

The deserters return at dusk smelling of sweat and dirt. "Freeloader," says one of them to me. Two others scoff when they walk past. I can't blame them; they worked hard while I rested.

Walver walks in last. "*Wie geht es dir*, Agnor? Lost your leg yet?" His eyes gleam with a savage type of hunger. He sits next to the tied family. "You could be having a much better time," he says to the mother, leaning into her. He takes her bound hands and licks them. "What do you say I take you for a walk? You can stretch those long legs."

The woman looks away, sobbing. Walver plays with her red hair and forces her head to turn to him. Her husband tries to stop him and screams through the gags in his mouth, but it only seems to entice Walver.

"We will have to find a more private place for our courtship," he jokes while everyone watches. The father manages to kick him in the chest and get in front of his wife.

Walver takes his knife out. "You're dead."

I push myself up and limp next to him. "Enough! Leave them alone."

He straightens his filthy uniform with care. The protective mail under his green shirt peaks out from behind his collar. He is at least twice my age and easily a foot shorter, but that doesn't faze him. He stabs a finger into my chest and pushes me back.

"Shush, *Circle*. You have no say." He slaps me hard. The strength I had grown used to is gone. "You are just a waste of air." He turns his back to me and walks to the woman. "My love, we will continue this later. The mood has been spoiled." He goes upstairs, where the living quarters are. Yana and he claimed the rooms. The rest of us sleep down here, among the animals and the feed.

Saxon comes close to me. "Be careful around Walver, man," he says, smiling like always.

"We should put him down," I grunt.

He scoffs. "Can *you* get us out of Jattaria safely? Get us through Sargena? Can you find the Jattaravkalt?" He shakes his head. "Walver is insane, but we need him. He is experienced and can find his way anywhere and through anything. Unless you can do that, there's no taking him out."

I look at the family we tied and threw in a corner. "What are we doing?"

Saxon squeezes my shoulder. "We are just making it through the day, my guy. Stay out of Walver's way. You are in no shape to fight, anyway." He walks to where his things are. One of the women in the group is there, waiting for him.

I hobble to where the prisoners are. "Are you all right?" I ask the woman, removing their gags. We are miles away from the next farm; no one would hear their screams.

"You need antibiotics," says the father after licking his split lips. "Cleaning that wound won't be enough. Keep us safe, and I'll tell you how to make some."

"I'll keep you safe."

His shoulders drop an inch. *"Danke."*

The family of five stays close to each other in their corner of the barn. I lie down near them to keep watch. A thin cloud of dust and hay particles lifts. The wind blows through the boards singing a lullaby, and I fall victim to my fever and exhaustion.

The sound of a struggle puts a stop to my restless sleep. Tears fall down the mother's face, and she looks pointedly across the barn when she sees I am awake.

"The man took him," she whispers. "He said he'd kill him if I made any noise!"

One of her eyes is black and swollen. I stand up, ignoring the excruciating pain in my leg. Walver is in the farthest corner, grunting and hitting something. I limp closer, using anything I can lean on for support.

Someone grabs my pants and pulls me back. "You can't stop him," says Uma, shaking her head as she lets go of my pant leg. "Don't be stupid! He'll kill you."

Her friend Sil is beside her. "Let it go." She looks away.

I free myself from Uma's grip and move forward.

"Stop fighting, or I'll grab that pretty daughter of yours," says Walver. Mounds of hay and animal feed block my progress. Some cows grunt from their stalls, disturbed by all this commotion. My leg pulsates and burns, but I gather strength from the pain and anger to override my weakness. I approach from behind and grab Walver by the neck as he is about to kick the man's back. I squeeze until I feel his spine.

"Freezing death..." He tries to turn and fight me off, but rage flows through me, giving me back my strength. Maybe this is what tapping into Fortitude feels like. I slam his head against a wooden pillar.

"I warned you, Walver." I smash his face again. "Leave." *Crash*. "Them." *Thud*. "Alone!" *Crack*. Each hit makes the barn shake.

He falls to his knees. "You'll pay for this," he whistles through what's left of his teeth, spraying blood everywhere. I bash his skull once more. His limp body crumples onto the dirty floorboards. He is wheezing through his bloody nose.

"Come with me," I say to the beat-up man.

He is shaking and bruised. "Thanks." He says. I bring him back to his family. One of his children crawls to him and hugs him. "Easy," he warns as he winces. They huddle together in their corner.

I sit with difficulty and watch them, determined not to fall asleep again.

"Hey, son," says the father after a few minutes. He nods at the sleeping traitors around us. "I heard them talk about the Jattaravkalt, that haven for criminals in Antares. Is that where you are headed?"

I nod.

He shakes his head. "You will never get there, boy."

"There is nowhere else to go." I take my sword and stab at the floor.

He shakes his head in disbelief. "Antares is cold as death, kid! It's hell for the likes of us!"

"There is nowhere else. The gods sent their demons to hunt us, *wiessen sie?* Titans can't be worse than a reaper."

"Reapers?" He breathes and looks up superstitiously as if checking for the flying demons. "They are real?"

I show him the burnt side of my jacket. "We are marked. Death is after me already, old man. I can't fight a demon. But a Titan?" I take the sword and put it before my face. "They bleed. They die," I mutter. My father was a Titan, and he died before I met him.

"So reapers are real. All this time, I thought they were legends." He shakes his head, and bits of hay fall off his reddish hair. He blinks repeatedly as if trying to clear his mind. "You don't want this path," he whispers urgently. He looks around, then at me. His bruised face looks sincere. "To get to Antares, you will need to go through Sargena. They have riding parties that gallop the Killing Woods day and night, searching for runaway Giants like you."

"I am aware."

"There are worse things than that as well," he whispers so low I can hardly hear him. "I heard stories."

"Stories..." I lean closer. Tales have always been my weakness. It's what made me close to Emma in the first place.

He looks at his trembling family. "Something else protects the Sargenina woods. It is because of these things that the forest is called the Killing Woods. Something old, as old as the Virtues and the Code itself."

"What is it?" I lean closer still, smelling the drying blood and rancid sweat on his filthy clothes.

"The spirits of the Colossi that died millennia ago and the lost souls of those who perished during the Shared Lands war. They stalk the forest, hunting invading Giants and seeking revenge." He shivers. "*Mapinguaris*, they call them." His light blue eyes set on something behind me, a thousand miles away.

"Just stories," I say softly, unsure of my words. I rub my hands on the boards beneath me.

"Maybe. Reapers were just stories, too. But you have seen them."

I bob my head, thinking.

"There is nothing good waiting for you down Cold." He stares into my eyes, maybe trying to push his truth through mine.

"Then I am truly damned." I lean against the pole, exhaling dread and fear, closing my eyes as I absorb it all. "You see, I'd like to be dead. There's someone I'd like to see again," I say, fingering the ring tying me to Emma.

"You are going anyway." He studies every inch of my face as if looking for a crack in my conviction. He sighs, perhaps understanding. "The medicine is upstairs, in the kitchen cabinets," he says finally. "A brown bottle that reads Antibiotics," he says, showing me with his tied hands how big the bottle is. "A green one that reads Ointment. Quickly. You might not have another chance." He looks at Walver, snoring on the floor.

Upstairs, I search the small kitchen. The air smells of baked bread and fruit pies, and the walls have colorless decorations. There are a few bad paintings done by a small child and a handful of framed pictures showing in poor black and white detail the faces of ancestors, perhaps. There is the mandatory portrait of the Highest, our glorious leader, although it is cheaply made and fading. A simple, austere house, like most in Jattaria. The doors to the two bedrooms are closed, so I inspect cabinets and drawers, looking for the medicine, but it has all been raided. Just when I am about to give up, I find it inside a box next to Yana's things in a corner.

I uncork the brown one and take a small sip. Its sweet and spicy smell almost makes me vomit. I pull a drop of the ointment from the other bottle and rub it on my wound, biting hard. The pain is so much, so intense that I get woozy for a heartbeat. I expect the ointment to burn, but it feels like an intense freshness, similar to chewing mint leaves.

I stuff the two bottles in my pocket. They clink inside my coat.

"What do you think you're doing?"

"Yana," I gasp.

She is on me before I have time to react. She grabs my neck. I swat a punch, but she takes my wrist and twists it painfully. "It's medicine! For the infection!" I grunt.

"Thief!"

She takes the bottles out of my pocket, opens them with her teeth, and smells the contents. She pulls back with a snarl. "Freezing death, this can't possibly be medicine. Get out of here!"

"Yes, Boss." I head to the stairs, but heavy steps approach from beneath. Someone is coming up.

Walver.

I freeze in place and wait for the inevitable as he walks in on wobbly legs.

Yana laughs. "What happened to you?"

He tries to speak but spits a tooth instead. He raises a hand and points a bloody finger at me.

"*He* did this to you?"

"*Ja*," he whistles through the holes I left in his smile.

"Well, I'm sure you had it coming."

He nods, but there is murder in his eyes.

"Go rest. Something tells me you need it."

He walks into one of the rooms and slams the door shut.

"I am impressed." She sits on a chair by the table. She kicks another chair toward me. I sit. Something like curiosity has replaced the disgust she had for me.

"He was hurting them," I explain. "Someone had to do something."

"And you, sick and broken, were that someone. Are you a vessel for Fortitude?" she murmurs, tilting her head, measuring me.

I shake my head. "I didn't study the Virtues or their fighting styles."

"You thought strength would be enough. Never felt the need to reach within for what the Virtues offer." She grunts.

I avoid her gaze. The truth is a bit more complex, but why bother explaining? I didn't have money for an instructor, books, or time to find an apprenticeship.

"I'll teach you," she says, to my surprise.

A moment stretches. I swallow and shake my head. "You would be my mentor?"

"Yes. I like teaching, and you have potential. I am trained in a couple of Styles of Virtue " She puts her hand over her chest. "I am a Golden Blade, after all. I can touch the Colossal Virtues the ancestor left in us. That's how I became what Jattaria wanted me to be."

It hits me then. "You are Yana Hensin. The Vulture."

"The one and only." She smiles. Her sharp face softens when she does, almost beautiful, more like the posters they made of her.

"You are a legend," I say, breathless.

"Was. I am a traitor now." Her lips stretch into a bigger smile, her hazel eyes narrow. "Do you still feel loyalty to Jattaria, even after what they did to us?"

A flush creeps up my cheeks. "They sent us to die like that. The high officers broke the directives and summoned the gods' demons." I look away, trying to find an answer in the gray walls. "But I can't hate Jattaria. Everything I am, I owe to this nation."

She chuckles dryly and taps her temple. "You were brainwashed, boy!" She waves her hand. "We are all programmed to serve and follow, like dogs." She grins menacingly with all her teeth. "It's an implanted attitude that guides your every thought."

She slides her chair closer to me. It scratches the wooden floor. "I like you. So innocent and hopeful." She whispers this as if it were a terrible secret. "Sadly, you can't eat innocence or take shelter in hope. Fortitude is what you need. Power to thrive, lead, and get where you need to be. I can give this to you." She plays with the medicine bottles, holding my life in her hands. "Agnor. That's your name, *ja*?"

I bob my head.

She sighs. Her expression shifts from amused to somber. "They betrayed us, Agnor. Jattaria failed us and we owe them nothing. They wasted thousands of lives for nothing, many of them kids I trained. It is next to impossible to breach the Fifth; how will we break the four other walls that come after?"

"We are only meant to stop them from building the Sixth Wall." My voice fades. "That's what they said in the School of War."

"Ah! Weaving truth into the fabric of lies is the ultimate way to deceive." She looks up to the ceiling and folds her hands on her chest. "We cannot stop them, Agnor. I have questioned prisoners, broken them with these hands." She makes two fists and studies them as if she had never seen them before. "You know what they said? The Fifth Wall is the weakest. Their equipment is poor, just in case we capture it. Most soldiers manning the strongholds are untrained criminals like the traitors we send to the mines in the Kjede mountains. Think about it! A tiny race of people wiped out an entire battalion of seven-foot-tall humans with the worst elements in their arsenal."

"That can't be true!"

"If you were the Highest, would you tell your country how weak it is compared to its enemies? You wouldn't. You couldn't. That's why you have been lied to since you were born. Manipulated to obey orders without question."

I touch my chest, where I keep my old letters. "Mother told me not to trust anyone but myself. Maybe this is what she meant."

"Wise woman." Her eyes open wide. The corners of her lips go up a fraction of an inch. I've let her in. Was it a mistake?

Yana stands up and gets behind me. "You belong with us, Agnor." She massages my tense shoulders with fingers as hard as pliers. "You are a traitor." She seems to taste the word. "Traitors. We all are." She chuckles softly, like a breath. "Once you are ready, I can show you how to reach Fortitude." She squeezes the back of my neck once more and walks to her room.

Before she crosses the door, she turns and tosses me the medicine bottles. I catch them in the air, almost dropping the ointment. I keep them against my chest and watch Yana walk into her quarters. She leaves the door open. Her shirt slides off her back, revealing the curves of her body. Many tattoos and dozens of scars trace the white skin on her small but athletic frame. Some scars are new, some very old. The way she stands there, looking over her shoulder, feels like an invitation.

Perhaps some version of me would step in with her, but not this one. Yana's power and youth spill from her sculpted shape, but it does not pull me. Not with Emma's perfume still dancing in my memory.

I turn to the stairs, make my way down to the stable, and sleep in the cold, itchy hay.

CHAPTER FIVE

TEARING

Regler Korps Officer

Thyra

Later that week, in Thyra's home

Beams of light cut through dust particles floating lazily in the air inside our shop. I try to catch some between my thumb and a finger. Dad's hammering and mumbling add music to the moment. The oils and cleaning chemicals mix their scents with the fresh air coming through the open windows and door. This is heaven. Working alongside my father, knowing that I need nothing else.

For just a moment, I'm the little girl I was days ago, and things are as they should be.

The small metal tube in my hand shines. "What's this for, Dad?" I ask, puzzled by the tool I'm holding.

"A spike-launcher to help miners climb."

"Can't they use a hammer?"

"Yes, but this is for emergencies. Sometimes you don't have time or space. Maybe you're falling, and it's your only chance to save yourself."

I manipulate the machine and wonder at it. So simple and useful. A six-inch-long canister holds compressed air and a powerful spring, and a spike shoots when the lever triggers the mechanism. "You made this?"

"Your mother designed it, and I made it for her. She fits it on her forearm plates and shoots them as a last resort. I thought a similar design could save lives, so I made this prototype. They have it so bad in the mines."

"The miners are criminals, *Isa,*" I argue. "Captured Edgens, thieves, and worse. They are supposed to suffer."

"Oh, Thyra, *sot flicka,*" he replies softly. "Some are sent there for just knowing the wrong people or being in the wrong place.

And everyone deserves mercy and a chance to live, don't you think?"

"Only *we* deserve peace. We should load them in the Dark Runner, so we never have to see them again. That life isn't worth living anyway. That's what Mom says. They say the same thing in school." The clever piece of engineering loses value in my eyes. Its purpose seems unworthy.

"The office said that as well when I brought this to them. They weren't interested. Most miners are over eighteen, *du weist*? Too old to be Appeasement Offers, so we can't put them in the Dark Runner. And who would work the mines if they don't? Me? You? They contribute in their own way. Life is all we have, my dear girl, even if some lives are more precious than others."

"Like the Highest's, our great leader!" I instinctively punch my chest with a fist.

"Or like yours." He squeezes my cheek with an oily hand. I look up and up until I find his eyes. From over his big belly, his bearded face looks down at me. He kneels so our heads are level.

"I am one more. I am only what I give to Jattaria," I recite by memory.

Dad frowns. "You are precious. My only daughter, and now my only child. I know you are angry and sad, and that's alright. Just don't let it settle and become a part of you. Don't let it define you. There will be joy and love again. You must believe this."

He tears up and guilt twists my insides. The lie is breaking his heart, but the truth would certainly kill us. They'd throw us in those mines next to condemned criminals if they found out. This is my burden. What Nefri did could bring shame and pain to my family, but I will keep the secret. Perhaps no one will find out.

I return the spike launcher to him.

"Why don't you keep it? Let it be a reminder that with Fortitude, a weapon can be used to save a life," he says,

Or that a tool can be used to end one.

I shiver. My thoughts can be so dark.

"I see your Virtue, Daddy." I hug the spike launcher close.

"Go. I'll put everything away," he says, ruffling my long hair.

I walk past the many shelves that crowd the space on my way out of the shop. Dozens of half-finished projects wait for our attention, patiently collecting dust. One of the shelves has Mother's old Army chest with the training gear from when she was a student. Now she is a High Officer, a First-Star, and her gear is much better.

I rummage through it and find the practice equipment I last used when Mother visited months ago. Unlike most kids in the village, I never practice in the public gym or fight anyone other than Mother. One of her many rules.

Lately, I find plenty of excuses to avoid practice and training sessions with my tutors, but today something calls me. It makes me grab my bundle and drag it outside. I drop it, and a thin cloud of dust erupts from it. I light a few oil lamps, set them in the yard, and then slip into the stiff leather pieces that make my protective armor. The plates still have the hearts and unicorns I drew on them, although they are faded and scratched. I connect them, along with their hooks and belts, then adjust them until they fit snugly.

The weathered wooden dummy is at the back of the yard. When we don't use him for practice, he is our valiant scarecrow protecting Father's garden. Its concrete base has cracks and is missing chunks, but it can handle another session.

"Hey, Woody," I greet the dummy. I touch its nose with the tip of my sword. "Bop!" I say, but this time I don't smile. Mother would be annoyed if she saw me being so childish. "You ready to take a beating?"

The face Nefri carved on it years ago gives me the same old crooked grin.

I hit my shield and start my exercises. Basic warm-up based on Fortitude's style, slow and accurate. This is a way of war based on defense and the perfect timing of devastating finishing moves. Solid footwork, strong stance, fast parries, deadly strikes. I build up to the more complex maneuvers, careful not to overdo it.

"This isn't dancing, Thyra. This is killing."

But I like dancing.

Mother's voice echoes from the past, opposite to all the teachings Dad gave me.

"Cut, kill, destroy," she'd say while teaching me to defeat any enemy.

"Heal, love, create," he would say while he taught me how to repair what's broken.

Love can't fix the anger and fear in my belly. They must be cut, killed, and destroyed. Thanks to Mother, I am familiar with the ancient ways of Virtue that can help me do it. She showed me how to reach for them and tap into that potential we all carry inside. It's a gift from our ancestors, destructive and precise.

I circle Woody, striking with rage and accuracy while progressively transitioning into the other styles Mother taught me. My muscles burn, burn, burn. The practice sword's grip gets sticky and slippery with sweat at the same time.

Each hit shocks my bones as much as it rocks Woody's solid body, but I am too far into the moment to feel pain. Anger flows out of me without the need for direction. It's aimed at Nefri for being a traitor. It's aimed at the Edgens for taking our land. It's aimed at the Aftergods for forcing us to live like dogs.

Kill. Them. All.

One crippling strike to the dummy's neck, then I move back into Fortitude's stance. My shield goes up, positioned between me and the target. My core is coiled and tense; my arm extends behind me with the tip of the sword aiming up. I always leave this stance for last because it's Fortitude's deadliest. *"Make this the last thing they see,"* said Mom. This is a killing touch and I let it spring.

Crack!

The blunt sword cracks the dummy's arm. I go down with the momentum, and Woody goes down as well. I regain balance and mount the dummy, as I would in a wrestling round. Its chest is between my knees, and it's perfectly positioned to take my rage. I smack it again and again and again with the sword, always between the eyes. There is no panic or need to stop. My instincts speak clearly, and my anger blurs my rational thoughts. The sounds around me are deafening, but I am in a frenzy.

Nothing else matters.

My weapon breaks; slivers sink into my palm. I keep swinging, punching with knuckles that are so used to fighting. Even after months without serious training, my bleeding hands remember. Woody takes all the damage without complaint, smiling stupidly. His chest is wet with my sweat and blood and tears. My voice breaks too.

I was screaming?

I stare at the broken sword in my hand, blood dripping from all the splinters stabbed into my skin. The blade cracked and stuck in the dummy's head.

I roll off Woody and lie on my back beside him, looking at the dark sky. Bugs fly about my head, attracted to my sweat and body heat. The stars float above me, indifferent to us insignificant mortals.

"Thyra?"

Dad's face is pale. Fear?

Why would he be afraid of me?

"I just got into it, Daddy. It has been a while."

He stares. "You were your mother for a minute. You had her fury. I forget how good a fighter you are." He scratches the back of his head.

"That must be it," I say, studying my mangled hands. How good could I actually be if Mother feared letting me fight other kids? I can't even fight a dummy without bleeding.

Dad helps me clean the cuts. When he is done, he grabs my gear and brings it to the shop, where we keep both the killing and the healing tools.

Love and death can feel the same sometimes.

The smell of butter, herbs, and tomato sauce fills the air in our small dining room. The dining table is set for two, but four chairs are waiting. Dad's creaks under his massive weight when he sits, rolls his sleeves up and whispers a quick prayer to the

Aftergods with folded hands, then throws a few words in for the Forsaken God, just in case he is still out there. Few Jattarians still remember the ancient deity the Colossi worshipped; Amberson Ener is one of them.

"Let it be," I say, repeating the last line of his prayer.

"Let's eat!" He stabs with his fork and brings a bunch of noodles to his face.

Knock, knock!

The entrance door opens. Must be the Regler Korps doing a random search. They don't need permission to enter a house, even if a high officer like my mother owns it.

"We are having dinner!" announces Dad with a full mouth. He doesn't stop eating for a second, but I almost choke. My blood feels like icy water. Did I leave Nefri's name tag on my bed?

Yes, you did. My brain reminds me.

I want to run to my room and shut the door. I force myself to eat and remain seated. The food tastes like mud. Why do I have to be so stupid?

"There is plenty of food if you guys are hungry," says Dad.

There are two of them, both covered from head to toe in black armor. One has a heavy limp on his left leg that anyone in town could recognize: Cartan, the local Regler Korps' First Star must be bored if he is doing rounds like a Circle.

"Sorry, Amberson. Can't eat on the job."

Dad gives him a look. This hasn't stopped him from joining us before.

"*Ja, jag vet.* Some deserters came through town. We caught and executed three already, but at least one more is missing."

"That's awful," says Dad. He bites his bread. "Are you sure you don't have five minutes? My little garden is growing the most delicious tomatoes."

Cartan smells the air. "You know what? It won't hurt to sit for a bite. I haven't had tomatoes in a while! Faz is selling them for five marks each, the bandit!"

Dad shakes his head. "A bandit indeed! I'll only charge you four!"

Cartan cackles a loud laugh and slaps his hip, pretending to wipe a tear from an eye even though he wears his helmet. "Kirk, my boy, come sit with the Eners and your old man."

Officer Kirk is skinnier and shorter than Cartan. He seems unsure of what to say to his superior, to his father. They are supposed to remain impossible to identify while on duty.

Too late for that.

Cartan removes his helmet and reveals his weathered face and balding head. He slams the helmet on the table and drops all his weight onto Mother's seat. The chair complains. Cartan wipes sweat from his face while Father gets him a plate with half a portion of food and a slice of bread.

"Sit down, kid," commands my father, no authority in his voice.

Cartan nods to the empty chair, and Kirk takes it.

"Thyra, get Kirk a plate," says Dad with a frown.

I jump off my seat. "Oh, sorry! Yes, right away." Did they see Nefri's name tag when they passed my room?

We would be in chains if they had.

I convince myself to breathe again and bring the younger man food and a drink. He has removed his helmet as well. He looks like Cartan except for the haircut, which resembles a lightning bolt and ends with a long braid. His left eyebrow has three wooden piercings, which is the fashion lately. His soft, young face has almost no beard, but you can tell he is trying to grow one.

"Thanks, young lady. I see your Virtue."

I sit and return to my food.

"So, Kirk, I've heard a lot about you! How are the Black Tops treating you?" asks Dad jokingly. Black Tops is a disrespectful term, but Dad has known Cartan since they were kids.

Kirk takes off his gloves and puts them over his helmet before answering. "Not a year in, but it has been very satisfying. Last month I helped dismantle a Waster cell aiding deserters in exchange for stolen Army equipment. Last night we processed those traitors we caught. Earlier today, we threw their families in jail. Busy but exciting!"

"Busy indeed, and there is still work to do," says Cartan with a full mouth. "We will find those other traitors. It's inevitable. Eventually, they try to cross to Sargena or end up with Wasters, and that's where the Regler Korps get them."

"Inevitable," I repeat. A freezing fear creeps through my veins. They must have caught Nefri's friends last night. It could have been us processed and in jail this morning. If any of them had spoken Nefri's name, Dad and I would have been dragged out of our beds and beaten to a pulp in a cold cell.

"We always catch them, Thyra. You don't need to be worried. But enough of that! What about you?" asks Cartan. "Dad is an engineer. Mom is a First Star in the Army. Which way will you go? Sword or hammer?"

Father bites his lip and looks at me with expectation.

"Engineer, sir." The wounds in my hands itch and hurt. "Hammer."

"If you have the brains to make it into the School of Knowledge, then you must do it. Few have what it takes to enter a non-military institution, and we need smart Jattarians like you to help us knuckleheads win our battles!" He pats my head. "Build us some siege machinery to tear down those walls and crush the Edgens!"

"Yes, sir."

"Selection is in a few days. Are you applying?"

"She is much too young," says Dad, patting my head. "She is only thirteen."

"In two years, maybe." A knot twists my stomach. I lose my appetite. What if Nefri gets caught before then? Or if I make a mistake and say too much? I will not be going anywhere but prison.

"What will happen to them?" I ask quietly. "To those families, I mean."

Kirk clears his throat and cleans the sauce off his mouth. "Jail until they are sentenced. Occasionally, those families with officers or influential politicians get pardons. Most likely, forced labor in the Kjede mines. Sometimes, we hang them along with the traitors. It's a good deterrent."

"It's grim but necessary." Cartan pats my hand softly, reading my expressions. He throws Kirk a warning look, and they change the topic. They chat amiably with my father for a few minutes while they finish their meal.

They put on their helmets and gauntlets as they stand up. Cartan steps to Dad. "I am very sorry about Nefri. Such a promising young man. I remember he and Kirk used to go at it at the gym when they were little. Not once was Kirk able to get him. Neither could any of the other kids, if I remember correctly. Lagas did a great job training him. A great loss."

The Regler Korps officers shake Father's hand and head for the door. The floorboards squeak, the door creaks open, then softly groans shut. We watch the night swallow them in their black uniforms through the window.

They didn't notice the tag on my bed and they didn't suspect my strange behavior, but this doesn't mean anything. Eventually, they will find out; it's *inevitable*. We'll be discovered and sentenced to backbreaking labor, dishonor, and death.

I clean and put the dishes away, then go to my room. The tag is on my mattress among some clothes, but easy to find had they been a bit more attentive. I snatch it and throw it under my bed.

It's too dark for someone my age, or any age, to be wandering the town. A few curtains open. People watch with worried frowns as I continue to the village's entrance. The gaslights throw weak light on the home and storefronts. The polished cobblestones on the road shine.

The air is still warm and pleasant, but I shiver like crazy. I don't want to see this, but I must. I have to see what Nefri threw upon us with his treason. The plaza is deserted, like everything else at this time of night. The center has a platform where bands sometimes play the national classics. There are no musicians up there tonight.

I come closer and hear the ropes squeal with tension. The soft breeze plays with the torn clothes of these three soldiers.

Their toes hang down, feet swinging softly as if performing an ethereal dance.

"They took their shoes off," I say. Dad used to do that to put me in bed.

I watch the hanging traitors for a little more, crying and wishing I could forget everything. I close my eyes tight; maybe when I open them. I will wake up from this nightmare. But I am still here and these young soldiers still hang before me, with their tongues out and their eyes blackened and bloated.

If they find out, it could be me up there. Worse, it could be Dad.

I cry my desperation, unable to control it. I scream into my wet sleeve until my head feels like it's about to split.

I punch the frame the bodies hang on and the fresh scabs from my earlier practice session open again. "I won't let this happen to you, Daddy."

I sneak back home before Dad is done with his reading. He comes to my room and finds me reading too. He hadn't noticed I left. He doesn't see my dirty boots peeking out from under my bed. "We better go to sleep," he says. I nod and get in bed. He tucks me in as he did when I was little, cupping my face with his warm hands.

"My dear Thyra. Such a wild little one."

"Heart, heart, heart."

"I love you too." He smiles and leaves. The door creaks and shuts softly.

I am wide awake. Kora-Elena watches from her cage, the black spikes on her back stand on end. Her three-foot-long reptilian body coiled tight, her claws flexed. The light that comes through the glass sparkles over her dark scales. She is defensive. Maybe she senses something is about to happen.

A thought has been growing in my mind, and now it's all I can think about.

Inevitable, inevitable, inevitable.

The word bounces around the walls of my skull. Nefri's secret will come to light sooner or later. The Regler Korps said it. It was a miracle that he didn't get caught when he came or that they noticed I was hiding something.

You must pay for his treason. Earn your family's redemption.

Hopeless. Whatever I accomplish as an engineer will not be enough to compensate for Nefri's crimes, anyway. No one sings for the engineers or makes statues to preserve their memory. Not a single engineer is mentioned in my school books.

School of War? They'll crush me. I should wait at least two years, train with Mother and go when I am more developed.

There is no time. Nefri could be captured this very night.

Maybe they'll forgive us because of Mother's rank.

But maybe they won't.

I would have to fight older, stronger, better-trained kids in a school where only half the students survive graduation.

Or wait in fear for the Korps to storm the house. Inevitable. All we can do is prepare.

Kora-Elena is right to be defensive. Something is about to happen.

"Come here, girly," I whisper, letting my gator crawl up my arm. She wraps around my neck and pushes her nose into the nook of my shoulder. I cover her with my scarf.

Careful as a mouse around a resting cat, I leave my bed, get as many clothes as possible in my bag, and escape through the window. I sneak into the shop and take my practice gear. The cruel winter is approaching, even if tonight is pleasantly warm.

One last look back as my childish dreams tug at me. Peace? Mother was right. War comes for us all.

Somehow, I must find Fortitude and be strong enough to survive the School of War and make myself into something redeemable after Nefri's cowardice.

My brother's tag, a handful of credits in my pocket, and ten years of vicious training with Mother, one of Jattaria's few Masters of Virtue. That's all I have to my name. I pray it's enough.

For my Father's sake, I will make it be.

CHAPTER SIX

EXODUS

Tertiary Lands

Agnor

Hours later, in the farm captured by Yana and the survivors

We load the last bundle onto the stolen cart on a morning much colder than the night before. Winter is still a few weeks away, but the bitter old man must be impatient to come visit. The horse looks nervously at all the strangers working around him or perhaps is aware of the coming winter. Saxon grabs the animal's head and whispers something to appease him, sensitive to the beast's moods. He has a small guitar hanging across his back, which he didn't have before. Another thing we take from this poor family.

"Hey, don't worry about them, Agnor," says Saxon when he sees me staring. "Arsen and I left money to pay for what we took. Some of the others did as well. Sil, Nova, Uma. Even Siff and Ingrid. Vinz said he didn't have any money." Saxon screws his mouth up, showing disbelief.

"You paid for everything we are taking?" I ask, doubting.

"Well...not everything." He ties his long brown hair in a bun. "We didn't have *that* much money on us." He returns to the group, playing happy arpeggios on his new guitar.

Of the five survivors who left to visit their hometowns one last time, only Nefri and Wanda came back. The other three got caught. Now only thirteen Giants remain, all eager to leave. If those they captured talk, we could have a squad of Black Tops on us any moment.

Luckily, the ointment and antibiotics are already working. I might not lose the leg after all. In case things don't improve, I have a rope, a stick, and a serrated knife hanging from my hip.

No need to be so negative, my love, whispers Emma's memory, making me shiver.

Arsen comes near; her black bandana keeps her ginger hair under control. She carries a jar with dirt and pebbles under her arm. "Thanks for what you did, Agnor. Protecting them," she says, her green eyes stopping on the family. "It's good to know there is Virtue among us."

I smile back. "At least I'm not just a burden."

She grins and punches my arm playfully. "We got your back, but be careful anyway, *ja?*" She squints and looks at Walver.

"Listen, Traitors," says Yana, cinching her worn satchel on her strong shoulders. "Get plenty of blankets; it will be cold down there. Take off your uniforms and armor and dress as civilians. Saxon," she calls. "Take one of the daughters with us. She will be our insurance." She eyes the family with a threatening stare. "No running to the Regler Korps after we leave, *wiessen sie?* We spot one black helmet on the road, and -" She lets the silence speak for her.

Saxon extends an arm to the oldest girl as if inviting her to dance. She comes with her chin up and her eyes set on Yana. "We will release her near the Sargenian Border," says Saxon to her parents. The father looks at him with hatred. "Your name is Zeeri, *ja?*"

The girl nods.

"I will take care of you," he whispers.

Walver throws his bag on the wagon's seat and starts to climb in.

"Let Agnor ride with me for a day or two," says Yana. "His leg needs rest." She touches Walver's injured face, black and blue and swollen from the beating I gave him.

He grunts and climbs down. Ingrid, Vinz, and Siff watch and give me the stink eye.

"Freezing bum," curses Ingrid.

"Come with me," says Yana, taking my arm. She helps me up. "Rest and enjoy the ride. This landscape and fair weather will become a thing of the past once we leave Jattaria."

"*Skynda!*" says Walver after throwing a quick look around. Yana gets the horse going. The wheels creak pleasantly as the rising sun warms my skin. The fresh, sweet breeze brings us the perfume of a new harvest.

This land's beauty is a thin veil; I have seen what's behind it, suffered it in my flesh., And still, it hurts to leave. Each moment, I feel farther away from Emma. But the world is out there, and she would want me to see it all. For her, I'll endure this hell. I'll tell her about it when we meet in Valhalla.

What did you learn? What did you see? she will ask, and I better have a good answer.

Yana leans back against the seat and watches the scenery peacefully, seemingly lost in the bird songs and the indistinguishable chatter and laughter of the Traitors walking around us. Saxon plays the guitar, singing a sappy tune while Arsen walks beside him.

Oh, Luck of Old, you left again.

You promised gold, delivered pain.

Bring back my love,

Oh, Luck of old,

Oh, Luck of Old...

He hums and keeps playing the guitar. I try to memorize those words, that rhythm. Emma would melt if I sang something like that for her.

"That's beautiful," says Arsen. "I never heard that one before."

"I came up with it today. Want to sing it with me?" He strums the instrument softly. Arsen smiles at him. Seeing them brings me joy. They are happy souls who found friendship and love even in these times.

"Life will be a freezing hell soon," Yana says softly. "There won't be time for songs when we cross to Sargena."

"You will keep us safe," I say, hoping. The idea of creatures roaming the Sargenian forests haunts me like the memories of winged reapers setting the forest ablaze.

She puts a hand on my good leg and pats it a few times. "I appreciate that, Agnor. Getting into the Jattaravkalt won't be easy either." Her hand rests on my thigh for a moment. Clouds seem to pass through her eyes. They are golden one second and light green the next.

"You are one of the greatest fighters in Jattaria. Why wouldn't they want you to join?"

"I imagine they will be reclusive. Antarians are pacifists, but they hate us as much as the Sargenians. Antarians have peacekeepers in every village and knights as big as Colossi in their cities to keep the peace. If the Jattaravkalt survived, it's because they know how to hide. Even Walver will have a hard time tracking them."

"I have faith in you," I whisper. She nods, her sight set on something far away.

After a minute of silence, I start thinking of my Giant mother, and how she had to return to Jattaria when my Titan father died. I hated her for so long. How could she break the Oath and leave our country in the first place? She was a traitor.

Here I am, doing just the same thing. Maybe she wasn't a traitor. Maybe she did it all for me.

She chuckles. "You are a serious young man, Agnor. *Franvarande?*"

"*Ja*, I am preoccupied. It's all those promises I made. I am alive because of my mother's sacrifice, and I promised I would not waste my life. I am what I am thanks to my country and those I lost." I try to scratch a ghost itch deep in my chest.

"There is an emptiness here. All I wanted was to be a soldier. Now," I say, gesturing around. "Traitor."

"I die, we rise." She considers something. "I'll find a place where we can belong. That's my promise to you." She whips the horse even though his pace is steady.

Her words appease me. It feels good to put myself in the hands of another once again. It was Jattaria and my leaders before; it's this rogue warrior now.

"You can call me Yana when it's just you and me." She elbows me softly. The sun makes her eyes look like molten gold. "You remind me of someone. He wasn't as big and not as shy, but his eyes were almost the same shade of green." She bites her lower lip, eyeing me. "Someone I knew before I became the Vulture." She doesn't smile anymore.

"Thanks, Yana." I whisper her name like a secret. Being so close to her is distracting. I almost forget she is a killer.

"One day, you may take Walver's place," she whispers back. "He is not himself lately." She squeezes my healthy thigh again, letting her hand linger.

My pulse quickens. "Yes, Yana."

Later that day, we find a depression among the fields to make camp. A small fire cooks the food we stole from the farm. We lay rocks around the firepit to put them under our covers later; few things are as pleasant as a warm bed on an evening full of stars. Emma and I would sneak out of school during nights like these and sleep among the trees with just the starry heaven above us. We only knew three constellations: Magnitude, Gratitude, and Servitude. We made up the others.

"It was a night like this months ago, by the sycamore tree just past the training grounds, when I went down on one knee and asked her to marry me." She took the ring I made, gave me a lock of her hair so I could make the ring now hanging on my neck. We could not stop smiling.

It was the happiest night in my life, says her memory.

Flying sparks distract me. Walver and Nefri crouch before the flames, Nefri chopping pieces of meat. He slices the fat and tosses it aside.

"You animal!" squeals Walver, slapping Nefri across the face. He picks up the dirty pieces of fat with his even dirtier hands.

Nefri glares at him. "It's just fat!"

"The best part!" He puts a pan on the fire and the fat inside it. It starts to sizzle immediately. "You'll see." Walver throws in a pinch of salt, herbs, and dry lemon peelings he stole from the family. The air is a poem of scents.

"You could have just said it, Walver." The eye on the brutalized side of Nefri's face wells up. He rubs his cheek, then fixes his messy black hair.

I turn back to the night sky. Shooting stars fly through the black heavens, the moon shines fiercely, and the soft wind sings.

"Here, Agnor," says Nefri after a while. Walver's handprint is red on his cheek. "Eat before you turn in." He hands me one of the bowls he brought and sits by me. "You seem to be getting better, man."

"I see your Virtue, Nefri."

He watches me as if contemplating what to say. "Smart move, getting close to Yana."

"We are not close, and it wasn't a move," I respond quickly, biting into the hot meat. "You are a First Circle, too, right?" I say with a full mouth. "Did we train together after Trials?"

He exhales noisily. Maybe his Trials were as bad as mine. Maybe he also had to send a friend to her death.

"*Ratt.* I saw you during drills. You're hard to miss, towering over everyone else. Where did you go to school before?"

"Ivai." My face gets hot. That's the worst of all Schools of War and most orphans in Jattaria end up there. His accent tells me he studied in the Primary Lands, where rich and influential families send their children. "You?"

"Solitude," he grunts, confirming my thoughts. "It isn't like they say," he adds hurriedly, throwing an annoyed gesture with his hand. "You were with the Intruders during the attack. How did you survive? We saw your squad get destroyed on top of the Fifth Wall."

"I jumped."

"You jumped -" His eyes gleam with the bit of light our fire offers.

"I could have stayed and gotten shredded."

"*Ja*, I'd jump too." He takes the last bite and chews it for a while. "You went to work on Walver's face last night. He probably looks better now," he chuckles. "Is that why Yana took you under her wing?"

I pull back an inch and look at him sideways. "He was beating that man. And I'm not under her wing."

He puts his hands up as if surrendering. "I didn't mean to offend you. I'm just curious why Walver is being treated this way after being Yana's second for years. That's all. Enjoy the rest of your meal, man." He slaps my shoulder, stands up, and holds out one hand. A tiny red and green ball wrapped in transparent paper sits on his palm.

"Candy?" I ask, taking it.

His eyes get shiny. "Yeah. My little sister gave me some when I went to say goodbye."

He leaves and strikes up a conversation with Ingrid and Vinz, who were sitting together until Nefri wedged in between, making everyone around laugh. He starts muttering jokes that have them cackling soon after.

Is it at my expense?

It wouldn't be the first time I was laughed at: no parents, no last name, no money. Being a half-Titan didn't help. Sometimes, the mocking got so bad I had to stop it with my fists. Emma would always be there after, healing my knuckles with her soft hands and whispering loving words. *We only need each other,* she'd say.

I pocket the candy next to my mother's letters and the vows I never read to Emma.

On the edge of the camp, barely touched by the fire's amber light, sits Zeeri against a tree. She is tied and gagged again.

Poor girl.

I look away and stare at the stars once more. One by one, they fade until I succumb to an uneasy slumber -

- that asphyxia interrupts.

Can't I get a full night of sleep?

A strong hand stuffs something down my throat while my arms are pinned to the ground. I try to punch and knee my attacker, but I'm trapped under my covers.

"Be still. You don't want my knife to stab you accidentally, do you?" A piercing pain tortures my side. "I don't like you.

I don't like how close you are to Yana. I don't like that you got away from me, you dumb beast. I'd chop you to bits if it weren't for her. One wrong move and I will gut you and feed you your own entrails. Understood?"

I mumble an affirmative response.

Walver's odor and voice give him away. I doubt he wanted to hide it, anyway. He pushes the blunt end of a weapon into my ribs, and I twist with excruciating pain. "And stay out of my way."

Suddenly, I am free to move. I don't.

Much later, I get my breathing under control and manage to sleep again.

It isn't restful. It isn't peaceful. I dream of winged reapers flying above me at night and angry Traitors with shiny daggers surrounding me. When I look to the sky, the threats on the ground come closer. When I look down, the flap of black wings gets louder. Wherever I turn, danger creeps in from my blind spot.

Death stalks me. Waiting. Watching.

CHAPTER SEVEN

KORPS

Mounted Korps

Agnor

The next day, on a side road headed Cold

One lonely cloud streaks across the blue sky, and the breeze smells of harvest on the road to Sargena. I can almost taste the sweet corn in the air. Maybe destiny is showing us the right way to go. Gods carve our paths in indecipherable and subtle ways. Although sometimes they aren't subtle and send winged reapers to burn it all with hellfire. I look over my shoulder and up at the skies. Those flying worms are up there, somewhere, searching for us.

I pull up the collar of my worn shirt to fight a shiver. The fabric is worn and rough, with caked dirt and sweat. We look nothing like the soldiers we once were, wearing only stolen clothes to blend in. An Army soldier doesn't belong in the Tertiary Lands, far from the Edgeslag, so we hid our armor and weapons under the cargo in the wagon.

Only Walver and Yana kept theirs. "In case there's a fight," she said, but I know better. She also wants the two of them to have superiority over us to prevent a mutiny.

The cart's wooden wheels crunch along the packed ground on the street. The horse's hide gleams with sweat, but our pace is slow and easy on him.

Saxon and Vinz lead the way, playing a song about exiled warriors. Vinz keeps the beat using his chest as a drum while Saxon sings. I watch the shapes he makes with his fingers on the fretboard and how he strums the strings. I try to understand and memorize them.

So when you march, you charge with your swords.
And when you die, you die for your lords.
-Mighty Aftergods-

So when you leave, because you are alive,

forget what you've seen and hold your heads high.

-New hope is nearby-

A few steps behind us, Nefri chats with Wanda, a tiny blonde with sharp indigo eyes.

"Who are you thinking of?" Yana blocks the sun with her hand. Her little finger goes up delicately, an indicator she grew up in the Primary Lands.

I inhale slowly.

She grins. "Oh. Young love. Nothing's stronger than that. I miss that feeling." She eyes me with a playful smile, touching my hand.

"Someone I lost," I reply, ignoring her closeness and wondering how she may read me so easily.

"Someone you loved? You might not be as innocent as I thought!"

I chuckle dryly. "She was very close, yes." And I think of Emma's laughter and how her hands were a little cooler than mine. She would always torture me, trying to steal my body heat, especially at night.

"*Was.* I'm sorry to hear that, Agnor. Tell me about her."

"We met years ago, so young. We went to school and the Trials together. I only graduated because of her. I was someone else before Trials. What a horrible event. Nothing about it is right."

I tighten my fists instinctively, my broken nails digging into my palms. Jattaria is insulted; shields go up.

"Oh, relax, Agnor." She rubs my shoulder. "But forcing children to fight one another for a chance to join the Army? That's culling."

"Culling," I savor the word. "What is that?"

"Sorry, I forgot how limited your education is. It must be appalling in the Tertiary Lands."

"I did well enough in class," I reply curtly.

"How many books have you read?"

"Three," I answer and my chest swells. "Jattarian Code of Virtues, Elementary Wisdom, and Battle Manual."

"The usual."

"It's all we had in the library," I answer, my chest deflating.

She clicks her tongue. "I have read many books, some stolen from the Edge. They call our Trials a culling. One half of the class fights the other, only the strong survive, only the strongest remain. The rest are made Appeasement Offers and die."

"We don't know if they die."

"They are called Appeasement Offers, Agnor. We load them in the Dark Runner and send them as a sacrifice to the After-gods. They die." Her expression is somber again.

"Why would you need to read more than those three books?" I insist. "All true knowledge is in them. Everything else is a lie," I say, sensing how weak my arguments sound. Emma would scold me. All I know crumbled down when the very officers we swore to follow used forbidden fire and brought the demons. To challenge the Aftergods in such a way, while knowing soldiers would be the ones who pay, is the worst of betrayals.

"And I guess Jattaria holds all truths. Isn't that convenient? Wake up, my boy. Let go of those lies before they kill you."

Truths outside the great books? It's hard to think there's more after Jattaria, but it is what Emma believed. She wanted to travel, even though it was forbidden. Her whole heart was set on this. "There is a whole world out there," I say, quoting her.

Yana closes her eyes with a smile, nodding softly. "Yes. That's exactly right, Agnor. Well said."

"Someone is coming," calls Sil, one of the more experienced soldiers in our group.

Yana pulls the reins and takes a long look at the tiny dot and a small cloud of dust in the distance. "A horse or a vehicle, far but approaching." She stands on the seat and puts a hand on my head for balance. Her plates clank as she moves, reminding me that if there's a fight, I will be very unprotected.

"Sil, take my place," says Yana, watching the approaching dot. "The rest of you get off the road and hide in the cornfields. We will follow the wagon and remain out of sight."

"Yes, Boss," Sil says. Sil is about thirty and excellent at staying out of everyone's way. She lets her auburn hair fall over her neck to cover a long scar under her jaw and changes her expression to something sweet and innocent. It's like she is a different person.

Yana barks orders and walks around the wagon. "Walver, grab weapons and go to the right of the road with these four. And keep Zeeri quiet. I'll take the left."

Walver obeys, disappearing into the crops. Sil and I get the horse going at a slow pace. Minutes stretch while we wait for the travelers to reach us. "It's a couple of riders. Maybe three," I whisper when I can make out their shapes in the day's fading light.

"Ice me," curses Sil. "They must be a patrol. Few can afford a horse, let alone three as big as those."

The sun reflects on a piece of metal: armor or a weapon. "Regler Korps," I announce.

"Definitely. Shhh...act normal," orders Yana from behind the foliage.

A minute goes by, and the two or possibly three riders are actually a team of five officers. They were riding in formation, the two Korps at the back hidden by those in the front. "Oh, freezing death."

"I'll do the talking," says Sil, putting a hand on mine. She plays with a pretty wooden ring, sliding it up and down her finger.

"You are married?"

She turns to me with a pained smile that reaches her eyes. Her gaze wanders in the mid-distance, then centers on me. "I am. I can tell you about him and my daughter later," she whispers with a smile and touches my forearm. "Shush now."

One of the officers pulls up next to me just a moment after. The stink of sweat mixes with the horses' smell.

The patrol rides by and turns, blocking the road. Sil pulls the reins and the horse stops. I grab the side of the wagon, trying to focus on its smooth wooden surface instead of the threats approaching.

Two Regler Korps stay at a distance, checking the immediate vicinity; the other three approach. They have their light repeating -crossbows pointed in our general direction. Their muscular horses breathe heavily and snort.

"How's it going," says the officer. Not a question, but a dry greeting. His helmet swivels smoothly on his shoulders. He must be scanning every inch of the cart and cargo.

"Nice and quiet. What can we do for you, sir?" Sil's voice is silky, her heavy accent is different from before.

The officer's visor blocks most of his face. I try to find a weak spot on his protective gear, but his dark cloak covers him almost completely. I doubt there's an opening anyway, and it doesn't matter either. I can't fight them in this state without weapons or protection.

"Where are you headed?"

"Back home," she replies sweetly. "We got all this stuff from a relative who passed last month." She looks at the bundles on the back of the wagon.

"Deserters were coming this way. Noticed anything?"

Sil shrugs. "You are the first people we've seen today, sir." Her tone is honey, no longer shy.

He nods and looks around. "Be careful, *ja*? They are around here."

"Give 'em hell."

"We will."

Sil smiles. "I see your Virtue, sir."

The officer touches his helmet and turns around. He signals at the others and they resume their march.

"Deserters!" a shrill voice screams from the crops.

Zeeri.

The officers aim their crossbows at Sil and me, but the Traitors send a wave of arrows first. One officer gets catapulted off his saddle when his horse stands on its back legs. The rest shift to a tight formation. The horses back up, stomping the ground. Another officer falls. His horse rolls on him, bones crack, and the officer screams at the top of his lungs.

"Get them!" screams the leader as he aims and shoots at me. I dive off the wagon and hit the road with my side. Red and purple take over my vision, but I push through the pain and roll under our vehicle. A storm of cries and weapons clashing erupts on this lonely road while I cower behind a wheel. Grains of sand scrape the skin off my wrists and lodge into my flesh.

Horses squeal and kick while men and women scream and cut at each other. I watch from under the cart as the Traitors charge and bring down the heavily armored Korps officers. Nefri and Walver wrap one with a rope and pull him to the ground. The knight goes down swinging, making them eat armored knuckles and elbows until he is neutralized. Even then, he struggles and screams insults.

Yana and Wanda have better luck with their mark, who only manages to land one hard blow on Wanda after losing control of his crossbow. The others gang up on the remaining officer.

The melee lifted a thin cloud of dirt. It settles and reveals the aftermath. The Traitors are bent over, forearms resting on their knees. They breathe hard and sweat harder, their clothes torn and their hair disheveled.

I crawl out from my hiding spot as Yana screams new orders. Arsen sees me and comes to help me. "Hang on, Big Guy." Her teeth are bloody. She checks me out quickly, then takes off her bandana to wipe her brow. Her hair flies freely into my face. "Can you climb up on your own?"

"*Ja*, I'm fine."

She nods and goes to help the others. Walver is bleeding from a cut under his eye. He looks about, panting with his tongue out and an idiotic smile. Nefri has a split lip and a bolt loosely hanging from a flap of flesh on his back, which Wanda is trying to address. Saxon lost a chunk of his ear and Vinz laughs at him while bleeding from a flattened nose. The rest are in similar shape, leaning against each other or sitting on the ground, trying to recover.

Uma triages everyone quickly, instructing Arsen and Saxon on how to treat the many wounds she finds.

"I got too used to fighting little humans from the Edge," says Ingrid. Her long black hair looks like an osprey's nest.

Siff checks her for injuries. "You are fine, Inny." She touches her friend's face with a sigh of relief. "You have to be more careful next time." Siff twists her back one way and then the opposite to crack her spine.

Vinz wraps Ingrid in his arms. They kiss and cuddle under a blanket. They must have forgotten they are married to other people. How quickly we forget the promises we made.

"Our enemies will only get bigger. Keep that in mind," says Yana. "Take their gear and tie them on their horses. Quickly," she orders. She returns to the wagon. "Walver! Make sure the girl doesn't do that again."

"Why didn't you jump down, Sil?" I ask as I sit next to her on the wagon. "Sil?" I shake her shoulder, but she doesn't respond. Her expression is relaxed and distant. Her mouth hangs open, blood trickles down her chin. The arrow's feather comes into sight when I lean forward, hidden between her teeth. The bolt had gone into her mouth, through her neck, and nailed her to the seat. "No," I murmur.

Yana yanks Sil from the cart. She lets the corpse fall, rips off a piece of Sil's clothing, and proceeds to clean the seat. The sound of blood against the fabric makes my skin crawl.

"Walver!" she calls. He comes dragging a beaten Zeeri, who looks worse than those of us who fought. "Freezing death, I meant to gag and tie her!"

Walver shrugs and shoves the crying girl toward us, making her fall. "I'll interrogate the Korps and find a safe way out of Jattaria."

Yana stares at him. "Make camp first; then you can get to work."

"Aye, Boss." He walks away and relays orders to the Traitors.

CHAPTER EIGHT

ALMA MATER

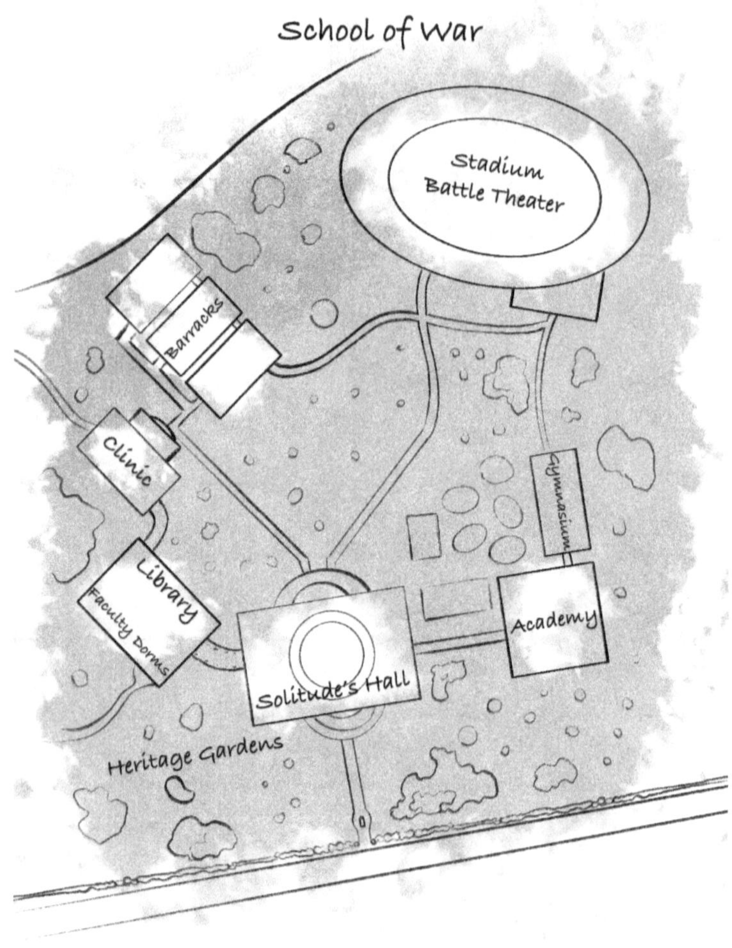

Thyra

Days later, in the ancient city of Solitude

Creamy clouds dance with the soft morning breeze. Birds of

all colors dive from the heights to play on the currents of thin air so high in the Kjede Mountains. A multitude of young Jattarians pass me to enter Solitude's School of War. This is the best academy in Jattaria, the one that offers the most honors, and the hardest to get selected for.

Kora-Elena stretches as she wakes up from her hours-long rest. Her claws pierce my clothing and scratch my skin. She didn't mind the bumpy ride or the noisy overnight train trip, but I did. Or maybe it was the fear and anxiety. I push the feelings aside. I spent all my money getting here; I have to make Selection, or I will have to walk hundreds of miles to get back home.

Solitude!

The incredible city was named after the Colossus Knight of Solitude's Virtue. The last Colossi abandoned the city after the Division and went down Cold, deep into the Ice Lands. Now it belongs to us. Unless the Edgens build the Sixth Wall. In that case, most of what's left of Jattaria will be lost.

Kora-Elena's claws dig into my flesh. I reach into my bag for some dried meat and feed it to her. She almost bites my fingers off. "Kora-Elena Ener! Behave!" She eats quickly, yawns, and extends the black spikes on her back. She starts snoring moments later. She is the only thing keeping me from breaking. I would explode with rage, but then who would care for her? She behaves so poorly no one would take her.

I walk past the wide iron gates and follow a cobblestone road to the main hall. Hundreds of students and applicants walk toward the large doors. Gardens roll for acres and acres on both sides of the path. Colorful trees grow here and there, and marble statues of our heroes stand on black pedestals everywhere. These represent the school's Golden Blades and national legends. One of Mother's apprentices has a statue here, too. Only the Highest has more honor than those depicted here.

There's a large white marble block almost as tall as me in the middle of the cobblestone path. The Spear of the Tried rests on top. Signs of age mar the block, but no rust corrupts the silver weapon. People going into school pass it and, as hurried as they may feel, they all give it at least a moment of attention. Some even reach out and touch it.

I grab it.

I am a Giant, the daughter of a strong new family line. I had dreamed of a peaceful life, but I will sacrifice it for glory.

The tradition is well known. A Tried Jattarian must lift the spear with one hand and hold it up while reciting the Oath. Only then does one truly graduate from Solitude's School of War, they say.

Few actually do it.

I will be one of those few.

I try to heft this massive weapon with all my might, but the spear barely leaves the marble surface. "I have to do this!" I grunt and give it my all. The spear hovers over the stone for less than a second then escapes my grip and falls with a jarring clang.

Students laugh at me. "Just a kid playing soldier," says an older girl to her friend. "Someone's little sister, never mind her. As I was saying, I must get my challenge this year. I'll find the Hidden Ring if I have to."

"Again with that, Lana," responds her friend. "You'll die lost in the mountains searching for a school myth." Their discussion fades into the crowd.

Everyone is larger, older, more experienced. I have never even fought anyone other than Mother. Nobody applies at thirteen for a reason: it's suicide.

I am dead anyway.

The man registering names looks at me again. He shakes his head and searches around the vast hall. I follow his gaze. Thousands line up to have a shot at being selected for Solitude's School of War. If I am to redeem my family's dishonor, only the best school would do.

"Hurry up!" yells the family waiting behind me. They are so close I sense their body heat.

The clerk hums impatiently. "Where are your parents?" He searches the main hall again, and I stupidly look around with him. White columns hold the high ceiling above us. Red, black, and white banners hang from the pale walls. Paintings of the Highest and his predecessors look down from above, watching over their children with the love only a father can feel.

"I am alone," I answer finally.

"You are too young," mumbles the clerk, refusing to jot down my name. He shoos me away.

"There is no minimum age to apply, sir. Selection's only requirement is to be less than eighteen years old. My name is Thyra Ener, and I want to apply." My voice is shaky. I am trying hard not to lose my patience.

"Get lost, kid! You'll get hurt or killed if I let you in."

"Ener?" repeats someone from behind him. A scarred older man who is missing half an ear approaches the desk. He has been overlooking the whole inscription process from behind, but he now stands by the table. "Did you say Ener?"

"*Ja*, Instructor Klausen. She wants to apply for Selection."

"Lagas Ener's daughter?"

"Yes, sir," I reply. Mother is well known, and my last name is fairly new. There are not many of us.

The white-haired man zeroes on me. "Thyra. You look just like your mother. And you are here because of your brother." My blood turns to ice. "Freezing death, girl," he curses. "Dying won't bring him back to life."

My heart works again. "It doesn't matter. Please, write my name on your list." I tap a blank line on the ledger where a name could fit. My finger should be threatening, but it shakes despite my efforts to steady it.

The moment goes on for an eternity. Instructor Klausen sighs. "Go on. The rules are clear."

I take my sealed packet and move forward. Signs on the walls guide the students, who walk down the corridors like cattle. There is a list of exams I must take in the next two days, and the first one is a written knowledge test.

Kora-Elena doesn't even wake up when I leave her on the bed assigned to me. She curls up in a ball by the pillow and keeps sleeping. I leave the barracks and find Klausen waiting for me. He scratches his clean-shaven chin and clears his throat.

"Miss Ener," he says finally. "I don't doubt your mother trained you well, but these are serious tests. If you pass, you will face life or death fights. Your name is written and your courage is exemplary, but there's no shame in walking away today and coming back in a few years when you are more, uhm. Developed." Instructor Klausen struggled to choose his words. My small frame must be underwhelming to a seven-foot-tall Giant like him.

"I can't wait that long."

"Just like your mother. Lagas was my apprentice, *wussten sie?*"

I stop and face him. Is this the man who made Mother cold and distant?

"She didn't tell me much." The insolence in my voice makes me blush. I can't hold his gaze for longer than a second at a time.

"I see." His starched gray uniform almost squeaks when he moves. The many medals on his chest ring and shine. "Young applicant, I am sure you will be selected. When you do, seek me. For now, please hear this." He leans closer. "The most important stage is the final one. Save your energy."

I nod, study his face for a moment, then move toward the auditorium where the first test takes place. Inside, about two hundred students are waiting to begin. A young assistant hands me the four page exam. I find a seat at a wooden desk with some very obscene carvings on the surface. Someone also tried their hand at a Full Jattarian Shield and failed miserably: the star is crooked, the circle more like an egg, and the diamond is almost a triangle.

When all the seats are taken, the instructor waves at the red-haired aide and closes the doors. Applicants left outside will have to wait for the next round. "Begin," commands the instructor.

We scribble on our papers as the minutes go by, pouring onto those few sheets everything we managed to learn from First School and family.

Who is the most precious being in the land?

Who are the enemies of Jattaria?

What is the greatest honor?

Only a fool would answer these incorrectly. The Highest. The Edgens. To die serving Jattaria. The following twenty questions are about as easy as these and are basically part of our Anthem.

The second half of the exam must be significantly more complex. This test is meant to measure applicants' potential. These answers are the beginning of my career. I could serve my ten years following orders as a Circle, leading on the battleground as a Diamond, or strategizing as a Star. My path through the Jattarian Army's ranks starts today.

The pressure builds in the pit of my stomach. I bite my lip and grip my pencil tight to keep it from trembling. I flip to the next page and read the first question.

What is the simplest way to take an enemy armored mobile unit?

I skim through the other twenty-three questions and shake my head. "Describe a battle medical assessment procedure, list basic life support measures for battle wounds," I read with a whisper. "List components of a standard repeating-crossbow.

Describe ballistic calculations for basic Army weaponry," I go on. I've been assembling crossbows since I was four and practicing projectile trajectory calculus with Mother for about as long.

This is stupid.

I finish quickly and turn the papers in before most applicants. Lots of kids exit the auditorium with their heads hanging low.

"I got less than half right. I'll be lucky if they let me clean the bathrooms," complains a muscular girl. "I always get confused listing the Jattarian Hierarchy and each rank's function."

"I heard that isn't so important," says her male friend, who stares at her with adoring eyes. "You'll do well."

"I am seventeen already. If I don't pass, I'll have to try one of the crappy schools of the interior with all those kids from the Secondary and Tertiary lands. Or try to join the Regler Korps, ugh." She pushes her palms into her eyes and sobs against the concrete wall. She slides down until she is sitting on the floor.

Her friend's face shows a trace of disgust at the idea. "Surely you can't fall that low. They'll let you in this time." But he doesn't sound so sure.

How dumb is she to have failed several times? Don't they go through all those questions with their parents every week?

The strength and speed tests are designed for more developed applicants, but Mother prepared me mercilessly, and the work at Dad's shop wasn't light either.

"Aftergods, let that be enough," I pray.

I stand in a line of about a dozen applicants while the proctors perform a physical examination. The cold floor tiles numb my bare feet. The electric lights are bright, almost painful. There is a faint chemical scent that I know will stay in my nostrils for hours. Posters with colorful illustrations of the human body cover the white walls. One compares Titans, Giants, and Edgens. Titans stand eight feet tall, Giants are about a foot shorter, and Edgens are below six feet tall. There are diagrams of bones, muscles, blood vessels, nerves. Mother drew similar ones during her creepy lessons to show me how to neutralize enemies and aid injured allies.

"You're just a kid," says the proctor before me.

"We are all kids, sir."

She grunts. "Go on, Ener." She hands me a paper with her signature and sends me to the exercise machines. The girl before me does pull-ups, bench presses, and leg presses under observation. I count her reps and study the proctors' expressions. The applicant gets an immediate pass. I perform about twenty percent worse than the previous applicant.

Two proctors discuss my results and give me the seal to move on after a brief discussion. "We hoped for a higher score, Ener. You should have tried harder."

"But I passed."

"Yes," says one hesitantly.

"Then why would I try harder? That would only make me tired."

The proctor shakes his head. "Be careful tomorrow, little one," he says, sending me off.

Making my way to the barracks through hundreds of loud students. They are obnoxious, discussing how to celebrate making it this far. The bitter smell of teenage excitement and way too much perfume is vomit inducing. Partying and feasting the night before the final stage of Selection? Absolutely not.

Jattaria wants good warriors, and its people love watching the next potential hero. One needs to deliver a spectacle. It's how the system works. I would love to party and eat all that delicious food I saw in the main hall, but I can't. One bite of the wrong food could get me sick and at a disadvantage tomorrow.

Instead of following the flow, I drag my feet to bed, lie down, and put my head on the rough pillow. There are a few applicants and students in the barracks, talking excitedly on their beds as they eat contraband food or play knights with fancy playing cards. I sigh and roll inside the sheets. My bed is scratchy, stinks, and it's also the softest thing I've felt today. Many sleep in hotels and in much better beds. Only the rich and the influential can afford such luxury, and I am neither.

Kora-Elena climbs on my belly and inside the covers, being extra harsh as punishment for leaving her alone all day. She settles her long, cool body on mine and proceeds to steal my body heat. Her cute snores lull me to sleep.

I curl up tight and close my eyes shut. With any luck, I will be asleep before the crushing thoughts of Dad and Nefri come rushing in.

Chapter Nine

A Price

Thyra

The next day, in Solitude

Winged reapers come flying to tear me apart. Those creatures from legend pull my limbs and dig at my organs for hours while a Korps officer questions me about Nefri. I won't give him up; I won't confess, even though the black monsters pick through my flesh and eat me alive. Fear but no pain. This is only a nightmare.

I wake up covered in sweat. Guilt, that's all. I harbored a criminal, and now I must pay. He has gone and forsaken everything my family stands for. I check myself quickly, using my issued sword as a mirror. I hope the black circles around my eyes are misleading and that I actually got some rest last night. I need all my energy today.

I shiver when my feet touch the cold concrete floor. Kora-Elena leaves my lap and makes a cave under my pillow. I reach for my bag and wrap my limbs with bandages and padding to soften the many blows I will receive today.

A battle is won before it starts.

The memory of Mother's advice is louder than the clamor of hundreds of applicants getting ready. I ignore them and go through today's tests. First, Applicants fight against coaches to check on general skill level and get rid of the scum. Second, two teams face off in a scenario prepared to rate communication and teamwork and get rid of more scum. Third is the elimination matches, in which we fight one-on-one against other applicants.

And the last of the scum leaves.

Once an inch of soft armor covers most of my body, I bend and twist my limbs to ensure my movement isn't too restricted.

I feel as stiff as Woody, my practice dummy. The steel plates will make it even worse. "I can't fight like this, Kora-Elena." I quickly shed a layer of padding and slip back into armor. "Fortitude, be with me," I whisper.

With my eyes closed, I let my other senses make a picture of what's around me. Workers prepare the stadium. By sunrise, everything should be ready. I hear them talking, walking, putting things together. Thousands will watch applicants bleed for a spot in school.

The sounds fade away. Pain lingers but becomes irrelevant. The doubt and fear, which I picture as pulsating yellow clouds, shrink until they're nothing but specks floating in space. My mind and body are quiet.

I've tapped into Fortitude's virtue before, feeling its power in my muscles and spirit, but there was never a reason other than facing my teachers and mother. Until today, every minute of torturous training was pointless to me.

Now, I am overwhelmed with purpose. Whatever the price, honor must be mine. That's how I save my father, my mother, and me from torture and death. That's how I bring honor to redeem my family.

The sheer size of this stadium takes my breath away. Banners hang on the walls around the arena where the applicants fight. Red, white, and black flags wave, displaying the Jattarian colors. Twenty thousand faces look down from those seats, cheering, eating, and enjoying the bloody games. Applicants step into one of the many rings on the sand to fight their qualifying bouts under the scrutinizing gaze of judges, students, and the general public.

An instructor grabs my shoulder and points at one of the many rings on the ground. "That's you, Ener. Good luck."

I walk to my first opponent of the day, spear and shield in hand.

The large boy smirks. He is an older student, probably volunteering for credits and a chance to be an instructor after graduation. He blows air through his half-helmet and shakes his head, measuring me. "Haven't seen one so small in a while. Maybe ever."

"Yes, sir." I wonder how many more times I'll hear the same comment.

He tilts his head. Maybe he is confused by my answer. "I am supposed to only *test* your technical skills, but there is only so much I can hold back. You sure you're ready?"

"*Ja.*" I step forward and let my leather boots sink into the pebbles of the extensive arena floor. The sun shines through the Kjede Mountain's thin air, hits my armor, and reflects on the sandy surface before me.

A hundred other applicants are fighting their qualifying matches already. They are noisy and distracting, one more than the others. Just a few rings away from mine, an applicant with a red scarf glides around his much larger opponent, dismantling his offenses a bit at a time. His style is art. That applicant is definitely being selected.

Don't let anything distract you!

"Ready?"

"Yes, sir."

"I apologize in advance." He hits his shield to start the match. "Five rounds." He tosses his head to move dark hair out of his gray eyes. His helmet makes the effort futile.

He steps forward with a spear in hand. His stance is loose, maybe too relaxed. I would usually spar and test him, but perhaps -

I swing my shield up and lunge from under it. The spearhead strikes his weapon arm. The clash sounds like my hammer smashing iron. I can't believe this simple move worked.

The spear is stuck in the armor at his elbow joint. I jerk it free. "Your point, Ener," he says, eyes wide. He rubs the spot I struck, shakes his arm, and tries closing his hand slowly. Hopefully, I debilitated him.

He hits the shield again; his stance is different now. Proper Fortitude Style, one of Mother's first lessons. He steps forward, swinging his spear and charging with his shield right after. He is still holding back, surely. His maneuvers are basic.

Lose a battle if it gives you the war.

If I wound his pride, he might fight without restraint.

So I take the hit.

Crash!

My helmet flies off my head and rolls on the sand. I lose my footing and fall on my back. His blunt spearhead is aimed at my bloody nose when I open my eyes. Tears of pure pain roll down my face as my sight returns. I didn't miss this part of fighting, but Mother made me bleed plenty of times. My whole body would be sore and bruised for weeks after each match. This is nothing.

"Your point, sir." I stand up slowly and collect my helmet. I empty it of sand before I put it on again. Other applicants enter and leave the rings around mine, some victorious, most defeated. The crowd cheers, following their favorites.

Has anyone in the audience placed a bet in my favor?

Who cares? Get back to fighting!

The third round commences. He deflects my light strikes for a minute, then commits to a big swing. I evade and land a devastating hit under the waist. He folds into the blunt tip of my spear. He curses, squats, and then curses some more.

Mother would never let a strike like that go through.

He starts the next round and stays at the circle's edge, carefully planning his steps. Each boot is well planted into the sandy ground. His spear follows me constantly as I close in. I throw my shield at him like a disc, get in range when he blocks it, and set up in a tenth of a second: knees cocked and ready to spring, arm extended back and prepared to sting with the spear. I jump to compensate for the height difference and finish him with a downward thrust to his neck.

Klunk!

That's my version of the deadliest move in the style of Fortitude. Mother is a purist, but even she would appreciate how well it worked.

The young aide takes a minute after that painful blow. "I am sorry, sir," I apologize, realizing how much he's suffering. I was often left crying during my training. I offer my hand and help him up.

"Well fought!" he concedes, panting. "That's some old-school dancing, Ener."

"My mom taught me."

"Some mother you must have."

I touch my knuckles to my forehead to show respect and follow the line of victors leaving the arena.

"Don't get cocky," he says as I walk away.

Hours later, I find myself in the middle of the next test, being shot at from every angle. The player to my right is eliminated before we reach cover, and a small group ahead of us is also taken out.

"Freezing death! Three down already!" I grunt.

I suck hot air and run even faster through boulders and obstacles. The arena is now a desert scenario with two teams of ten fighting for domination.

"You three!" I yell to teammates a few steps behind. "Move behind that box and suppress it so I can pinch from the left!" It's a simple maneuver that could eliminate an annoying enemy posted in a strong position. That would give us a break and some space to rearrange our attack.

The three applicants nod, transition, and begin firing bolts to give me a window. Somehow, they are following my orders without question. I dash and make my move. The pebbles roll under my feet as I run at my target. As soon as he is in sight, I stop and bring up the old crossbow they gave me for this exercise. Good thing I cleaned and oiled it before the match.

Snap! The bolt flies straight into the opponent's shoulder, bouncing off the steel plate and spinning out of sight.

Around me, the audience roars. The master of ceremonies screams through the amplifiers. "Black helmets take one opponent out and advance! Well done, applicant Thyra Ener! White helmets started strong with three early eliminations, but now they're retreating! It's seven versus nine!"

I zig-zag, dodge, and dive while advancing deeper into White Helmets territory, finding cover just as a handful of arrows whistle past me. I reload, peek to place my next target, and attempt to channel every Virtue in a half-second prayer. With honed efficiency, I zero my iron sights on my target and release the latch. The buttstock pushes back into my shoulder, and the bolt flies up.

Thunk!

The flat arrowhead bounces off my opponent's armor, and he throws his arms up, surrendering. An aide escorts him out of the battle stage.

"Great shot by Thyra Ener!" screams the announcer. "It's eight White Helmets left against seven Black Helmets! Scratch that! Two more White Helmets are out, Jattaria! What a marvelous spectacle we have before us!"

My team rushes to fill the gaps left by the opponents. "Hold your positions!" I yell, realizing what's about to happen.

It's too late. Two teammates get shot on their backs by hidden White Helmets. My team spreads out while three White Helmets perch atop a small wooden tower in the center.

"Black team is down to five after a terrible tactical move!" yells the announcer.

They'll win the match if I don't do something, but I feel clumsy even without the padding under the plates.

Forget the armor!

I unhook the arm plates and let them fall to the sand. My range of movement is twice what it was before. Breathe. One, two, three, go! I dash out of cover, climb a small rock, and bring the crossbow up. The Woodstock clanks against my helmet as

I move it to my shoulder. I aim higher and to the left to compensate for wind and gravity. My target is only half a helmet, but that's as good as it gets.

Snap!

The bolt whistles as it pierces the air and hits the player.

"Fancy move by the Black team just when the White Helmets were taking hold of the field!" yells the master of ceremonies.

The other opponents on that tower turn their attention to me. *Thack!* One gets shot from the right side of the field. My teammates are finally getting their act together. The surviving player jumps off the tower and gets tackled by one absurdly large Black Helmet player.

"Triple elimination! Five versus four! Black team has White retreating!"

"Hold!" I yell, raising my hand to get their attention from across the scenario. I signal a move, something basic from Battle Maneuvers. They look at each other, shaking their heads. Too bad. A Sledge Power Run would be a sure way to kill that single opponent near them. "Push forward, close to the edge!" I scream. This they understand.

"Black team is on the offensive, and they take out one more!" booms the announcer. "Oh! It seems like the Black team lost one, too! It's a trade, and we have four versus three!"

This is my chance.

I charge from the opposite side, shooting mid-race. Hit! But now they know I am coming.

There's nothing they can do now.

I dive between them, slashing savagely as I land. I dodge their clumsy attacks, easily finding ways to cut high and low in a rushed attempt to perform Solitude's Last Stand. Metal clashes against metal, ringing loudly in my ears. Mother would be embarrassed with such a brute display, but they eat blunt steel and the heel of my boots. I deliver a dozen strikes within seconds, leaving them crying and begging me to stop.

"Three kills by Thyra Ener!" the announcer says, his voice echoing loudly through the stadium. "Black team is victorious!"

"Yeah!" I lift my trembling hands, blood dripping from a wound on my elbow. I hit armor during the melee. It would be nothing if I had not gotten rid of the plates.

I'll deal with that later. A little cut is worth this.

I walk past those we eliminated. I got six of them. They are all bloody and covered in dirt, and some have cracked noses or broken bones. I can cause so much suffering.

Cut, kill, destroy.

"Black Helmets win the match!" roars the announcer. "Thyra Ener! What a daring applicant! What a great match, ladies and gentlemen! This young one is a true Jattarian!"

The rest of the teams go through the second phase of the day. Those who failed will try Selection another season or apply to a lesser school. Only the best make it into Solitude's School.

I will be one of them.

The underground anteroom is full of anxious kids like me. They check their gear and pray as parents or trainers give them a last-minute tip that will likely be forgotten by the time they walk through the doors and into the arena.

The announcer opens the mic, taps on it a few times, then speaks. "It's time for the third and final stage of the day, ladies and gentlemen!"

Occasionally, there is a death during Selection. They try hard to avoid this since every Jattarian child is precious. They become fighters, engineers, or take one of the hundreds of Appeasement Offer spots. The Aftergods don't care if the offers are wounded, half dead, or unskilled. All they want is breathing children, and every year we oblige. Such is the Jattarian way.

"Some lives are more precious than others." Dad's sweet voice comes through all my exhaustion and anxiety as I gear up for the next test.

"Hey, Little Stinger," calls someone from behind me.

I turn. The boy is older, half a foot taller than me. A short red scarf wraps around his neck. He is the one I saw fighting during the first stage, the one with stylish moves. Brown hair and hazel eyes in a strong, youthful face. He is definitely a Dedicated, one of those rich kids who get most of their education from private instructors instead of school.

"I saw you in the first stage today. That was impressive dancing. It was the Swift Scorpion, wasn't it?"

"A version of it," I reply, tired of all the jokes already.

"You made it look pretty, that's all."

"Thanks. I have been practicing for years."

"Ha! That's funny."

"Why?" I look him in the eye now. "Why do you think it's funny?" I ask a bit defensively.

"Well, you look very young, and that move is advanced. If you practiced the Scorpion for years, how old were you when you started? Seven?" he chuckles and shrugs.

"Three," I answer.

"Oh." He gets serious. "I see. You must be a Dedicated." He touches his chin.

"I am not!" I reply, taking a step back.

"Hey! There is nothing wrong with that! Most of my friends are Dedicated. In any case, good luck in the final stage." He waves casually and walks away. "Not that you need it."

"Good luck to you too."

He shakes his head. "I'm already a student. I volunteer as an aide." He gives me a handsome smile I won't easily forget.

The minutes crawl. Applicants get called, and they leave through the wooden doors leading to the arena. Then the announcer screams. "Thyra Ener, the youngest applicant in Jattarian history!"

I get up and get my things.

All for you, Daddy.

Two proctors motion me through the wooden doors and walk up the ramp. The electrical lights are blinding, the fervor of the audience deafening. The desert scenario is gone and the rings are back. About fifty matches are happening.

The announcer speaks again. "Thyra Ener ranked seventy-three out of two thousand finalists. Neros Gergen, ranked seventy-three last, is her opponent."

The audience responds with loud clamor. I approach with a spear and a shield, stopping an inch before the ring. The ground crunches and gives under the soles of my armored boots. Leather, padding, steel, and rubber add weight to my body.

A thick cloud of dust lifts from the ground thanks to the many young Giants fighting their final tests. The lights turn the dust cloud into a spectacular show of shadows and ghostly shapes. The smell of dirt and blood and the sounds of screams and violence stir the rage inside me.

Every minute someone walks away a victor and someone else a loser.

One more moment to prepare before I face this menacing kid. His score might be low, but his anger could compensate for it.

He couldn't possibly be angrier than me.

He paces around the ring, screaming threats and swinging a deadly-looking flail. "You are mine, Ener!" His voice is deep but cracks at the end.

Just a nervous teen. That's all it is.

I drop my spear and step into the arena with only my shield. This idea has to work. I can't afford a single hit with so little padding under the steel plates. Neros is so large that even full armor wouldn't stop a blow from him.

"She is going in unarmed! What a crazy child!" thunders the announcer, and the audience joins him with a loud "Oh!"

My opponent looks surprised, but only for half a second. He charges confidently and gets carried away. His swings are large and powerful, but slow and predictable. In a duel, one usually tests the opponent before committing like he is doing. His attacks are not dangerous in the least, but he is wasting his energy anyway. I angle my shield and let the flail's ball scrape it. The impact of steel against wood is loud but harmless but Neros seems entranced by it.

No fancy moves. This isn't dancing. This is killing.

He tries but his swings are awful. My footwork is far superior, but I must remain focused. I let him graze my shield again to keep him engaged and try to guess the trap he is setting. There is no way he isn't doing this on purpose. No one would be this dumb in a fight.

His breathing gets louder as his exhaustion grows, and we are only two minutes into the fight. I am tired, too, but only a fraction of what he must be feeling inside that heavy suit and after all that effort. Sweat pours down my face, into my eyes and mouth.

I force him to travel all around the circle. He steps on the rope, maybe forgetting the mental map he made of the ring. He will be careful not to make the same mistake. His parents and trainers must have taught him how to do all these things, forcing him to do drills until it's second nature.

He lets the chained ball rest on the ground while he catches his breath, but I don't let him. I leap forward, wait for his attack, then step out of his range when the swing comes.

His chain clicks with silvery tones every time he moves. I circle him, preventing him from resting. I throw feints, half charge, and pretend to test his range despite knowing it well. I am defeating him without the need to touch him, channeling every lesson on Fortitude I learned from Mother. Endure and wait for the right time, then strike once, strike true, strike to kill.

So I keep waiting. But his shield arm hangs low. He isn't preparing a surprise attack. This is the actual limit of his skill.

He isn't a tenth of what Mom was when she was holding back.

He swings again, and I dodge it easily. I maneuver behind him, take the spike launcher out of my forearm plate, and release the safety with a quick flick. I hide it behind my shield and wait for him to face me. The long tool is ready to shoot; I only need an opening.

"Come on, Ener! Stop playing," he says, spreading his arms, almost without breath. He is done.

I aim at his sternum and squeeze the trigger.

Bang!

The tool jumps in my hand and hurls two pounds of steel into my opponent's chest with a loud and powerful blast of compressed air. Neros slams onto the sand with a spike on his breastplate. He pulls at the metal rod, but the spike is firmly lodged. "Cheater," he manages to say. "You dirty cheater!"

I did not cheat. I read the school rules many times, as I assumed everyone else did. We are allowed to bring one shield and one non-lethal weapon to the ring. Neros is alive, therefore the launcher isn't lethal. I dulled the spike and lowered the air pressure to make sure.

Two aides go to Neros and inspect the spike on his chest. They give the judges a thumbs-up.

"Legal victory! Thyra Ener is victorious! The youngest Selected in History!"

I move out of the ring and leave defeated Neros behind, who wails when they remove his chest piece and reveal the bloody mess I left.

"I could have killed him!" I say, horrified. I step toward him, but one of the aids stops me. "I need to apologize!"

The instructor pushes me toward the balcony where the other Selected watch. "I've seen worse, Ener. Take your place among your fellow students."

I climb the stairs, forcing myself not to look back. I knew this was a hard place and that I needed to be tough, too. I didn't know so many would be hurt in the process.

The other Selected welcome me with cheers and handshakes. "Can't believe you made it," they say, eyeing me up and down. They bring food and drinks, and we watch the rest of the matches from this balcony. I take bites of food I can't taste and sip drinks I don't enjoy. I can only think of the suffering I created.

That's a problem for another day.

Today, victory is mine.

Chapter Ten

Talks with Nefri

Agnor

Two days later, into the Tertiary Lands

We waste precious hours. We could be in Sargena by now,
but instead we sit, hoping this handful of trees hides us from

passing Korps. A large search party will come looking for the five prisoners. We had better not be here when they do.

Zeeri wheezes, struggling to breathe. Walver beat her within an inch of her life and tied her so tight I fear she'll be cut in half. She cost us Sil and put those Korps' lives at risk, too, but she is a scared kid.

An onyx-owl flies overhead, hooting to tell her crying owlets she brings a meal. The orange sky turns purple, then blue. Stars dot the dark sky. The few conversations around the fire quiet as the night advances. I stay up longer, chewing on a blade of angel-grass and humming one of the songs Saxon sang earlier to try to cover the sound of soldiers being questioned.

I walk away from the group. A bit farther on, Nefri is busy with Wanda, and they are not exactly quiet. They are so close that one couldn't slide a paper between them.

"You are out of your mind," breathes Wanda between giggles.

"Maybe, but let's do it anyway."

"Behave!"

"It's hard with you around, Wanda!" He slides a hand behind her neck, through her golden hair.

They keep talking, their heads closer and closer.

I go farther and find a spot, then unfold the two letters. The pale moon provides barely enough light to see, but I have memorized what they say.

Mother's words were drawn with a trembling hand. I caress the papers with a new love for her. Who knows what horrors she faced to escape Jattaria? All she had was faith and Virtue.

The two small stained papers are wrinkled from when I crumpled them in a rage.

I held on to some of that anger until recently.

I bring the notes to my nose. I imagine a flowery smell for her hair and something warm and homey for her clothes and skin. Bread and honey, perhaps. What I actually smell are the places where I have been. School, battlefields, bootcamp, the orphanage. Smoke, sweat, blood, and dirt.

"We loved you, Agnor. You made our lives whole. You are Antarian, like your father, but you belong in Jattaria too. I pray you grow strong and virtuous like him and find someone worth dying for."

I wipe my eyes before any tears fully form, fold the little paper with care, and look at the other letter.

"Have a life you love, my dear Agnor. Trust no one before yourself, and follow your heart. We die, you rise, my dear son."

"Letter from a loved one? How can you read with no light?"

"Nefri!" I fold it quickly and stuff it in my chest pocket. "What are you doing here?"

"I saw you awake and thought I'd come chat and kill some time. You are always alone." He sits on the ground by me with a grunt and puts some leaves in his mouth. They smell like mint.

He wraps his shoulders with a heavy cloak. The high crops around us make waves with the breeze, the leaves ruffling when they rub against one another. *Rish, rish, rishhh...*

"No reason to be embarrassed, Agnor. We all lost someone. I lost friends, my father, my mother, and my little sister."

"Thought you were busy," I quip, changing the subject. I am not about to open up to Nefri.

He shrugs inside his cloak. "I pushed my luck and Wanda put me in time out. So? How's life at the top?"

"Not as sweet as one would think. I got enough threats to keep me up at night." I look up at the stars. Nefri does, too.

"You are playing the game wrong, friend."

"Friend?" I try to sound sarcastic.

He chuckles. "Yeah, why not? You are honest and annoyingly trusting." He tosses out those compliments as if they were insults. "Are you aware of what she is doing?"

"Yana?"

He nods. "She is playing us all, giving us a bit of what we want so she can take what she needs. Yana makes us compete for second place, so we don't aim for first. I don't mind and neither do the other Traitors. But you? You are so hungry you confuse crumbs for a feast."

"Ouch. Don't hold back, *ja*?" I toss a pebble at him. "You are wrong about her, anyway. She cares."

"As I said, honest and annoyingly trusting. Think, Agnor. Remember how she treated you."

I do.

"She is using you. *Ser du ikke?*"

"What can she possibly want with me? I'm a wounded First Circle who doesn't know the first thing about Virtuous fighting."

"Yet you stopped Walver. You *stepped up*," he chuckles and softly slaps my injured leg. "You took a stand when everyone else stood back. They like you, man," he says, jerking his head toward the Traitors. "Yana sees your potential, and it's in her nature to use it. You look like a Titan, and we are headed into Titan territory."

"She changed her mind about me, that's all. Everyone did."

"Yana was my mother's apprentice. Trust me; I know what she is doing because Mother taught me to do it, too."

"Your mother trained Yana Hensin?"

He blows an annoyed sigh and lets his head hang back. He contemplates the skies again.

"Ener. That's your last name, *ja?*"

"*Ja.*"

"I know about you. A new family line with ties to the Colossi."

"Every family claims to be related to the Colossi, man. And how do you even know this?"

"I have no last name," I admit after considering it briefly. "So names matter to me, and Lagas Ener is a pretty famous one. She made a reputation out of nothing. Any orphan would dream of doing the same."

He snorts. "What matters is that Mother taught me how to spot it and use it to my advantage."

"Spot what?"

"That hunger for power. Yana has it, you have it, Walver too."

"I don't want power, Nefri."

"*Ja, ja*. I am sure you never dreamed of being a High Star or maybe even becoming the Highest one day."

I flush violently.

He smirks. "You're in the middle of their game and can't get out. You humiliated Walver. He'll end you the moment Yana loses interest in you. Stay close to her. At least for now."

"Should I kill him, then?"

He looks up, shakes his head. "Couldn't, shouldn't."

I sigh. "Saxon said the same."

"We need them. Walver's crazy," He taps the side of his head. "But he can make things happen. And no one fights like Yana. No one. We will not survive Sargena, much less Antares, without them, and *if* we want to join the Jattaravkalt, we certainly cannot get rid of them."

I study his face, his posture. He isn't concerned. "*You* are playing their game."

He slaps my shoulder. "*Ja* and my move is to keep you alive. Ultimately we'll need someone like you more than we need them."

"I doubt I will be of much use in this shape."

"Then get better," he answers with a smirk. "Keep Yana happy, Walver at bay, and let's use them to stay alive."

"She offered to teach me how to fight."

"Let her. Take what you can from her. Every person is a teacher, and every moment a lesson."

"Freezing death," I whisper, thinking that Emma would have loved that phrase. She would repeat it, taste the words, and squeeze their meaning.

"Heavy, right?" Nefri watches intensely. "Things will get grim. Be ready. Give Yana what she wants. And build up those muscles," he pokes my bicep. "Muscles aren't Fortitude, but they help."

Dark clouds close in. Distant lightning warns of a coming storm. Thunder rumbles, and leaves rustle in the strong winds. I wish the sun would turn black and spare me from this sight, but a promise is a promise. I told Emma I'd bring her stories.

Walver works on the prisoners with sadistic pleasure. The Korps are tough. They are nameless entities and that lets them operate without concern. Faceless under their armor, they can be brutal then forget what they've done when they remove their protective suits.

Anonymity is their biggest strength, but with greater strength, he breaks them.

Walver interrogates with his hands and a few words. "Name," he says calmly while slowly twisting the subjects' fingers, stripping a section of their skin, or sticking twigs into their toes. They all identify themselves and their partners at some point. He questions them separately, with patience, and systematically. He writes every answer in a little notebook that was clean when he started. Its pages have crimson stains now.

"Patrols' routes and schedules?" he asks them. "Checkpoints, caches, stations?" He digs deep into their flesh and minds. He pulls bloody bones from their hands and needed information from their lips. "Safe routes to leave Jattaria? Best passage through Sargena?" He jabs splinters into their eyes or pulls exposed tendons with his pliers. Walver doesn't mind doing this arduous work alone.

Yana watches from the wagon as Walver finishes his work. Her neck muscles work under the skin. I touch her shoulder.

"Yes, dear boy?" She grabs my chin with her first finger and her thumb in an almost intimate way. She seems thankful to be distracted. Behind her, the storm rolls closer.

"You offered to train me. Did you mean it?" I give her a sheepish grin, and she seems so pleased.

"Absolutely, Agnor. I'll need you to be a good fighter if you are to be my right hand." She looks at Walver, and those words seem more meaningful now that he is covered in Jattarian blood. "It wouldn't hurt to get strength back into those muscles, and it would keep me in shape as well."

"I see your Virtue, Yana."

"Climb on, now. Let that leg rest." She looks up when a gust of wind blows her hair. "A storm is coming and it's time we leave."

"Yes, Boss. Jattaria doesn't feel like home lately." I eye Walver. "First, I must do something." I walk away and take my knife from the sheath. As I walk to Zeeri, I mutter a prayer and a new oath.

I'll play their game, but on my terms. Every word and action must be aligned with a purpose. Only then will I have Fortitude before adversity. I should die before forsaking this Virtue, for that is true failure.

The scriptures of the Code of Virtues come to mind from the depths of my memory. I kneel before the poor girl, who sleeps against the tree, breathing through a broken nose. Her clothes are filthy, her skin is split open and infected.

"What do you think you are doing?" Walver rushes to my side and grabs my shoulder. I stand back up and touch the serrated side of my knife to his jaw, cutting skin.

"She is free to go," I growl. "We don't need her anymore."

"I warned you, Agnor. I told you," he mutters. "Don't get in my way."

The cut on his cheek grows half an inch longer. "No," I grab his face and bring it close to mine. "*I* warned you."

He retreats with his lips curled into a snarl and his hand at his short sword. He eyes Yana, and she shakes her head. Walver turns around and leaves, cussing and swearing an oath of his own.

"Zeeri," I whisper after cutting her free. I bring my canteen against her broken lips. She opens her less-swollen eye.

"Agnor. Thanks," she sobs. I let water trickle down into her mouth, then clean the wounds on her face, and rub the ointment her father gave me. She doesn't react.

"Treat your other wounds, too," I say and put the bottles in her hands.

The flasks are almost empty, but the medicines are strong. They worked for me, they will work for her. They have to. I squeeze them and force myself to let them go. The healing wound still hurts like crazy, but she needs them more than I do.

She nods and puts the bottles in her pocket. "I see your Virtue," she croaks. I leave her with my rations of food and water.

Gods, let her live.

The Traitors watch me silently. Walver glares with the madness of a starved hound.

Yana stands up on the wagon as I sit next to her. "We are leaving shortly. Nefri, Walver, Arsen, Nova, and Saxon, lead the way in the Korps' suits in case we encounter more patrols." She looks around. *"Skynda,"* she says when they finish putting the Korps' armor on. We are absolutely committed now, and Yana does not mind everyone being armed and heavily armored.

But Walver stays back. He walks casually to the men and women he questioned. They defiantly watch him approach, knowing what he is about to do.

I get up.

"Hold hard, Agnor," says Yana.

"You can't kill them! Just leave them here! We are two or three days away from the border. They won't be able to stop us."

Yana shakes her head. "It's too risky. Sit."

I do.

They are so close I can smell their sweat. The grass around them is brown with gore. They are missing teeth and fingernails; some might never walk straight again. Walver unsheathes his blade and puts the tip on a boy's shoulder. He is about my age and has some crazy blue haircut fashioned like lightning bolts. He had three wooden piercings on his eyebrow, but

Walver pulled those out. Walver chuckles and angles the blade. The metal reflects the midday light and flashes into my eyes.

He looks up at Yana, waiting for a last-second signal.

Nothing from our leader.

Walver pushes his weapon an inch into the unarmed Jattarian. I jump off the wagon, landing awkwardly, then regain balance as I rush him. I leap and swing to stop him. He spins and elbows me in the gut, jerking my knife out of my hand in one swift move. He kicks me in the chest, knocking me to the ground, leaving me struggling to move, to breathe, to think.

"You do not learn, Agnor." Walver approaches, weapon pointed at my throat. Death is before me. I look at Yana, who could be made of stone.

"Enough," she orders.

"He challenged me." Walver raises his sword again.

Yana is beside him in half a second, wrapping her steel around his, yanking his weapon off his hands with an impossible technique.

"You challenge me, Walver. I said enough."

He glares for a minute, then his expression changes suddenly, like the page of a book. There is no anger but a pleasant smile under his ashy eyes. He arches his back as if stretching after a delightful night of rest. "Ahhh!" he sighs. "What a beautiful morning. That smell of blood and harvest." He breathes in slowly. "But we better go. You heard the boss. *Skynda!*" He climbs on one of the horses we stole and heels it. The rest follow.

I get up, watching the five Traitors in Regler Korps' uniforms ride off.

"You weren't going to stop him," I mutter accusingly.

"Leaders must make decisions like that sometimes," says Yana, looking at the prisoners. "I told Walver to kill them." She takes her sword. "I passed the sentence. Should have carried it too." When she approaches the prisoners, they seem ready.

When Yana is done, we leave five Korps behind us. Soon, we will be out of this country and, hopefully, all this guilt.

CHAPTER ELEVEN

CHOOSE YOUR BATTLES

Gymnasium

Thyra

A month later, in Instructor Klausen's office

Long, shiny curls of golden hair fall from my head. I choke back a sob and keep my chin high. The sound of shears by my ears makes me shiver, but I hold still. I focus on the lingering smell of tobacco and coffee and try to forget. There is no mirror in this room, for this is not *Frau* Ursula's parlor but a teacher's office, and this isn't a trim but a removal.

"We should have cut it weeks ago when you got Selected. I should have made it a requirement before I took you as an apprentice. It's an obstacle, and you already have enough of them as is." Instructor Klausen pauses his work and looks down at me.

"I won. I was Selected." I blow some strands that landed on my nose and push aside the painful memory of Neros struggling to stay alive. From the corner come the gross sounds of Kora-Elena having her lunch: a bird I knocked down with a stone earlier today. Her black eyes are squinty and suspicious. She doesn't seem to approve of my new look.

"You defeated an applicant. You'll need to win a Challenge to qualify for Trials against skilled students with years of experience. What will you do then?"

"Choose well. Some First Year student," I retort.

He knocks my head softly. "Challenging First Years is frowned upon."

"Frowned upon like thirteen-year-olds applying for Selection?" I know all the rules, but they seem different in practice. I don't know the customs of this place, but I am learning. There are ways around everything, it seems.

He points the scissors at my heart, perhaps guessing my thoughts. "And what about Trials or when you fight at the Edge?"

"The Edgens are weak, small, slow. We are already a superior race, instructor."

"Yet they remain undefeated through the centuries. *Miksi*?"

"Because the Aftergods favor them."

"Now you are speaking sense. Is luck enough against the gods' favor? What about superior weapons?"

"No, Instructor."

He nods.

"I taught your mother the Swift Scorpion, but she couldn't perform it as well as you when she was your age. She was too fiery, too wild. Your father must have given you a more balanced spirit. That and this bright hair that could be spotted a mile away." His voice is even, soft, and hard to interpret.

"I see your Virtue, sir," I reply, just in case he was giving me a compliment, trying to hide the lump in my throat. Thinking of Dad is a sure way to start crying, and I cannot afford this here.

"Lucky for you, you don't have to worry about a challenge. Challenging a First Year, especially one as young as you, is dishonorable. Now wipe that smirk off your face and list every mistake you made yesterday."

"All of yesterday?"

"Just the last training session will suffice. Go on."

I take a deep breath. He seemed unhappy with everything I did, so I go through every move I had made after I stepped into the gym. "I misstepped once, over-extended my arm in a lunge, left my guard open for too long, and was predictable when defending *and* attacking."

"It all comes down to timing," he says, touching his chin. He looks at my hair one last time, then nods. "Choose your battles; pick your strikes. Each one must have a purpose. A battle that starts too late has a different outcome than one that begins at the right moment. A strike that starts too early does not have the intended effect. Learn it and apply it to everything you do. Your mind is soft but flexible. We have years to give it shape, but we must start working on it immediately. Understood?"

"Yes, sir." Except I don't have years, but months. Trials are at the end of the year, but Nefri's truth might come to light before then.

"And stop holding back during training."

This takes me aback. "You noticed?"

"Of course I noticed, Thyra. I am your instructor. Stop pulling your blows."

"I thought we were supposed to," I say defensively, but I blush with guilt. Since Neros, I have been unable to fight the way Mother taught me. Against her, my best was not even close to enough. Here, against these opponents, even a measured effort causes significant damage and suffering. Mother kept me from training with other children so I wouldn't be soft like them.

"We have practice armor and weapons for that. Next time you step into a ring, you give it your all."

"Yes, sir."

"Good. Clean up here, get lunch, go through the course schedule I prepared for you, and go to the gymnasium for exercise. Tonight, we begin your apprenticeship in full. I'll be there after I finish my Third Year lecture."

"What's this lecture about?" I ask, eager to know what he teaches the more advanced students.

"I'll give you my notes tonight, like always. Focus on the tasks at hand."

I get off the chair and start sweeping my hair up while he leaves the office. The remains of his breakfast are still on his desk, enough to satisfy the hunger I developed this morning. I snatch the bread and stuff it in my mouth and finish my work, steal one of his books, and return Battle Engine Maneuvers, which I stole a week ago.

Mother had already told me most of these moves. She knew I loved the idea of driving one of those huge machines, wonders of engineering. All that power at one's fingertips, a thing of dreams. Motivational posters and paintings all around the school have stoked my childish hopes of one day commanding one of those tanks to battle.

But I must hurry. "Come, Kora!" I call, taking a quick look at my reflection in the window glass. Half the length of my hair is gone and my sides are shaved. I look older, at least. My gator climbs up my arm and settles down on my shoulders. I gather everything and take a deep breath.

The gym is on the opposite side of campus, but I already know the shortcuts. If no one catches me, I can run through the proctors' and instructors' restricted corridors and save a few minutes. If they catch me, I'll have to lie and smile my way out of it again. It's getting easier and easier either way. Easier even than when Mom made me sneak around town, stealing things from all the shops on Main Street or entering into people's homes and taking their things. It was fun as long as I didn't get caught.

She would make me sneak back into those homes or shops and return everything after. I often put things in random places, like apples among oranges, or hang paintings upside down. Once, I intentionally returned two pans to the wrong houses. I giggle every time I think about that.

Good times.

Now, I run from one end of the school to the other, sneaking from corridor to classroom, from office to dormitory, from ground to window, until I reach the hall. The paintings and decorations here are exceptions to the typical Jattarian architecture. They are magnificent, colorful, and inspiring when everything else in the country is gray and sober. I have been through these corridors a dozen times and still get lost in their art and beauty. I push a little door meant only for instructors and enter the main hall. A small group of adults waits at the large entrance.

A more prominent figure with light blonde hair stands at the back. He seems out of place with his old leather jacket and working shirt. He looks about, lost and confused. That's a man falling apart. I find myself walking down the Graduate Stairs, which only the Tried are allowed to use, and approaching the sad man.

"Daddy," I say, surprised, and pull his brown sleeve. Dust falls from the creases of the fabric. This is the only jacket he owns. He brought the smells of the shop with him and the best memories I possess awake.

"Thyra," he says and turns to me. He wraps me in his massive arms and breaks down. His red-rimmed eyes tell me he has been crying already. He sobs loudly. I let him hug me. Little by little, he calms down. Kora-Elena complains. She got squeezed during our hug. My hands look ridiculously tiny on his big face and messy beard.

"Why did you leave me?" he asks, looking at my short hair. "I have been worried for weeks! Why didn't you tell me where you went?"

"Sorry, *Isa*. I thought you would try to stop me." That's half a lie, but the lessons on deceit make it easier. Everything Mother taught me, how to lie and sneak around, comes back to me like fresh knowledge.

"Why are you here?"

I can't answer.

"It's because of Nefri, isn't it? He is gone, my girl. Come back and learn to be an engineer like you always wanted!"

But I shake my head and take half a step back. "No, Daddy. I have been Selected. The only way out is through the Trials."

"Thyra, please! You don't know what you are saying. They will make you fight your friends and send half of you away! *Weist du niche?* They send the winners to war and the losers as sacrifices!"

Parents and instructors frown at us. Patriots are suspicious of this type of conversation, especially in the School of War.

"Sorry," I whisper. "I must stay. Thanks for coming for me. I miss you."

He starts sobbing again, bringing me down with him. A thousand questions begin to attack my determination. Will this anger last long enough to get me through Trials? Did I waste my precious last days in this violent School instead of spending them with my dad?

Too late.

"I'll make you and Mom proud. I will do everything Nefri couldn't do and more."

"But I am already proud!"

"I love you," I whisper, grabbing his face. His prickly beard tickles the palms of my hands, but not in the fun way they did before. I want to go back home with him, but I know what I must do, and I can only do it here. "I am going to be fine. I have to go, Daddy."

"You can't even go have lunch with me? I came all this way."

And I want to. So bad. But I have no time. Every minute I am not training means I will be less prepared to win during Trials at the end of the year. My family's future and his life depend on this. "Sorry, Dad."

Once more, I turn away from him. This time is much harder. His crying is loud and miserable, but I can't turn back. My secret drives me forward. "Heart, heart, heart," I hear him say.

I manage to get through all my classes and tasks of the day. After a sad, lonely meal, I drag my feet to the gymnasium and hope I can find a way to not think about Dad. I climb to the top of the bleachers and set up with my books and Kora-Elena at my feet.

Students fight with heavy gear in the many rings on the gym floor. Others work out with weights and machines. I sit high on the bleachers, crying while I try to both read and watch the kids' sorry attempts to fight with a Virtuous style. I am surprised they don't hurt themselves.

A few rows down, a beautiful girl flirts with an older student. I have seen this one around campus, always surrounded by boys and girls, clearly more accustomed to luxuries than most.

She looks me in the eye. *Crap.* I hide behind the book.

"We can meet later," she tells the boy, who reluctantly leaves. She fixes her skirt, her shirt, her hair. A picture of perfection. She climbs the bleachers and sits next to me. "You are crying."

"I am fine. It's nothing," I say and wave her away, doing my best not to appear rude.

"Homesick? There is no shame in that." She touches my short hair, frowning. "I am Erika," says the girl, looking pleasant again. The bruises along her jaw do nothing to mar her dreamy face.

I swallow hard and shake her hand. Strong, rough, firm. Her knuckles are raw, and her palm callused. Like mine. "Thyra," I say with a small voice.

"Oh, I know who you are. Your mother's name is all over the school, and you were the only thing everyone talked about for weeks. Was about to get jealous." She elbows me softly.

"You are brave to apply so young." She touches my arm gently. "Fourteen?"

"Not yet."

Her eyebrows go up a smidgen. She considers something for a second. "You will be more than fine."

"Thanks, Erika. That's nice of you."

She gifts me with a gorgeous smile. "I always see you alone. You don't have to be, you know? We could be friends!" She squeezes my arm just a little. "I can introduce you to some of my friends, and maybe you will find someone *you* can be close with."

I look up with a sliver of hope, but then I remember. Cut, kill, destroy. "I won't have time for friends."

Erika's breathing stops with a little gasp. "You are something else, aren't you?"

"You are not trying hard enough!" complains one of the fighters across the gym. Tall and full of himself, he walks around his opponent, touching his sword to the inadequately flexed joints. "You had three chances to go through my guard. Pay attention!"

"Sorry, Oniv. Let's try again."

"You can do this, Kar," says the boy, Oniv, as he resumes his duel.

Erika turns to follow my gaze. "Have you met them?"

"No."

"You'll like them. Just don't get too close to Oniv." She giggles and winks at me. "He is sort of mine."

"What about the boy who just left?"

"Mikael?" She fans her neck with her hand. "Just a toy," she purrs, winking at me. "Don't worry about that. Just give Oniv space to breathe, I'll take his breath away later." Her smile would disarm a siege engine.

Below, the two boys resume their practice. The one Erika claimed moves in a familiar way. That's the aide with a red scarf. He called me Little Stinger.

I close the book and lean forward, planting my elbows on my knees and my hands on my cheeks. I study the two boys' dance. No, battle. They battle. They throw brutal attacks at each other's weak points, clashing with force and deadly intention. That's how Klaus wants me to fight.

Oniv moves like a black viper. His small shield is another weapon. Kar, his opponent, is slower, larger, and lacks proper technique. He has no way to stop Oniv's attacks.

"He is gorgeous, isn't he?" says Erika. "He is one of the favorites this year. Definitely *my* favorite." She smiles beautifully. "Watch out for the ones he hangs out with, too. Arvo, that huge kid in the ring behind them, is Undefeated. If no one beats him by the end of the year, he will get the Golden Blade." She stares at the blonde boy and bites her lower lip for half a moment. "He is quite the specimen, isn't he?"

"Sure," I say, but I can't stop looking at Oniv.

"My point again, Kar. Mind your stance!" He chuckles and his voice sounds like music.

"Not everyone has your skills!" responds Kar.

"It's practice." He eyes the clock on the wall. "Let's get going. The class will start soon."

"Oh!" I say. "I forgot!" I stuff my things into my backpack carelessly.

"Lovely meeting you, Thyra. Hang in there, *ja*?" Erika kisses my cheek in a very Primary fashion and walks away. "Let me know if there is anything you need!" I swing my backpack, throw Kora-Elena on my head, and race to the training spot before Klausen arrives. If he sees me come after him, I will do push-ups and crunches until I pass out.

I run across the gym, dodging fighters and people working out, and almost bump into Oniv and his friend. Kora-Elena goes flying forward when I stop, scratching my neck and shoulders. Klausen catches her mid-air.

"Barely on time, Thyra," he says, handing the gator back. Klausen clicks his tongue and points his chin up. "Do you want to be my apprentice? I can put you in regular classes if you prefer."

"No, instructor!" I blurt out, almost interrupting him. "I will not be late again," I say, looking down.

"My schedule is getting full, so we will have lessons as a group instead of as individually. Oniv, Kar, this is Thyra."

They turn their heads toward me. "We've met, Grandpa," says Oniv.

He didn't forget about me, and why must I blush this violently? And did he say Grandpa?

"Don't go easy on her because she is small and young. Go through your warm-up drills and recite the foundations of battle. Commence."

"Good to have you here, Little Stinger," says Oniv with a smile.

"Hi," I respond with a small voice. I look away and reach for my hair to cover my face, forgetting it's been cut.

"Enough talking! This isn't First School. Begin!"

Mother was as tough as Klausen. These routines are almost identical, showing how out of shape I became without her pushing me to train daily. We strain our muscles to new levels of exertion in each circuit. Heavy breathing turns to grunts, then to growls, and eventually to screams. My brain struggles to remember the basic principles, but at every break, I find myself watching Oniv as he gracefully performs all the moves.

"Thyra, you recited that principle already. Focus! Start from the beginning."

"Sorry, Instructor Klausen. A wise warrior chooses to battle only when victory is certain."

"And what if you are forced to fight, Thyra?"

Every muscle in me spasms with exhaustion. My stance falters; I miss my strike. His staff hits the back of my leg hard enough to sting. I scramble for the answer.

"Each battle is a series of smaller events, student. Choose when to deliver each strike. Choose when to execute that skirmish."

"Yes, Instructor."

The two boys chuckle. I blush again and glare at them. Oniv's smirk is soft and friendly, and the anger and frustration become a warm tickling feeling at the base of my sternum. Then I think of Dad and ropes with traitors swinging at the end and the feeling turns to cold dread.

"And so, Miss Ener, always be ready to kill, or the right moment might find you unprepared. Give your all, or they'll take it all."

Chapter Twelve

Tale of Siff's Last Stand

Agnor

Later that day, near the Sargenian border

The Traitors and I sneak out of Jattaria at night, stealing between guard posts, disguised under stolen armor, and wary that the Regler Korps might take us at any moment. Walver plans every route, every meal, every step, and takes us out of Jattaria safely. We cross rivers, scale cliffs, and wind our way through a narrow valley near the Kjedes. I march, head low, my eyes fixed on the ground ahead. Every step is treacherous; a slip could be deadly.

I bump into Saxon. "Careful, buddy," he says, smiling. He is looking up at the snowy peaks and the orange morning sky.

I take a slow, deep breath. "First time I've seen something like this," I whisper. My breath condenses in the cold air.

He smiles and pauses there with me. "Sometimes you just have to stop and find the beauty around you, man." He extends his hand toward Arsen, standing a few feet away.

She takes his hand and rests her head on Saxon's shoulder. "That's pretty," she says.

Boots wet, face red, and hands trembling, I watch dawn break over those peaks and try to remember every detail. Emma and I were never this far Cold. She'd want to hear of how the wind howls between the rocky walls, how the water clings to stones like clear pearls, how the flowers tuck their petals when it's dark as if they were embarrassed of being caught out so late.

Walver calls with a birdlike whistle.

We resume our march, catching up to the rest of the group a hundred yards ahead of us. The journey stretches for days, which get colder and colder as we leave the warm side of the continent behind and forge deeper into winter.

My Titan blood seems to yearn for it. Despite the exhaustion, and the hunger, and fear, I feel a deep excitement. Something is calling me to go Cold, back to the land of my father.

Walver's maps are good, but they are still mostly based on estimations. He got us out of Jattaria, but now, days into Sargena, we are guessing our way through the Killing Woods. He plots our path, somehow keeping us away from wandering Lanzas patrols. These mounted soldiers hunt intruding Giants like us with bloody efficiency, and we cannot afford an encounter with them.

We saw these Titans patrolling the woods far away a few times. They wear green cloaks with patterns that meld into the foliage, but Yana and Walver spot them every time. After a while, I learned to spot them too. There was something else one night. Big, noisy, wandering through the trees. Maybe it was a mapinguari, that monster the farmer told me about.

I tremble just thinking about it.

Walver stirs the little fire with a stick, trying to coax as much heat from those logs as possible. Horse meat roasts above the flames while orange sparks fly with the bitter wind. Some wild mushrooms and herbs fry in fat inside a tin cup. He adds a pinch of precious salt.

The horses get as far away from the smoke as the ropes allow. We are cooking their fallen brother, after all, because we are running out of everything. Food, health, time. Siff, faster than the rest.

"They were your friends, Siff," says Yana, facing away from the group. Her voice cracks like a whip, yanking my attention back to the horrible scene developing. "You've known Ingrid and Vinz since School. You knew they were going to leave, yet you said nothing."

"I didn't know!" cries Siff. She is down on her knees. Her body heat melted the bits of ice immediately around her. Her stubbled scalp is torn to shreds. Walver's meticulous work didn't change her answers. Siff's answers didn't change Yana's decision.

"Maybe you didn't know, but you were going to leave too. That would have been fine, except you were taking half our supplies." Dead leaves and snowflakes swirl around them. Yana raises her sword above Siff's head. Before we left the Army, they called her the Vulture. She's after death. "You'll die quickly."

Siff puts a broken hand up. "At least let me fight you."

Walver sneers. "You'll die even faster!"

Yana puts the sword down and motions for Siff to stand. Walver tosses her his sword. Siff gets on her feet, takes the blade and tries the weapon's grip. She wraps her cloak around her arm and puts it up defensively.

"Ready?" asks Yana.

"Father, I am coming to you," whispers Siff. She crouches into a stance resembling Solitude's Last Stand, a style for fighting several enemies when alone. She does stand on her own, after all.

"I'll take that as a yes." Yana dashes forward, dodging Siff's low jab and swinging high. Yana's steel goes swiftly through Siff's neck, slicing bone and flesh, leaving only cold air. Another Traitor's life ends. Siff's body collapses, hitting the ground knees first, spraying blood before the heart gives up. Her head falls from her shoulders and rolls away. Blood pools in dark contrast with the thin layer of snow.

We were twenty when we left the Edge; now we are nine. At this pace, we will die long before we get to the Jattaravkalt.

"Let's try this again," says Yana, demonstrating the fighting form. She makes me practice daily, but today, she is meaner than usual. She is taking her frustrations out on me. "And try to pay attention!"

"I can't fight and listen!" I complain, barely avoiding a jab but eating the next two. I have been enjoying my time with her more and more, even when the sessions get harder each day. She pushes me constantly and doesn't wait until I've learned the previous lessons before beginning the next.

"I am trying to make you understand, Agnor!" She hits my ankle. "Each fight, each decision, must be part of something bigger." She ducks, deflects my attack with a quick flick of her short sword, then pokes me in the sternum. "To master Fortitude, to truly grasp that power inside of you, you must align your efforts with your life's goal. What are you here for? What are you meant to be? Tell me!" She smacks my ribs.

"I don't know!" I swing wildly, missing and opening my guard. She slams her blade against my back, knocking the air out of me.

"Then find out! Without that, your efforts will be aimless and dispersed like flames in the wind."

"Flames in the wind," I cry, panting. I parry a thrust to my gut and throw a half-decent slash at her head. She deflects it with ease.

"You must be a forge, concentrate all that heat, make it useful." She walks around me, probing from all angles. She finds a way through my defense and I take the punishment. The lesson intensifies every time I fail, as does the pain.

"Your stance is wrong. Flex your knee and tighten your core." She repositions my limbs. "Let's try the Swift Scorpion from Fortitude's Way of War. A strong and accurate overhead thrust to finish weak or debilitated enemies."

"Swift Scorpion," I repeat softly. Everyone wanted to learn this move in school. I let my arms hang. "I can't master something *that* advanced."

"Mastering? No. You can probably manage this dumbed-down version I developed. It's still risky. You leave your whole body open for a moment just before you strike." She shows me. She hides behind her shield, extending her sword arm behind her like a scorpion's tail. She leaps at me, swinging her shield to her left and leaving her chest open. A moment later, *Slam!* She stings with her sword, forcing me to take a few steps back.

"If you do not move fast, you'll get killed in a heartbeat." She shows me again, this time at the speed she would use during a fight. Half a second. *Crash!* My shield splits, and I fall to the ground with a numb arm.

Lazy sunbeams make their way through the dense woods as the sun rises and the session progresses. She lets the light bathe her tired face after a few rounds. It doesn't seem to bother her eyes, which look dead like bits of glass. "Not bad," she says, putting away her gear.

"It will take me years."

"Your leg doesn't seem to bother you anymore."

"A mild throb," I say, breathing hard. The wound is now a shallow hole covered with light-colored skin. Her training agrees with my body. I am far from beating her speed, technique, or quick thinking, but the gap closes.

I lean against a tree and breathe through my mouth. Every fiber of my being hurts.

She finishes putting her things away. "Find your reason, your purpose, Agnor. It will help you focus and make you stronger. Only then will you find Fortitude."

"How? Everything I wanted is gone." I punch the bark with my glove. Emma was my reason. Now, I have a promise I don't know how to keep.

"You are in this world for a reason." She stays there as I recover my breath. Her expression gets serious. "I had to kill Siff. You know that, right?"

I say nothing.

She grunts and shakes her head angrily. "She robbed us! Without the food she planned to take, we would have starved! What did you expect of me?"

But I don't respond.

She punches the palm of her hand. "I am trying, Agnor," she growls. She drops her shoulders and sighs. "I am trying."

"You can't fall apart. We need you."

She collects herself. "Right." She wipes her cheek with her sleeve, leaving a red streak of dried blood on her white skin. Siff's blood. "Do tree-stabs for an hour."

So I hit a dead tree for an hour with a weapon that must be completely ruined by now. Downward-cut, uppercut, slash down, slash up. Swing left, swing right. Stab. Again. The bark on the trunk is gone. The tree's white core bursts every time I hit it.

"Hey."

"Agh!" I swing at the voice. "Freezing death, Nefri." He snuck from my blind spot. "What do you want?" I blurt out.

"Just checking on you."

"I am fine." I remove my gloves and rub my sore hands. A couple of squirrels dart before us and dash into a bush. "What do you really want?"

"I am worried about them," he admits quietly. "Walver, more than anything."

"Did he get you while sleeping?"

"No. What?" He squints. "Did something happen when *you* were sleeping?"

"Not like that, idiot! He only stabbed me a little bit."

"As long as it was *only* a little bit." He massages his forehead with his eyes closed and eyebrows high. "Walver isn't well. He is sick, and he'll do something stupid just to prove himself. This weather is really getting him, and he has been mad-dogging me since we left Jattaria. I think he's after me."

"So?" I say, annoyed. "We can't kill him, remember?"

He shrugs. "Rescue me if necessary, my brave prince?"

"Sure, Nefri. I am ready for him." I flex my swollen arms.

"So buff and handsome." He blows a kiss at me. "I see you followed my advice."

"Yana doesn't go easy on me." I turn my arm to expose all the bruises.

"My mother was the same." He tries a smile, but it's all wrong. His gaze is troubled. For a second, he looks at Wanda, sitting by the fire and working on her crossbow. "So. I am not sure finding the Jattaravkalt is our best path, *du vet*? Maybe we'd be better on our own."

"There it is. *That's* what you wanted."

He tilts his head. "Busted."

"We stick together or die alone. We need them, remember?"

He looks at me. "*Ja,*" he says, sounding unconvinced. "We stick together." He pats my arm. "Anyway! We are about to leave. Come eat something. Walver says he found a path."

He goes to the Traitors, who welcome him to the fire. Uma is talking to Nova and Wanda while she writes in her notebook. Arsen tries to sing while Saxon plays a new song. Walver stirs the pot of food, and Yana sits cross-legged by a tree, serious and silent. I collect my things and sit by the warm fire. A few yards away, Siff's dismembered body freezes in a pool of her own blood.

Walver's path has taken us to the edge of the continent. The air changes as we cross the Cadena mountains. The forest changes the closer we get to the sea, losing its stuffy, dense scent, and gaining a sharp, salty quality to it. We find a lonely path away from the main road, and as we travel, the horses start to get anxious. They whine and buck and bump each other.

"What's wrong?" complains Wanda. She rearranges the wool cap she wears under her helmet.

"They smell something," says Nova from her spot in the cart. "The city of Fortitude is close. Could be people coming from there. Or maybe travelers from Madeiro." She destroys the pronunciation of that exotic name.

Yana stands on the empty cart and looks at the grounds before us. "This place is full of wolves, big cats, and bears. Or that huge thing we heard some nights ago. Have your crossbows ready. Agnor, you lead. If anyone can pass for a Titan, it's you."

I look around. All of them are fair-skinned and under seven feet tall. "Yes, Boss." I heel my ride and move about half a mile up the road. The horse steps sideways and pulls back every few yards, whining and snorting loudly. "Easy, boy! We are alone here." I rub his neck.

But the smell.

We break out of the tree line and find ourselves on the edge of a breathtaking ridge that falls to the Raging Sea. Waves explode against the sharp rocks, spraying salty mist but doing nothing to cleanse the hot and putrid smell that intensifies as we continue along the ridge.

Then I pull the reins and come to a stop.

Nova pulls up next to me a few minutes later. Her horse whines and stomps the ground. Wanda and Nefri appear on my other side on foot.

"Ice me," he whispers when he sees what I am seeing.

The landscape can't compensate for the cruelty before me. How will I tell Emma about this in the afterlife when I already wish to forget about it?

"Sargenians are inhuman," says Walver. Even *he* is appalled by the sight.

Saxon, Yana, and Arsen approach slowly. Arsen covers her mouth with a gloved hand. Saxon looks away and retreats to a tree a few steps from the ridge, holding his stomach.

A shallow pit holds close to a hundred smoking corpses. Some of the skeletons are small, some tiny. The littlest ones cling to larger ones. The charred bones still hold tissue. Fat and flesh crackle and drip in black and red chunks. Skulls with empty eye sockets scream silently and forever.

"This fire is from last night," says Saxon with a throaty voice. His eyes are red and shiny.

Uma covers her nose. "Some were burned alive. The way their arms are wrapped around the remains, the open mouths, the hands in fists," she points at different bodies.

Yana is expressionless. "This is how they dispose of Giants in Sargena. No wonder they call this the Killing Woods."

Arsen picks up a handful of ashes and pours it into the jar she carries. She wipes a tear with her sleeve, then goes to Saxon, already strumming a heartbreaking song about ashes and burning love.

Mother risked this fate twice. Once when leaving Jattaria and again when coming back to save me. How terrible was her life that she braved this? How did she allow herself to love my father, kin to the people that can do this to other humans?

She must have been a truly great woman, more capable of loving than most. What did she get in return? Forced labor in some mines, dying a nameless slave next to the rotting bodies of war prisoners and deserters. Deserters like me.

A lonely tear freezes on my cheek. "I love you, Mom." The wind carries my words and the dust of these dead Jattarians away.

Chapter Thirteen

A Tale of Mapinguaris and Legendary Lanzas

Agnor

Weeks later, deeper into the Sargenian country

The tall trees sway and sing pleasantly. The scents of pine resins and wildlife slip into my nose so strongly that I can taste them.

Now and then, the branches allow some moonlight to filter through. Small critters rush away from us. Birds of prey dive from above after a meal with nothing more than a whisper of feathers and a flash of talons.

Yana, Walver, and I crawl slowly, creeping up to the edge of this low hill in the middle of the Killing Woods. My belly is cold and wet, and my back hurts, but I stay low. A steady drizzle falls on us, making us colder and colder.

"Hold!" says Walver, who has led the group all day. "Something is up ahead." He crawls forward on his own.

Walver gives the all-clear a minute later. I slither to him with Yana. "There they are," he says triumphantly. "Vinz and Ingrid. I have been tracking them."

"Freezing Death, Walver!" hisses Yana, punching him in the ribs. "What the - why?" She peeks around the tree and looks at the bottom of the hill. I do the same. Sure enough, there's a small fire down the shallow valley with two bundles around it.

"What do you mean why? To kill them!" He readies his crossbow. "They betrayed us."

"No," she says firmly. "You made us waste a whole day chasing them? You useless idiot."

Walver frowns, then his eyes open wide. He looks at me with terror. No, past me. He lowers his head and pulls his hood. "Oh, no..."

Thump. Thump. Thump.

Three huge ape-like shapes walk through the trees a hundred yards behind us. They are ten feet tall shadows with glowing eyes and spikes on their backs. Their strides are long and heavy. They snort noisily, spitting clouds of steam from their big heads.

"What is that?" whispers Yana. Walver covers her mouth.

The things come closer, closer. *Thump, thump, thump.* Their steps make the ground tremor as they approach. One of the things stops and growls, its voice like a low crackling. They are right on top of us, dripping oily water from their furry backs.

I close my mouth and hold my breath as the dark monsters communicate. Blood rushes to my head, making my eyes throb. Thick black fur hangs from their bellies, dangling above our heads and dripping rain.

They continue down the hill, circle the small fire, then close. Vinz and Ingrid move in their sleeping sacks, awoken by the loud stomps of the beasts encircling them.

"What is this?" I hear Vinz say.

"RYAGHHH!!!"

The screech makes me jolt. One of the monsters grabs Vinz by the neck, then slams him into the ground. His screams end abruptly. Ingrid manages to avoid getting grabbed and even shoots her crossbow at one of the beasts. The third monster stomps her, breaking her legs.

"Freezing death!" she curses, but a long, spiky arm spears her through. The beast tosses Ingrid's body and bellows again. The three monsters lift their heads to the moon as their howl dies down, then continue down the valley.

"We have to get out of this country," says Yana, crawling backward.

"Mapinguaris," I say.

"Whatever they are, they killed Vinz and Ingrid for us," grunts Walver, grinning like a madman.

We get on our feet and go back to camp as fast as our legs and lungs allow. Low branches scratch at my face and arms as I dash through the wilderness. Even Yana seems terrified, racing a good distance ahead of me.

"What was that?" Asks Wanda when we reach camp. "Freezing death... what was that!?"

"More things wanting to kill us," says Yana through her teeth. Her eyes are as wide as the moon. I exchange a look with the rest of the Traitors, wondering if they see the same thing I am seeing. Wondering if they, too, are watching our best hope of survival come undone before our eyes.

The morning greets us miles away from where Vinz and Ingrid died. Their deaths replay endlessly in my brain. Words rush and jam as I try to spin a story for Emma that makes at least some sense to me. I lean against the root of an ancient tree, picking bits of bark and jumping anytime a leaf falls.

Yana and Walver perch on one of the lower branches, spying on a nearby town. Cava, according to some signs we passed. It hangs from the ridge of a cliff, defying gravity and sense. The white walls and tower surround the lower parts of the hill, fortifying the city. There are hundreds of austere houses around it, with streets running through them like straight veins. Even from here, we hear the sound of activity. Shops full of supplies welcome buyers and trade away while we starve outside those shiny walls.

"We can't go in," says Yana. She chews her nails, bloody and torn already. "And we don't have time, anyway."

Walver's eyes are sunken, his skin is pale, and his oily hair sticks to his skull. Nefri was right: this weather does not suit him. He stands like a gargoyle, thinking, observing, plotting. They call it the Rectitude's Clarity, a state of mind in which one can see all paths and all consequences to one's actions.

"Let's go, then," croaks Walver after some time. "Have Agnor drive the wagon with a few of us hiding behind and jump the first Titan we see." He scratches his beard. "His huge head might distract them."

"My head is normal-sized," I growl.

"Sure is, Huge Head." He rolls his eyes.

"No one calls me that!" I look around at the Traitors, but nobody meets my gaze. They actively avoid it, in fact.

He chuckles.

Yana chews her lip. "*Ja*. That works." She looks at the white tower, the Guardias' barracks. That city is a fortress. "We have to get going. Walver, Saxon, Arsen. Get in," commands Yana. "I am going, too. Keep it clean if possible."

"*Ja*, Boss," we say at once.

The hours go by with nothing but critters running around us. The Traitors whistle every few minutes to let us know their position away from the road. The woods are not dense enough for them to hide, so they stay away. Grass grows on the road, and the one set of tracks I see is at least a day old. "We will be lucky if we cross anyone before sunset."

"Maybe," says Saxon. He starts playing his guitar.

There was a boy on the Sargenian roads,

Head was so big he could cover the sun.

He changed the tides with his massive bone dome,

His name was Huge Head but also Agnor

I steer into a big hole. This is not a song I'd play for Emma.

"Hey! Be careful, Agnor!" complains Saxon through his laughter.

Walver grunts and kicks my chair. "You are probably scaring them. I'd run away if I saw your ugly mug approaching."

"Shh!"

"You shush, Agnor!" says Walver coughing.

"I think I see something. Someone's coming," I say, letting the eerie silence in the woods settle again. The tall trees look down, swaying. Animals seem to get quiet. The air is still.

"Hold your fire unless necessary," says Yana. "A fight would attract attention."

"Any moment," I say when we are only fifty yards from our target. The reins tremble with my hands. These Sargenians are eight-foot-tall warriors who kill any Jattarian regardless of age or intention and burn them in open graves.

Breathe in, breathe out. Get it together.

"Two riders. Male and female." I tap my foot nervously. "Walver, Yana, and I can cover them. Arsen and Saxon, you approach and neutralize them."

The Sargenian wagon swerves to their right to make space for us. The driver is old and nods as our eyes meet. The woman next to him is middle-aged, maybe his daughter. She looks tired but offers me a little courtesy too.

"Now!" I pull out my crossbow and aim it at her. The four behind me spring out of cover. The Sargenians' hands go up in surprise, their dark green eyes open wide; Eyes that watched loved ones live and grow, eyes with wrinkled skin around them, maybe from lots of smiling. "Freeze!"

And Walver shoots.

Those friendly eyes close when Walver's arrow sinks into her sternum. She grabs for the rod buried in her chest, but it kills her quickly.

"No," I sigh.

The man turns to his dead companion. Walver shoots him too. "It was them or us," he says before the man exhales his last breath.

"They weren't armed," I mumble. "They surrendered."

Yana grabs Walver by the neck, but he yanks himself free. "No half-measures, Yana! We can't take the risk!"

She shakes her head rapidly. "Get the wagon. Quick!"

"They didn't even move," I croak, still aiming my crossbow at the dead woman. "She surrendered. They weren't going to give us trouble."

Yana grabs me by the shoulders. "It doesn't matter!" She says, her eyes about to pop out of their sockets. She is pale and trembling, unhinged. "We have no time to waste, Agnor! Those things -" she says, throwing a finger up the road, where we come from. "We can't risk staying here!"

We drive the two wagons down the same road after tossing those Sargenian bodies behind some tree. "Animals will take care of them," says Yana, looking into the distance past the trees and down the road, where I imagine she sees safety for all of us.

Walver makes a quick inventory as we roll down the empty road, apparently unbothered by all the killings and danger on our heels. "Not much. They had some money." He discards the purse, tossing it by the road. "Flour and other raw ingredients. Bread and bait." He shakes a small tin barrel and reads the inscription. "*Fogo de Alma.*" He removes the cap, dips a finger in the liquid, and then smells and licks it. "Liquor! This will keep us warm." He smacks his lip.

"It will have to be enough. We must get out of this country, away from the villages." She looks left and right. Her left foot taps the wagon's floor repeatedly.

"Yana," I whisper, leaning into her. "You are on edge. Get it together." I grab her elbow.

She pulls free. "How?" She whispers through gritted teeth. "Didn't you see those monsters? Or that pit full of Jattarians? Isn't the smell still in your nostrils? Don't you feel the Guardias closing in?"

I swallow hard and look at Nefri, who seems more worried than me. "Nefri, Uma, Wanda, and Nova can come to this wagon. Yana and the rest can stay a mile behind us and get some rest."

"Not a bad idea." She holds my hand with her cold fingers. "I see your Virtue, Agnor."

"Someone's coming," I say after hours of riding through these back roads. It's already dark, and I look twice at a far dot down the road to make sure. "One wagon, two travelers." It was bound to happen.

"This doesn't feel right," says Wanda. "Yana's lost it." She looks back and tries to spot our second cart, which must be some twenty minutes behind.

"She is trying to do what's best for us," I say. "Those things that killed Vinz and Ingrid freaked her out. They would have freaked anyone out..."

"So she is scared," says Nova. I picture her trying to make herself smaller, invisible.

"Scared or not, we need her," says Nefri, sounding irritated. "We have to take this coming wagon. Wanda and I will take the rider to the right," says Nefri. "Nova and Uma take the one on the left."

"No shots unless necessary," I say. "I mean it."

They rearrange under the tarp and get ready.

"Almost," I say without moving my lips.

A large black horse pulls a large transport with an oval and a line painted white on the side. Two young female riders throw a bored glance in my direction. They wear long green coats with hoods pulled back.

Then I remember. A shield and a spear, the Guardias symbol. "Oh, no..." I choke. "Stay," I grunt, but the Giants behind me have already jumped from under the tarp.

"Hands up!" screams Nefri, but the riders dive to the other side of their wagon and pull muskets from under the seat. The Lanzas fire as soon as their feet touch the ground.

Phoom!

An invisible force tears through us, disrupting air and whistling sharply. Its a slug traveling at sonic speed, missing us by inches.

"Get cover, Agnor!" Nefri shoots. His bolt bounces off one of the soldier's chest. The other Guardia peeks out from behind their vehicle, takes aim, and fires at me.

Phoom!

The blast punches my eardrums inward. Hot air dishevels my hair when the bullet rips by. Nefri pulled me back at the last possible moment.

I fall into the shallow ditch, air blowing out of my lungs.

Nefri drags me closer to him and Wanda. "Nova!" I call. She jumps just as another shot goes off. She is in mid-air but suddenly twists. Her chest bursts out, spraying guts on the ground. Nova's dead eyes stare at nothing while steaming blood pours from a hole the size of a fist. Uma closes her eyelids with a shaky hand.

One of the wheels explodes when hit by steam-musket fire, and our carriage collapses. The horse is already on her side, dying from massive wounds.

"*Voce vai morrer, cachorro de Jattaria!*" screams one of the Guardias as their bullets destroy our cover one chunk at a time.

"What now?" asks Uma as splinters fly in every direction.

Nefri puts his back against the remains of the cart. "*Blitzkrieg*. It takes them five seconds to reload, enough for Uma and me to rush from the right side if you two cover the other."

"Nefri!" complains Wanda. Another chunk of wood explodes beside my face, tearing my skin.

"It must be us. You are too cute and little, and Agnor is too slow and ugly."

"Don't get shot in the face. It's the only good thing about you," says Wanda with a choked sob and kisses him.

"As you wish." He crouches and digs his toes into the ground. The leather tips of his boots scrape against the icy road. He takes a few breaths and waits for his target to shoot. Uma readies on the other side, tucking her long brown hair in her helmet.

Phoom! Slivers burst near Nefri's leg.

They leap forward and into the burst of splinters and snow. Wanda shoots from above our cover, I from the right. Bolts fly close to the Sargenian soldier, but she doesn't even flinch. Her musket's cannon swings until I stare down the black mouth of its barrel. Steam explodes from it as it hurls its deadly bullet straight at me.

My crossbow comes undone as the projectile makes its way through it. The wood frame unravels in my hands, drilling splinters into my palms. The bow arms go flying, attached by the string. The fan shoots sideways, spilling its stored bolts. The bullet continues its trajectory into my shoulder's armor plate.

The force slams me like a horse's kick. Overwhelming pain cancels out all other senses.

Light returns, then sound. First, the orange sky through the foliage above us, then my heavy breathing. Steps approach. Nefri comes into my field of view.

"I can't move."

He kicks my leg - it hurts like crazy.

"Freezing death, you fatherless piece of..."

"Did you feel that?"

"Of course I felt it!" I whine.

"Then you can also move. Nap's over."

"Guardias?"

"Taken care of," says Nefri, cleaning his brow off sweat and dirt. "Hurry up."

I try fingers and toes first, then hands and feet. Arms and legs last. Every stage of my minute-long recovery is a world of pain.

My entire skeleton feels like it was dismantled and roughly reassembled. My bones fall into place noisily when I sit up. The arm plate is a mess of twisted metal sunk into my flesh. "Ice me!"

"Steam muskets hurt, man," he answers. "I am taking one. Now get moving. Everyone for miles around must have heard these blasts." He helps me stand, then kicks my butt. "*Skynda!*"

I walk by the pile of boards that used to be our cart. The dead horse's leg twitches every few seconds. Nova is pale and still like a doll.

A few steps away, by the Guardia's vehicle, Wanda kneels before Uma. She sits against the large wheel, breathing rapidly, her organs hanging from a gut wound. Wanda tries to remove her clothes, but Uma stops her with a pained gesture. "There is nothing you can do." She reaches into her coat and produces a small book with leather covers. "Take it." She looks at Wanda with watery eyes, then dies with a sigh.

Wanda covers Uma's face with a bloody handkerchief and kneels before her, looking down. "I die, we rise, Uma."

"I die, we rise," say Nefri and I.

"What do we do with Yana?" says Wanda after a while. She puts the medic's notebook away, and a dry flower falls from between the pages.

Something tightens within me. "Why?" I say shortly. The idea of losing Yana put me on Edge.

"We have lost too many because of her and Walver!" says Wanda, throwing her arms up.

"Nothing. We need them," I say, trying to push that emotion aside. Maybe being so close to Yana is making my thoughts scrambled.

Wanda turns her hands into little fists. "They'll get us all killed!" She breathes a few times, then opens her hands. She looks into Nefri's intense blue eyes. "Once we are in Antares, we leave them." She comes closer until she is a foot away. A terrifying fire burns in her stare. She touches my chest, her hand like a blade. "Who will you stand with when the time comes?"

For just a moment, I see Emma before me. I blink, and she is gone. "What do you think?" I ask, breaking eye contact with Wanda.

Nefri frowns. This may be what troubled him when we spoke days ago. He fumbles for words for a moment. "We need a plan."

"*Ja*, I forgot. Use them, use me." I take a step away from the two and look down the road, wondering how far are Yana and the rest.

"It's life or death, Agnor." Wanda looks pointedly at Uma's body. "Yana is all about death."

"I'll stand with you," I say. However twisted, Nefri has been straight with me from the start.

Wanda sighs, her frown dissipates. "Glad to hear it. You two take care of Nova. I'll take care of Uma."

I nod and walk to our little friend, broken by the remains of our wagon. "If I am with you, we should stop the mind games," I tell Nefri, mentally preparing for the grim job ahead.

He touches the right side of his chest. "My heart is in the wrong place, but my intentions are good," he says solemnly.

"That doesn't make sense," I grunt.

"It does if you don't think about it." He punches my arm playfully, but his face looks stormy. "If it helps you feel better, Wanda is using me too."

"You don't seem to be having a bad time."

We lift Nova by the ankles and wrists and bring her into the woods. Her protective plates rattle when we put her down a bit into the trees.

Nefri rubs his hands, cleaning them of Nova's blood. "I would die for Wanda, *du vet*? I'd marry her in a heartbeat." He touches a pocket on his chest. I bet he has rings in there.

"Then marry her."

He bites his lower lip. "What if she says no?"

I spread my arms out. "Who else is she going to be with? Walver?"

"Saxon is good-looking. I bet you don't look so bad after a shower and a proper shave. A change of clothes wouldn't hurt, you know?"

"I am wearing the same clothes as you."

"But I look good in them."

"Just ask her." I think of Emma. "Don't wait. Trust me."

His sad expression deepens. "You'll stand with us, then? Can we truly count on you?"

I nod.

"I see your Virtue. Glad you went through this hell at the same time as me." He chuckles dryly.

Wanda calls us. Behind the carriage, on the ground, sit the two female Sargenian soldiers, tied, gagged, and looking at us with murderous anger. They are as tall as me, with strong frames and skin as tan as mine. "I thought you killed them."

Nefri shakes his head. "You said not to."

Wanda takes Nefri's arm. "Yana will be here any second. What do we do?" She looks at me.

I clear my throat. "*I* think killing them is unnecessary, but *you* call the shots."

Wanda shakes her head. "If you say no killing, then that goes."

The wind of the Killing Woods snakes through these ancient trees, making us shiver. I look at the bloody horror spread about me with the creeping certainty that this is not the worst to come.

CHAPTER FOURTEEN

A TIME TO STRIKE

Thyra

Somewhere in the Kjede Mountains, miles from Solitude

Summer is over.

I must find my way back to school. I must survive the Kjede Mountains. I must make it through this exercise and find our way back. I must seek Fortitude, master it and grow in it. I had lost sight of my purpose. I have been in school for months now, training, learning; I must put it all to use or die. If my strength isn't enough, my friends will lend me theirs. The Code of Virtue demands it.

"Are you all right, Thyra?" asks Kar.

"Exhaustion, heat, hunger. She is delirious. We are almost there, Little Stinger," says Oniv dryly. He is so close to me, yet not close enough. "Just a couple of miles."

"We must stop the Edgens," I respond, my brain making weird connections, not processing what's around me properly. "The next century is near," I say, as if suddenly realizing. "We will be victorious this time! Fortitude! We have Fortitude."

"She is crazy," says Kar. I hear him clearly, but *he* is the one not making sense.

A thin layer of ice covers the gardens when we reach campus. We enter through a hole in the fence, then keep going. The rising sun extends a blanket of warmth that enlivens our beat-up limbs. We wandered all night through the Kjede mountain system, looking for the checkpoints so we could finish our exercise. Nearly forty miles walked since we started a day ago.

Oniv holds my elbow to give me support and takes a few dozen pounds of weight off my legs. Kar carries a handful of my things in his backpack and that helps, too. They didn't ask, they just acted when they saw I couldn't go any longer.

We walk against the sunrise, into the weak beams of dawn. We tread through the gardens, past tall trees and statues.

"We are almost there," says Kar. He drags his feet and leaves long tracks on the frosty grass behind him.

"He said he'd meet us by the Colossal's fountain," says Oniv. That huge fountain is one of the few marvels left by our ancestors. Here and there, one can see proof that this land was once home to the Colossi.

"Klausen will make us get in, the sadistic geezer," complains Kar.

"I wasn't going to." It's Klausen's smooth voice behind us. "But now you will."

"Grandpa," says Oniv. "Where did you come from?"

The fresh morning dew is all over his travel cloak and light backpack. His white hair is unusually messy but still pretty neat. "I can't send unsupervised children into the wild." He yawns.

"You were watching the whole time?" I ask.

"Creep," grunts Kar.

Klausen ignores his comment. "Yes. You have lots to learn, but you did well. Keep going. You are late and still have six hundred yards to complete the circuit."

Kar shakes inside his towel. Klausen made him get in the fountain, and the bath took whatever strength he had left. He is a pathetic sight, and I owe him greatly. "I see your Virtue, Kar. Take my coat."

Oniv is already wrapping his scarf around Kar's neck. "Hang in there, man." He rubs his arms.

Kar's blue lips tremble. He nods a few times, then pulls the coat over his nose.

The ground crunches under the heavy steps of our instructor. He looks like a deadly spear, always sharp, always ready. His jaw is angled and looks like it could cut paper. "Enough rest, kids. Eat up and go to your first session at the gym." He hands us small buns filled with butter, dry coffee, and sugar. He calls them carb-bombs. The butter drips and makes my hands shiny and slippery.

So be it. I devour the bombs while tears of joy and suffering mix on my red cheeks. He gives an extra serving to Kar.

"Go on now," says Klausen.

The shaft of my spear is dirty, bloody. I push against inertia and gravity, and the weapon's blade sneaks through Oniv's guard. Like a snake, it finds its way through the tiniest possible opening and hits my mark. Klausen said to go all in and now Oniv grunts with pain.

It landed on his ribs and would have pierced his heart if these weapons weren't toys.

His counter-attack comes when my defense is compromised. His short lance flies at my neck like lightning, stopping an inch before hitting. *He* held back. The match is over.

"Point for me," says Oniv, taking his helmet off. His black eye keeps swelling and swelling. We thought he lost a tooth, but he only chipped it. He puts all his weight on one leg. The other must be strained after that lock I did on him during our Suggested Stillness session. Beat-up as he is, he won the last round.

"Stop pulling your strikes," growls Klausen in my ear. "He deserves all your effort, and you must push your limits." He straightens up and looks at the three of us. "What did you learn today, students?"

"To not be disrespectful to you, sir," says Kar, whose skin is still bluish.

"To work as a team," I say.

"To not pull back," says Oniv.

"Fortitude!" he says. "Fortitude to stay in the fight, then wisdom to strike when necessary. Now, go rest."

We gather our gear with hurting limbs. We complain and grunt every time we move, and once everything is put away, we stroll to the dormitories. We walk by the spa. Tempting, but rest is much needed. I have class in three hours.

"I'll see you guys later," says Oniv, headed to the spa. "I need a massage after today." He winks at me. "You hit hard, Little Stinger."

"I was thinking the same," I say. Exhaustion is suddenly gone.

Go to sleep. He is with someone else, anyway.

Kar stops for a moment. "I am out. It was fun, despite everything."

Oniv bumps his shoulder. "That mountain cat you shot was great food. Good thing you were there for us."

"I guess I didn't do so bad," he says through a yawn. He turns around and slumps his way to the dormitory doors. "See you later."

"That guy. So insecure," says Oniv. His gaze follows Kar.

"He'll be fine," I say and touch his arm. His muscles are tense like steel wires.

"Yeah, I shouldn't worry. You are all right, Stinger." He grabs my shoulder. "You going in?" He jerks his head toward the spa.

I nod. He guides me in with a light hand on the small of my back. A warm shiver expands from where he touches me.

The spa is full of students in white robes and towels. We change and meet again to look for a good spot. Twenty or so therapists wait at the sides of the baths, ready to assist. The air is hot, humid, and scented. It nearly puts me to sleep, but I can't rest with my heart beating the way it is.

Other students walk in groups. Most of them keep their modesty in check with these bathing suits they give us, but now and then, some idiot will streak through and dive into one of the pools, splashing everyone and creating laughter and commotion when we are supposed to have peace. There are at least a dozen signs on the marble walls forbidding that behavior.

"This hot pool is empty and has eucalyptus scents. Is this fine, or do you prefer another one?" He looks at the other tubs in the room.

"I love eucalyptus," I lie. "It's my favorite."

"Then this one is perfect!" He waves me in and makes a show of looking away. I quickly drop my robe and step in. I've never been to a place like this, but I can see that students don't care as much about their privacy as I do. Typical Primary Land behavior.

Your body is Jattarian property.

"Shh!"

"Shh? Are you shushing me?"

"Oh! No, sorry. The temperature surprised me, that's all."

"Can I turn now? Can I come in?"

"Mhm," I confirm. The water is up to my neck, hot and slightly oily. My tense, injured muscles soften and relax.

"Oh, Valhalla!" he says when he gets in. He sits on the underwater bench next to me and spreads his arms. His forearm is behind my neck, resting on the pool's edge. He puts his head back and closes his eyes while he breathes deeply. Little by little, I let go of my legs and let them extend. I had them against my chest.

"Why are you here?" he asks. His tone is soft, his voice relaxed.

It feels like a bucket of cold water.

"I have to be." My secret is mine alone. Maybe that means never letting my guard down or letting anyone get close.

"But why so early? I applied last year at fourteen and even that was too early. Grandpa said I should have stayed out of school longer, prepared myself more, let my body grow strong to have a better chance during Trials. Older kids do better."

"I couldn't afford to wait. I have to fight and earn glory. For my family line," I respond quietly. "And for Jattaria," I add hurriedly.

"I understand." He says. He straightens up and looks at me. The moisture of the air beads in his brown hair. Droplets form on his face. I am tempted to brush them away with my fingers. "You want to train for as long as you can before you are seventeen."

I sigh and nod. Every Jattarian must go through the Trials before turning eighteen. The earlier one gets into school, the more years one has access to good trainers and facilities. Wealthy families like Oniv's have personal trainers and teachers, and they can enter school in their late teens. That isn't why I enrolled so early, but it's a good lie.

"Mother trained me, but she has been away. I have to get an education like the rest."

"Oh, right! Lagas Ener. Grandpa always talks about her, his favorite student. No wonder he broke his rule to take you in."

"Broke his rule?"

"Oh, never mind. Forget I said that."

Silence stretches awkwardly. He avoids looking at me.

Did I say something?

I sigh, irritated with myself, and bring my legs to my chest again. My toes brush against him. I chuckle nervously. My bathing suit seems to get tighter and tighter.

He smirks. "You'll do well, Stinger."

"You'll do better. You are the best in school."

He makes a funny, pretentious face. "Not so much. Curi challenged me at the beginning of the year, and I lost my claim to be undefeated. She beat me with a flying submission. I was stupid for not choosing spears as weapons! That's fine. I didn't really have high hopes of remaining an *Ubeseiret*."

"You didn't hope to be a Golden Blade? You are lying."

He rolls his eyes, then laughs. "You got me! But what can I do? It's too late now. Have you had any fights outside of class?"

I shake my head. "I haven't. It's a good way to stay undefeated!" I say with half a smile, feeling lame.

He shows me the tattoos on his back. Five marks for all the times he won a challenge this year. "You will have plenty of fights next year."

I don't have years; I have weeks. "Maybe I should look for that Hidden Ring place and get my challenge there."

"That's just a story Last-Years tell to scare the First-Year students. Many people try to find it and end up dead in the Kjedes."

"But what if no one challenges me?"

"No one wants to challenge a First Year, especially someone as young as you."

"I'll be fourteen in a few months," I say, hopeful but also hurt. I don't want him to see me as a kid.

How he sees me isn't that important. My feelings distract me. What matters is getting a challenge and winning it to qualify for Trials. I need to find a way to qualify for Trials, and fast.

I shake my thoughts off. "Maybe I can challenge someone."

He shakes his head, then lets it rest on the edge of the tub. "Be patient. Plenty of people will notice and want to fight you in your second year. It's what happened to me." He elbows me softly and looks me sideways. "I'm getting a massage."

"Me too," I say, despite myself. He leaves the pool and wraps himself in his towel. I get out and don the robe quickly. He takes my hand and tugs on it to get me going.

"This way," he says, smiling. He calls two masseuses with a gesture and brings me to two empty beds. We pass many students relaxing and getting their treatments. One of them seems to catch Oniv's attention.

"Erika?" He goes to her.

"Oniv!" she says and turns to him. Mikael, that boy I had seen her with before, lies in a bed beside her. He blushes and looks away without interrupting his massage. Erika gets up and comes to us. "I'm surprised to see you here. You are always training and never having fun." She puts one of her toned arms around Oniv's waist. "I was getting rearranged by Sasin," she says and looks pointedly at the bulky masseuse. "Thyra, I see you chose to ignore my advice and get close to my boy. Tsk, Tsk." She wags a finger at me.

"Oh," I say, trying to come up with some explanation. Nothing comes to mind.

"She is kidding, Stinger. I belong to no woman," he says, but the way they look at each other contradicts him.

"You belong to me, Boy. See you around, Ener," says Erika sweetly before dragging Oniv away. She looks over her shoulder. Her glare is not sweet but cold and vengeful.

Chronicle of Our Arrival to Antares

Agnor

Near the border between the Sargenian and Antarian nations

A blue tower stands defiant against the cloudy skies. It reaches up and seems to meld with the heavens. Sun comes through the fat clouds, reflecting on the tower's polished sides.

Magnitude.

Another ancient city, as old as history, lies only a few miles away. I hum the children's song about the brave Virtuous Knight of Magnitude who traveled the continent teaching the Code. Who didn't dream of being this legendary paladin, founder of the marvel before us? He was the largest of the seven Knights of Virtue and stood for what mattered most in life: Honor.

The other six Knights never really caught my attention, and I don't recall their bits of the song. Solitude, Fortitude, Gratitude, Certitude, Rectitude, and Servitude.

Opposite to those seven Knights of Virtue, here we stand. Seven killers, deserters, and thieves. The Soldiers of Treason, they should call us.

We look like specters, worn out and consumed by fear and hunger. Walver has regained some of his strength thanks to the stolen *Fogo de Alma*, a potent drink that gets one's blood boiling. I tried one drop and couldn't stay still for a day, let alone sleep. Now he stands on a rock, his sight fixed on the distant city. He chokes a bottle with his left hand, his thumb caressing the cap.

His eyes move slowly, scanning the huge gap scarring the land. The Gran Caida splits the continent from Raging Sea to Sullen Sea, a natural border between Antares and Sargena. The city of Magnitude forms a massive bridge between the two nations and offers the only passage for hundreds of miles over the fall. The ancient Colossi left this marvel to the world before they vanished.

"There is no way through, Boss. Those walls are too tall, the gates too guarded, and the city too populated. There are hundreds of Titans coming in and out. We must go to the coast of the Sullen Sea." Walver rechecks his map and notes, although he must have memorized it all by now. "That's the safest way."

"That's at least four more days in Sargena." Yana looks displeased, checking behind her back with shifty eyes. It's like she can't wait to be out of this country. She bites the flesh around her fingernails. "*Skynda!*"

The silent march goes on for days before the Gran Caida break starts to narrow. The vegetation shifts. The woods thin out until vast crops cover the plains. Saxon takes a few pods and grains. "They are tough. Probably need time and some proper cooking." He chews on them slowly but does not seem to enjoy them.

The temperature drops every day, and the wind seems to get meaner, biting cruelly as we progress slowly. Gusts of air blowing ice and snow punish us as we advance, edging the terrifying abyss.

We keep going, surviving each hour of hell. Sargena appears to have a hold on us and will not let us leave. Frostbite takes bits of us every night, hunger drains our energy, but we move on. I search the cliff walls, looking for some unknown flower or creature I can tell Emma about, hoping for one last story before I finally succumb. Fat hares streak across the road now and then, scared by us or some predator. Black foxes chase after small prey. Unlike the orange ones we have in Jattaria, these are bigger, with fur as black as coal, and little white-tipped tails and ears.

On the edge of the Caida grow purple flowers that look like skulls. "Death Blossoms," says Wanda when she sees me pick one up. "Uma has drawings of those in her book. They are good for infections." I snatch a handful.

"How can anything grow in this cold?" I ask, shivering, but not as much as the others shake in their coats.

Yana peaks from the vanguard. "This is the Eternafrost, the eternal ice lands. Anything that survives this weather must be tough. Like Titans, the Colossi and the mammoths they supposedly rode."

Eventually, the fall becomes so narrow that dozens of wooden bridges are able to span the chasm.

Walver seems unhappy with all of these passes, until he finally settles for one. "This one is far from villages and busy roads. We'll cross it after nightfall."

"But the pass is so narrow, the horses will freak out," says Wanda.

Saxon approaches the faithful beasts. "We blind them."

So we wait, and at sundown, we cross the risky bridge. The flimsy wooden structure bends and creaks under our weight but holds. The horses walk steadily, trustingly. The poor things.

When my feet touch Antares, an enormous load lifts from my shoulders. I feel it along my spine: a lack of pressure. This is where I was born, after all. I was a baby when Mother was exiled, but my body seems to remember.

I am home.

Not a day in this country, and we are already criminals here too.

"Hush your face, *frau*, or I'll silence you forever." Walver stuffs a sock into the homeowner's mouth. Her husband passed out after Walver clubbed him on the neck. He ties them together to a post in their basement. He proposed killing them, but Yana didn't allow it.

The house is like a palace, but it isn't bigger than the others we saw. There are sofas with cushions as fluffy as sheep and as soft as air itself. The floors are made of a dark sort of wood, and the walls are richly decorated with paintings and even photographs. Colored photographs.

"A telegraph," says Arsen, spotting a little machine by the entrance. She cleans her hands with her black bandana and runs a finger over the device's plastic frame. Plastic, as rare as gold in Jattaria, seems to be an everyday thing around here. How much did our culture devolve when the Colossi left? How costly was our dedication to a losing war? We could have lived like these Antarians, but we chose death.

Saxon whistles when he sees the communication machine. "Expensive. We had only one in our village," he says. He touches the button a few times, making the telegraph buzz. Next to it, there is a notepad with written messages. A waste bin under the little table has discarded bits of paper, where the communications printed.

"Unbelievable," I whisper, wanting all this to be available to us.

I sit at the table while Walver cooks in the kitchen. He sings and dances while working on a dozen dishes. "Tonight, we feast like kings." He brings plates and puts them on the table.

Pie filled with cheese, eggs, and tomatoes, stir-fried vegetables, and roasted chicken glazed with molten orange candy Walver made himself. There are pineapple muffins with little bits of crispy bacon sprinkled on top.

Walver puts his hands together. "Thanks for this blessing, you bastard gods. You gave us nothing without making us suffer a whole hell before. Gods of misery, I wish you all to die horribly, with bursting blisters on your eyes and burning sores in your privates. But first, let us eat."

"Let it be," we say. The blasphemies concern me, but not more than my hunger.

We eat and drink noisily. When dinner is over, the table empties. I take a hot bath in one of the many bathrooms. The luxurious house creaks as the Traitors step on those old boards and find their beds. Then it's quiet.

After my bath, I wander into the living room. The fire in the fireplace crackles softly, pushing waves of warmth into the room. The living room has a ridiculous library with at least a hundred books on the shelves. There are rolls as well, but not made of paper. Some other way of storing information I have not seen. I turn my attention back to the books and touch the spines as I read the titles, printed with detailed lettering using inks that gleam like metal. There's a little yellow one between two giant tomes. I run my finger over the words and feel the grooves. There is a drawing of a butterfly on the cover. "You would have loved this, I'm sure."

"I would have," answers the memory of Emma, with a smile that reaches her eyes.

I lie on a sofa close to the fire with the book against my chest, cover myself with one of the many blankets, and immediately fall asleep.

The next day, we leave before the sun is even halfway up. We've fill the wagon with food and blankets and put on every coat we found, hoping it would help us face the sadistic weather.

We make slow progress across the endless Antarian fields until we find another isolated house, then retreat a good distance away until the sun is down. Even during the day, the cold is brutal. The wind blows from the Raging Sea, bringing humidity and fast-traveling clouds that dump ice and snow for a few minutes before moving on to torture others.

Yana hugs her arms under the heavy coat she stole. She is in a good mood, but the cold might change this soon. That, or Walver, who is whispering things to her for the tenth time today. When I try to get close and hear what he says, he stops and goes away.

"What does he want?"

"The Jattaravkalt. But that's not the problem. It's the way he wants to do it." Her eyes close, and she trembles. She sips the liquor from her bottle. Her cheeks flush.

"He has been right a few times," I say. "Got us out of Jattaria and through Sargena, right?"

"This would get us killed."

I shift my weight and rearrange the armor under the huge jacket I stole. "We are in no rush, Yana. Maybe we find a barn and stay through the winter."

"It's what I am thinking," she says, nodding. "I doubt we will find the Jattaravkalt before the summer."

This house is even larger than the previous one. The wind whips with rage, and a dense mist makes our clothes wet and heavy, but we wait. There are lights in some of the rooms still.

Then, the last light goes out, and we slip in. The door and windows are unlocked. As soon as I am in, the strong scent of flowers hits me, almost making me sneeze. We take our shoes off and glide across the floor like hungry and shivering ghosts. The wind outside masks our steps.

Nefri, Wanda, and I sneak through a corridor and head upstairs while the rest secure the lower level. We enter the first room and find a couple sleeping. Nefri throws a noose around the woman's neck; I do the same with the man. We pull hard. They try to scream, but their throats are too constricted.

"Stop struggling and you will see the morning sun," says Nefri.

A few minutes later the family of four is tied and secured inside a cleaning room. Walver is already whistling while he prepares another meal in the kitchen. "Oh, kiddies, you will be sucking them chubby fingers for days after you try what I am making. Oh, kiddies! You will be singing praise for old Walver!"

After a dinner of baked potatoes filled with steak, green onions, and cheese, I almost feel like doing so. He brings apple pie dusted with cinnamon and pepper powder, and I almost start crying. The Traitors cheer as he slices the pie and serves it to us on delicate plates.

I fall asleep faster than the night before, the book I took from the previous house still unopened.

The next morning, it's clear the fields around us have been harvested already and offer no proper cover. Last night, we tried to sleep in the open, but a flash storm almost killed us. Now we know how unpredictable the weather is, so we eye the house on the next hill. We have more food than we can eat, but it will be useless if we freeze in the middle of some fields.

Saxon and Arsen walk to us from the back of our little caravan. I pull the neck of my new jacket up and tighten my cloak. I touch my cheek, freshly shaven, and wonder if putting on that cologne was a good idea. Yes, I smell fantastic, but my skin burns and is too sensitive.

A long howl travels through the fields, making my bones chill. "Wolves," I grunt.

"They have been getting closer," says Arsen. She breathes heavily and looks sick.

"They might be after the horses." The three Antarian beasts sniff and eat frozen grass. We took them to replace the ones we brought from Sargena, who wouldn't have survived a single storm.

"They are after us," says Walver curtly. "We need to find the Jattaravkalt soon. We are exposed! Vulnerable to animals and who knows what else."

"Calm down," says Arsen. "We sent Wanda and Nefri to check the area. They'll return soon and we can get into the next house."

Walver shakes his head and leaves, muttering to himself.

Saxon brings me to the back of the wagon and takes out three blankets and tarps. "I saw one of the farmers do this." He throws a blanket on one of the horses, then the tarp. I do the same with the second one, and we work together to cover the third. "I'd do this type of work until I died," he says, petting the horse. He takes apple cores from his bag and feeds them to the horses.

"Not a bad way to make a living, away from all the fighting and dying."

"Isn't that the truth?" he says, smiling. He is missing a few teeth, which somehow makes him more handsome. He pats my arm. "You are a good man, Agnor. Don't blame yourself for what happened on the way here. Zeeri, her family, the Korps, those merchants in Sargena, the things we have stolen, and even breaking our Oath."

"*Ja?*" I rub the back of my neck. "It haunts me."

He looks around, then whispers. "Ingrid and Vinz asked us to go with them, but we didn't like our chances away from you, *du vet?* You have given us hope, even if you can't see it. You are a decent young man, even when the world gets cold and ugly." His eyes wander away, scouring the landscape. Frost covers the hills, trees, and fences. They gleam as if made of glass. "Life bites at you, gnaws away your goodness. I ended up becoming a man I never thought I'd be," he whispers, as if dreaming, "but I also won the most precious thing."

Arsen works a few yards away from us, folding her coats and wrapping her gear. She wears that black bandana as a scarf, covering half her face. A single lock of fiery red hair escapes her wool hat.

"Thanks, Saxon. I am glad I met you, *wissen sie*? I am glad you two found each other. You have been so nice to me." I struggle with the words. I've only opened up with Emma before and I've had to guard my words every other time. With him, it feels so easy. His accent, his handsome but friendly face, and even the way he stands with his arms hanging at his sides. He simply invites closeness and trust. "It has not been easy. I lost the one I trusted the most back in Jattaria."

"I remember. I saw her at your feet when we pulled you out of the forest. Emma, you called her." He puts his warm, calloused hand behind my neck. I can picture him being a great father. "Just know we are with you." He winks and leaves me by the horses, wondering.

I walk around our little camp and find Yana studying the house. A huge tractor is parked next to one of the barns. About a hundred golden-back deer streak across the harvested field, hopping over fences, stopping to graze. Some tangle in quick fights. They are massive, their fur sleek and shiny, and their legs muscular and thick. Life in the Eternafrost continues to amaze me.

"Hey, there," says Yana without turning.

"Hey." I sit next to her on the crispy grass. My butt gets immediately cold despite all the layers. "Tent is ready if you want to rest."

"No. I want to make sure everything goes smoothly. And the sun feels nice." She stares at the house for a while, then her gaze wanders. She frowns. "What are they doing?"

I follow her sight. "Wanda and Nefri," I mutter. "They are back early."

Yana gets up and puts her hand to her eyes. "They better have a good reason to leave their post."

Chapter Sixteen

Description of a Descendant

Agnor

Near an Antarian village, that very night

Yana plays with a stick while she thinks. She snaps it in two.
"All you bring is terrible news, Nefri."

"That's what scouts do, Yana. Did you want me to keep it to myself?"

Wanda and Nefri are still panting from their run. Wanda takes a desperate bite of food and chases it with tea. "Antarian Titans are pacifist, but it seems we pushed all their buttons. They sent Pacificadores and a Descendant." She cleans crumbs off her chin. "We have to get out of here."

Saxon and Arsen huddle under the same coat. He blows steamy air into his cupped hands. "We haven't done anything that bad!" He says. "No killings, just robbing here and there."

"Walver almost killed two of them," says Nefri, leaning on his knees and catching his breath. "He always goes too far."

"Shut up! I need to think," orders Yana.

"What is the big deal?" asks Walver. "Just some Titans."

"Are you stupid, Walver?" says Nefri. "It's a Knight Descendant and a team of Pacificadores! It's not just *some* Titans! It's a *Colossus* with a *bunch* of Titans!"

"They are Antarians," I retort, leaning on hope. "They are not warriors. We are."

"Knight Descendants aren't Antarians," says Arsen. "Knight Descendants are Helarian priests, and they master all Virtues and can change the course of a war." She curls her lip viciously. "We are dead."

Yana paces around us, touching her face and fidgeting with the stick she broke. "We can't stay through the winter if they're already looking for us."

Walver straightens. "Maybe it's time we do something different." His voice trembles, probably with excitement. "Maybe we head into the storm instead of away from it." He grins a yellow smile full of gaps.

"No," says Yana. "We proceed as planned. Prepare to take that house tonight."

"Why?" asks Walver, smile gone. "Are you scared? Maybe the brave should lead, then."

Yana looks around. The Traitors' eyes all focus on her, waiting. She is not the Vulture, the legend she was when we left Jattaria. She is terrified, and it shows. "This is not the time," she mutters.

Walver walks away. The rest of the Traitors disperse.

"Agnor," she calls. "Get your practice sword, will you? We still have a few hours of light. Help me get something out of my system," she orders.

"Yes, Boss." I fetch my gear and throw on some heavy armor over extra padding. This will be an extremely painful session.

Yana waits for me in another group of trees, where four field fences converge. She is stretching her neck and back.

"That suit will slow you down, Agnor."

I give her a one-arm shrug.

"A man your size can afford some extra protection, I guess. Step in the circle," she says, drawing one on the ground with her blunt sword. "Let's play a game."

That's new.

Restless fingers squeeze my sword's grip; the leather of my gloves squeals. "Sure," I say quietly. "I'll do anything to be a better fighter."

She lets her coat slip down her back, reminding me of how she stripped back in that farm in Jattaria.

She wears no armor, only a light shirt and her sword. Her strong frame has grown lean after this grueling journey, accentuating her narrow waist. She looks up at me with hazel eyes that gleam like gold. Warm sunlight softens her scarred face. Her hair, longer than when we left, falls over her shoulders. Suddenly, I want her. I blush but can't stop staring.

She frowns and checks her posture. "Really, Agnor?"

I swallow hard. "Sorry." She can read me so easily.

"I thought it was just me." She approaches, her hips swaying slightly. She throws the sword to the ground, where it sticks. She comes within a yard, making me blush even more. She steps closer and can't stop looking at her lips, then at her eyes, then her lips again. "Kiss me," she says softly.

I hold her face and lean into her. Our lips touch. Her taste weakens me, making me starve for more. I close my eyes and let her guide me. I lift her up, her powerful legs wrap around my waist, and I hold her light body close to mine. Her hands cup my face, keeping me close. She plays with my long hair, then undoes the buckles of my armor.

There is no violence to her now. Softly, she draws me to the ground, inside the circle she drew, atop the jacket she was wearing.

Afterward, she lies on my chest and rests as our breathing slows. She rearranges the coat covering us and the cloaks we used for bedding. Stripped as she is, nobody would know she is a killer. Even with the dozens of scars and tattoos on her skin, she'd fool me. She grabs my arm and wraps it around her.

A minute goes by, then five. I move to stand, but she stops me, pulling gently with her hand. "You are so warm. Is it because you are part Titan? Is that why you are handling the weather better than the rest of us?"

Talking about this usually bothers me. But with her, I feel at ease. "I think so. I am not proud of being a Titan, but it serves me." The first words that have come out of me in quite some time.

"Keep your arms around me. I like this feeling."

"That's surprising."

"That I want somebody to protect and care for me?"

"You don't need anyone to protect you."

"I like to think someone would."

For a second, I consider her words. I wonder how many have gotten this close to Yana. "I would."

But I plotted against her. I planned to take everything I could from her. Our hearts are within inches of one another. How could I hide what's in mine? How could I hide it from myself for so long?

Yana's fingers play with my coat and tickle my chest. Her hand emerges with a folded paper: My vows to Emma, which she never heard.

"Can I read it?"

"Yes," I answer, hesitating but for just half a second.

She reads the few clumsy lines I wrote months ago. They are about me keeping Emma safe, giving my life for hers, conquering the world together, and striving to bring her joy. She puts it back where it was.

"She asked me to see everything."

"For when you meet later." She breathes softly as if understanding. "I used to love stories. I would read every book I found, talk to any soldier or traveler - then eventually, I decided to see it all myself." Her words break through my ribcage and grip my heart, squeezing it sweetly, painfully. Why does every step have to hurt this much? Everything reminds me of Emma. Could she, the one known as the Vulture, fill that hole in my life?

There's a whole world out there. Her voice is soft in my memory.

"I'd like to hear those stories."

She chuckles. "Of course, Agnor," she whispers, casually, unknowingly asking if she can occupy this space that has been empty for months. "I had a letter like yours, too." A finger runs along my collarbone. "I could tell you what it said if you want." Her voice gets smaller. Her eyelashes brush my chest.

"Tell me."

She clears her throat. "You always were elusive. I didn't know your face, your shape, or your name, but I knew you all the same. I knew one day I would find you. One look is all it would take for me to recognize you. I would be yours there and then and would pray to the gods you would have me. They favored this poor man, and you gave me your hand. You have given me everything, my perfect one. I'll wander through war, fearful and brave: fearful to never see you again, brave because I have you to fight for."

The two of us breathe quietly and let the songs of nature go on around us.

"Who sent you that?"

"It was from my father. He wrote it days after marrying my mother and died the night he sent it. Mother died with that letter in her hands a years later, and I kept it. She'd tell me stories of him, of the times they were together. I always asked her to tell me how they met, dreaming I would find someone too, but I lost the letter during a mission and stopped believing soon after."

"But you remember all the words."

"They came back to me when I read yours. That's the girl you lost?"

"Emma. Those were my vows, but we never married."

She tenses up slightly.

"That is why you're so heartbroken."

I swallow. Shut my eyes. Emma's memory tearing me apart, Yana's warmth putting me back together.

"That's why you keep going. You promised it to her." She scratches my chest with her short nails, making me shiver.

I nod. "I swore I'd bring her stories."

"What happened?"

"She died in my arms when we attacked the Fifth." My chest seems to cave in and shatter. Burning splinters burrow deep into my soul.

"Heavens, Agnor!" She pushes herself up and looks into my face. "And you were never with a woman until now?" Her voice is sad with this realization. She lies down again. "I am sorry I took that away from you. It should have been with someone you love. Someone who mattered."

She begins to stand, but I don't let her go. "I can't imagine it being better than this, Yana. In this cold and after so much suffering, feeling something so sweet is heaven. Things have been falling apart, but it's better when you are near."

"You put your faith in me, and I keep failing." Shiny tears roll down her rounded cheeks. "I am giving the Traitors everything I have and more, but I am losing. I lost sight of my goal, and my strength left me. I..." she bites her lips, shuts her eyes tight, "I have been so afraid. Since we left Jattaria. Being hunted by reapers, Regler Korps, those murdering monsters in Sargena, the Guardias. I lost something."

"You'll find what you lost. I'll be here, next to you." I close my eyes and let that sink in. Peace. That thought brings me peace.

She rests her head on my chest again. "I promised I'd help you find your Virtues, and I will. I have not forgotten."

I sigh loudly. "I need a clear purpose to find Fortitude, and I need Fortitude to achieve it. It's like a circle, a wheel I must climb while it's already in motion."

"You have Fortitude already," she says, tracing the First Circle tattoo on my forearm. "You couldn't have defeated Walver in your state without it, or stopped him from killing those Regler Korps. It comes out when you protect others."

"Maybe." I play with the idea in my mind. A smile comes to my lips. "A protector for those I care about. Your protector."

She hums. "In a while, I need you to let me fight you. I want to find a way to defeat someone much larger than me, and you will have to give it all. No holding back. Can you do that?"

"I can."

She pulls back a few inches and looks at me again. There is so much pain in her thoughtful face. Where is the killer who led with an iron fist? I pull her close and kiss her again.

She turns so our bodies meet again.

CHAPTER SEVENTEEN

STORY OF A WEDDING IN ANTARES

Wedding

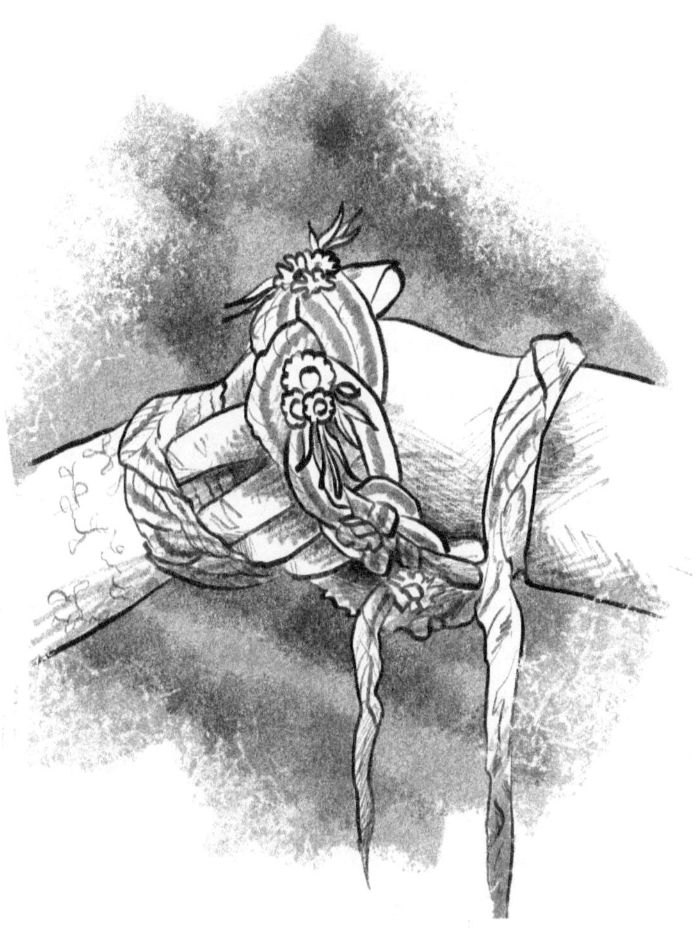

Agnor

Minutes before sunset, in the fields near an Antarian village

The sun sets behind Yana. Sunlight wraps her lithe silhouette and seems to swallow her as it dies. She arranges her hair and ties it in a ponytail, puts a fluffy hat on, then her heavy coat. She takes a deep breath and lets her head hang from her shoulders. A sensation intensifies in the pit of my stomach, climbs slowly to my chest.

I'm done for. I know this feeling.

Walver anxiously taps the sword hanging from his waist. Wanda and Nefri hold hands, their foreheads touching. Saxon checks his armor for the third time. Arsen rubs dust from her jar between her fingers. A deep frown darkens her usually pleasant expression. Her red hair flaps like a frost-cardinal's wings.

"Skynda." Says Yana.

We leave the small refuge of trees and run toward that house. The sky turns indigo as we reach the door. Yana is with me. The rest take to the windows and the back entrance. The house is made of brick, thick wooden beams, and columns with pretty bushes and plants around it. We stomp on the plants, stick close to the walls to avoid being seen, and open the door.

"Quiet," whispers Yana, as if I needed the reminder.

There are lights on, but the weather is too rough for us to wait outside, so we break in when the Titans are still awake.

The house's main door leads to a small entrance hall. To the right there is a dining room and a kitchen. An enormous

Antarian with shoulders as big as boulders eats a sandwich in a green robe. "We are supposed to notify them now, right?" asks the man with a mouth full.

"Yes. About this time," answers a woman I cannot see. "Finish your dinner first. Do you want some carrot juice? There is some in the cool room."

Yana signals me with a twitch of her chin.

We crawl behind furniture, get ready, and spring. The Antarian man's eyes widen. I clock him in the jaw. A cage with a dozen or so birds sits in a corner. They flap their wings and screech in panic. The man falls to his knees and his eyes roll up. I catch him before he hits a chair with his face.

The woman shrieks. She is about forty, as tall as me, and wears her brown hair tied in a bun. Yana jumps over the kitchen counter and knees the woman in the jaw, silencing her. She wraps the Titan's neck with her legs and puts her to sleep in seconds.

"Mom?" yells someone from the second floor. I turn to the sound, but Walver is already on his way. A second later, someone hits the floor. Nefri and Saxon go up.

"Did you have to strike him that hard?" asks Saxon.

"These Titans are tough," answers Walver, chuckling. "Can't risk it."

"Just help me tie him up," grunts Nefri.

"We better do that too," says Yana, anxiously scanning the room. "Wanda and Arsen, go put the horses in the barn before they freeze to death."

"Yes, Boss," says Arsen, putting her hood back on. The two leave the house, letting a cold gust of wind in.

I push the door closed. It's heavy and looks expensive. This home is a proper mansion. There are decorations made of expensive metals and with rich handcraft. The paintings are as large as those we had in School of War but far better. Even the smell is decadent. "How can they live with so much when we must die to have so little?"

"I don't know," growls Yana.

I finish tying up the man and putting a gag on him. "We'll worry about the knight in the morning, Yana."

She nods, checks the windows on the main floor, and goes to one of the chairs in the living room.

Walver delivers another amazing dinner. Grilled steak with baked carrots, onions, and sweet potatoes. There is cake and coffee and another drink they call *yerbamate*. By the end, my belly bulges painfully. I stifle a yawn and rub my eyes.

"Look at this," says Arsen. She grabs the paper on the big table. "Roamer alarm. Six-hour notices."

"Roamer?" says Saxon, taking the piece of paper from her. His long hair hangs wet from the shower he just took.

"That's what Antarians call Giants," answers Wanda. "Roamers, because we are always wandering."

Yana gets up from her chair by the fire. "The man was about to send a message when we came in." She looks pale, absolutely terrified. I have never seen her like this. She runs to the room where we bound the Titans; we follow.

The huge man is awake, glaring. Yana rips the gag from his mouth. "What's this?" She shows him the paper.

"We were supposed to send an all-clear message to city hall hours ago. Now they know you are here. They are coming for you," he says, smirking. His jaw is blue where I hit him. Yana strikes the same spot, knocking him out. The woman and the son scream, muted by the gags.

"Freezing death," says Yana, rubbing her fist.

Walver starts laughing, rubbing his hands on the pink apron he put on. "Finally!"

"Shut up, Walver." Yana goes to the living room window and touches the glass. It is already covered with a thin film of ice. The wind makes the windows and doors rattle. "We are stuck here." She bites her lip.

"I doubt they'll come with this storm," says Saxon. "Even a Descendant can't survive this."

"And they don't know we know," says Wanda, looking around at the Traitors.

Nefri shakes his head. "There were at least a dozen Pacificadores in that village we scouted. If they know we are here, they will send all of them."

"I am not worried about the soldiers," says Yana. "It's the Knight Descendant."

"We can kill it," says Walver, grinning.

"No killing," I say, punching a wall. "No more unnecessary killings, Walver." I look at Yana. "Maybe we should run. If we escalate this, they'll send even more after us."

They look at me, but I look at Yana. "We fight," she says. "If Walver is right, taking down a Descendant will get the Jattaravkalt's attention."

"Better than looking for them," he says, picking his brown teeth with one of his knives. "This country is huge, and I don't know where to start." He spits some bits of food at my feet. "We are trapped. No time for half-measures. If we fight, we fight to kill."

"We spare them if we can." Yana throws me a quick glance. "They might come tonight, maybe tomorrow. Nefri and Agnor, take the first watch. Walver, start preparations."

Walver touches his forehead with his knuckles. "Into the storm, after all."

Nefri taps the glass with a knife. "We have to leave Yana and Walver. Kill them if necessary. This has gone too far."

"We can't kill Yana. I won't let that happen," I whisper with my face against the window frame. There is nothing to see but darkness and snow.

Wanda sits on a chair by the bay window facing the other side of the house. Only the fire illuminates the decadent living room. The smell of strange wood burning is a sedative that I can almost get lost in. "I knew this would happen," she says, throwing me a suspicious look.

"She is going to kill us all. *Du weist das*, Agnor?" says Nefri. "Doesn't matter if you are in love with her."

"I am not!"

"Sure, sure. Then I am not madly in love with Wanda." He winks at her and blows a noisy kiss.

"Aww," she says and then kisses him.

"Alright, calm down, Nefri," soothes Wanda after the longest, most awkward minute.

"How do you know?" I ask.

"Agnor," says Nefri, and I can sense the coming wave of condescension. "You, my friend, are as subtle as a cat in heat. Those big, sappy green eyes looking at her longingly. Might as well write it on your forehead."

Wanda nods. "She has had her sights on you since we left." She blows air noisily. "Men. So clueless." She hits Nefri's knee.

"What did I do?" He complains, smiling.

"Nothing yet, but give it time." She thinks for a moment. "Can she beat the knight?"

Nefri nods slowly and puts a breadstick in his mouth. "My mother said Yana was the greatest fighter she'd seen. You were in her squad for months, Wanda. What do you think?"

"She's never fought a Knight Descendant," she mumbles. "But she is a Golden Blade with lots of combat experience."

"She has been training with me to get used to the height and size of Titans."

"So it is possible," states Nefri.

"Where do Saxon and Arsen stand?" I ask.

"They are with us," answers Nefri. He sighs. "I didn't know Yana was your type, Agnor."

"Am I that easy to read?" I squeeze one of the soft pillows.

"Like a children's book," says Wanda. "She is lonely, you are cute."

"Hey!" Says Nefri, a bit too loud. "What about me? Am I cute?" He slides closer to her and pokes her ribs.

"Yes, of course." She kisses his nose.

He throws me a murderous look. "Cuter than him?"

"Barely." She sticks her tongue out.

"So, hurting Yana is not an option." Nefri finishes the breadstick and takes another one from his pocket.

My mouth gets dry. "Not for me."

Wanda breathes onto the glass and draws circles in the condensation. "What about Walver?"

"He dies," I answer almost immediately. "If we set him loose, he will kill every Titan he crosses. We put him down."

They look at each other. "A necessary killing, *ja?*"

"*Ja.*"

Nefri slaps his knee to settle the issue. "Good talk!"

"We could be bounty hunters," says Wanda. "I am sure there's demand for that type of work." Her whispers are barely audible now. "Walver could be our first job."

Nefri's looking at me. "You are half Titan. That's where you come in. You pretend to be a small, ugly Sargenian, and talk to the Antarians."

"I was born here, so I guess I am Antarian. This could work."

"We'll see," says Wanda softly. "For now, we must survive." She stands up and goes to the cooling room, where Titans keep all their food. They don't need refrigeration with weather like this.

"Did you see the Descendant?" I ask.

"No. We heard Pacificadores talking." Nefri noisily eats another stick. Wanda comes back with a pitcher of juice and two cups. She gives me one and fills it.

"How did you plan all this?" I ask them, scratching around my ear. "I struggle to keep up with what's happening now, and you see so far into the future."

"That's because you are a dummy," says Nefri, tossing a piece of bread at me. "My sister and I had a wooden dummy at our house. It had a smile carved on its face. We'd beat the living crap out of Woody, and it would still be there, smiling. You remind me of it."

"Nefri! Be nice." She pinches his leg.

He smiles, but there's pain in his gaze. He is thinking of home and family. "We play games before we go to sleep," he says, quickly changing the subject. "It's a good way to wind down after-"

"Shut your face!" She elbows him, turning red. "Until you marry me, don't even dream about it."

"I dream about it, and often! But you are right. We should be married." He turns to me. "Would you be a witness?" He stands up and comes to my side. He holds my arm and looks into my eyes. *"Bitte?"*

"Yes," I answer. His stare is unnerving.

He returns to her, reaches into his pocket, and takes out two rings made of thin wire and strands of brown and blonde hair. He kneels before her. "Would you have me as your husband?"

She kneels with a huge smile. "Yes!" She kisses him. "Finally!" They put the rings on and whisper promises I can't hear.

The sting of jealousy digs deep as I watch these two enjoy something I'll never have. The twisted thought tries to steal this moment from them, but I won't let it. Emma would love to hear this story.

I walk to them, take their hands, and bow my head. "Do you take each other as husband and wife, to love and protect for as long as life lets you?"

"We do," they say at once. They hold their left hands and exchange their rings, staring into each other's eyes.

"Hey, lady of mine," says Nefri in a sweet whisper.

"Hey, my lord," she answers. Their foreheads touch.

"I declare you husband and wife."

They kiss, and I leave them to sit by the fireplace. I take the vows I had made for Emma, read them once more, then put them in the fire. It's time I let go. I won't find Fortitude in the past.

Nefri touches my shoulder. "Thanks, Agnor. We see your Virtue." He hugs me. "You are a true friend."

Wanda kisses my cheek. "We are eternally grateful."

"Congratulations."

Outside, the storm crashes against the house.

Chapter Eighteen

One Within

Hidden Ring

Thyra

In Solitude's School of War

Klausen fixes his old yet immaculate cap and squares his shoulders. His brown winter uniform gives his lanky body a presence and authority that makes it *almost* impossible to disobey him.

There is no way I'll hike another pointless circuit in the desert this time. I have my own circuit, and it's one I better keep secret. It's vague and might not be technically a circuit, but it will have to take me where I need to go. I will go to every mine in the Kjedes if I have to, but I will find this ring. I will get my challenge and my victory.

There are enough stories about it; it must be true. It's the only way I'll qualify for Trials in time.

I hunch my head down into my shoulders to shield my face from the cold wind whistling through the school gardens. At this point, I don't bother asking where lessons will take place. Every week he makes us do a new circuit, longer each time.

"You leave soon. Make sure you do better than last time."

"I thought you couldn't let kids wander in the mountains unsupervised," says Kar, his voice cracking before he finishes the sentence. A lot of the boys seem to have that problem.

"Is that what you are, Kar? A kid? I had hoped after these many months in school you'd be something more."

Oniv grunts and glares at the old man, who sighs and looks up as if asking the gods for patience. Dad would do that when a client got too needy.

"Perhaps this time you'll learn you are more than you think, *soldier*." Klausen puts a hand on Kar's shoulder. "Come, now." He gestures toward a pile of equipment on a folding table loaded with dozens of damaged weapons, armor pieces, and tools similar to those at Dad's shop. "Take two of these broken objects and fix them before you return."

I lean in to inspect them. Oniv puts a hand on my back, and peeks over my shoulder. I feel his breath on my neck and that's too much. I step to the side. Erika's friendly warning and threatening look are imprinted in my mind.

Klausen watches for a moment. "Choose your items," he says, doing a small flourish with his hand.

Oniv chooses protective gear. Kar steps up, gives me a quick look, and picks a backpack as his first item. It's big enough to hold supplies for everyone. His generosity makes me feel warm and fuzzy, and I nod with a smile when he looks at me again. I pick a spear and a sword. Dad would be mortified if he saw my preferences, but I cannot think of him.

"Very interesting," says our instructor when I step back. He makes three piles, each with two items. "These items generated negative responses," he mutters. "Kar," he says, tapping the pile of weapons. "Oniv." He pats the clothing. "Thyra," he says, resting his knotty hand on two broken gadgets.

My stomach sinks deep. Bile fights its way to my throat. He didn't give us what we chose, but the one we avoided most.

"Grab these items and do these routes." He hands us maps. We each get a different circuit, but all are relatively close to school. "Do not come back until you fix these items and can explain your aversion to choosing them. Go." He sends us away with a firm flick of his hand. He looks vaguely at the sky. One of his fingers taps quickly against his side, a break in his otherwise stony disposition. Maybe he is nervous about his grandson's fate. Maybe he is worried about all of us.

It doesn't matter. I left home because I couldn't wait for fate to decide my life for me. I am choosing my battles.

The Hidden Ring might just be a myth made up by students, but if it's out there, I must find it. The clock is ticking, and a squad of Regler Korps might storm our house any second. When this happens, I better be a valuable Jattarian, I better show them I am a promising soldier and a brave citizen. I might never do enough to compensate for Nefri's betrayal, but I will die trying.

I crumple the map Klausen gave me and toss it. When he is a speck in my sight, I veer toward my destination. I take the long knife I hid in my backpack and hook it to my belt. This journey is for me alone, and I am ready for it. I will find the Hidden Ring. I will get my challenge. When I return, I will come with the mark showing I am Trial material.

After sunset, after three more blisters pop on my feet, and after I've lost sight of the last city light, I stop. My knees give up. My limbs shake from cold or exhaustion, maybe both. The sand of the Kjedes rides gusts of cool air and hits me cruelly.

My hunger adds its complaints while I search for refuge in the pale moonlight. Following rumors might not have been a great idea after all. None of the two mines I checked had the white ring the stories mentioned. I have no clear path to follow or any idea of what to look for. Nothing more than a purchased map that could be nothing more than a made-up drawing sold to gullible First-Years.

This side of the mountain offers little shelter, so I throw my things on the ground in the shallowest of cavities. It's barely big enough for my backpack, but it will have to do. Before me are the Kjedes, majestic and brutal, like jagged claws bursting from the land, tearing at the darkening sky. Everything around here is death, but tonight I will rest.

Except the cave is hissing and getting louder.

I twist away, unsheathing my knife and slashing up in one motion. A huge reptilian head springs out of the shadows flashing two long white fangs. It comes for my neck but bites the edge of my weapon. Its jaw splits in half, but its massive body hits and throws me off balance.

I fall on my butt and catch my ankle between two rocks, twisting it. I bite my tongue to keep the screams in and shove the headless body away. It still coils, uncoils, and lashes against me.

"Freezing death," I curse between clenched teeth as I free my foot. "At least I have food now."

I grab the enormous viper's tail and drag it back to my shallow refuge. I build a fire with all the sticks I collected on the way here and let snake steaks cook while I tend to my many other needs.

A gash on my ankle requires cleaning. The dozen or so blisters on my feet could use some attention too. I drink a tenth of my canteen. Icy cold, soothing bliss runs down my throat. For a few seconds I forget the day-long torture I chose to put myself through.

I heat the smallest amount of water possible to clean my wounds and pray I wasn't wrong to chase the Hidden Ring, which sounds more and more like a school legend.

I take clean socks from my bag and put them on. The dry fabric feels like healing ointment on my hurting feet. I am safe from the wind, and the fire throws some heat my way. The numbness recedes and gives way to the feeling of a million needles pricking my skin. My stomach growls, adding to my general discomfort.

The snake meat sizzles close to the fire, almost ready. These Kjede monsters are larger than I imagined. This is truly an inhospitable land. No wonder we send the Wasters and traitors here. This place is hell.

Which reminds me of my task.

My gear is bundled before me. Enough to sustain me for a week. The two items Klausen made me bring are somewhere in there. I fish them out and watch the firelight dance on the tools' rusty surface. It would take less than half an hour to clean and reassemble them.

The serpent-like guilt inside me slithers again and makes me shiver. If I could only slay it the way I killed my dinner.

I put the tools away. I can't stand the sight of them. I can't think of Dad and how hurt he must be. If he knew why I left he would understand, but he can never find out. Nefri's treason is my secret. At least until he is caught.

I bite the chewy steak. It's almost like fish, but I think I overcooked it. Now it's almost impossible to eat. I gnaw on three thin strips, then give up before I puke. I save the rest and end the day with a taste of bile in my mouth.

Close your eyes already. There is nothing left to see today.

But stars flicker in the dark sky. One of them seems to touch the horizon line. Too low to be a star. Solitude? No. The city is in the opposite direction. Something else -

Gray clouds threaten to make my third day in the Kjedes worse than the previous two, but there's no time to waste. I rub my limbs awake, pack my stuff, and leave in a rush.

Two nights ago, I saw a fire. A distant one. Nothing else could have made a light like that here. That's my destination, and I must keep going. The map they gave me was almost right, so I march toward that light until I can go no longer.

Noon comes. Noon goes. The day grows darker, and I don't seem to be any closer to finding the Hidden Ring. Maybe I was seeing things...

No! It's there. It has to be.

The moon throws the most feeble of lights on this darkness. A mist falls incessantly. Water creeps into every crevice of my clothing and has me quivering. But I will not stop.

Not until I die.

Waking up fast, I unsheathe and point my knife at the voice. A pair of eyes stare at me, then a person materializes from the blackness. A short man with dirty light armor and Jattarian weapons. "What are you looking for, kid?" says the man.

"The Hidden Ring. I am looking for my challenge. Is it you?" My heart beats like a blacksmith's hammer. My senses are hyperaware, my muscles unbearably tense. I get out of my sleeping bag.

"No," says the man. "Another guard saw you a couple of hours ago. If you had kept going, you would have found the mine." He points at a torch down the rocky valley.

The soldier, whose tag reads Hugo, walks away. I roughly pack my things and follow. His stride is smooth while mine is unsure. We go deeper into a valley. People appear around us. They emerge from a few mine entrances. Some of them carry torches, all wear shackles. Giants and Edgens pour out of the mountain, crowding the dark valley. "Arin gets very enthusiastic about the challenges. I bet he called every worker in the mine. "

"One of these prisoners will be your challenger," says someone else. Another man, this one tall, skinny, and young. "This is the Hidden Ring."

I thought there would be some structure built by long-gone Giants, perhaps with columns in ruins and torches around the fighting area. This is a barren valley full of half-dead prisoners. "And you?"

"A student. Gunnav." He turns to see me with curious lime eyes. "Perhaps you have the courage I don't."

"How long have you been here?"

"About a year."

"A year? Here?" I look about, wondering how he survived. "How old are you?"

"Seventeen."

"Then you better return or you'll be an outlaw." I squeeze my weapon's grip. "You must go through Trials."

"I have been wandering too long, afraid of doing what I must," says Gunnav. "I thought it would be easy."

We keep walking down the mountainside. I turn away and inspect the miners. All wearing ragged clothes and tired expressions.

The guard answers the question in my mind. "Some are Edgens, most are Jattarian Wasters and deserters. We had a Titan years ago."

"It escaped?"

"No one escapes," answers Hugo. He waves his hand slowly. "The Kjede mountains are worse than the mines."

Gunnav touches his face. "If they win they get the mark. Hidden Ring fights are rare because only a few students make it here. Most give up or die or get eaten by the mountain beasts. Vipers, lions, or insects are the usual suspects."

The miners surround us when we reach the valley's bottom. The disparity in sizes is huge. These full-grown Edgens are no taller than me at thirteen. How can they take our lands and kill our soldiers?

More and more witnesses join, wearing their shackles and chains. Some guards here and there watch with interest. Hugo waves at some of them. "We get one or two students every year. This is the most fun these miners get." The prisoners stare and whisper to one another. The murmur grows louder and louder until one of the Edgens raises a torch. Everyone then falls silent.

Hugo points at the person holding the torch. "You got your opponent. *Licka till*." He steps aside and melds into the crowd.

'Good luck?' I won't need it.

"I challenge you, young Jattarian. That's yer weapon?" asks the prisoner as approaches me.

I inspect the long knife in my hand. *"Ja."*

The man with the torch squints and looks me up and down. He is old, close to forty. He has fiery red hair with a matching beard and wears a ragged and discolored outfit. I recognize the uniform from paintings of the Edgens' typical clothing. He throws the torch into a pile of wood and a bonfire slowly grows. This is what I saw the other day.

Light pushes outwards from the fire and touches the ring's edge. White and gray bones mark the Hidden Ring's large area. Old, broken melee weapons lie mixed with human remains. A corpse, fresh by the looks of it, lies at the edge of the circle. I shiver realizing I could die here.

"She came a few nights ago and failed," he whispers. "Her opponent earned his mark. I am ready to earn mine. Are ye?" he asks and aims a bony hand at me. The strange accent is thick and stretches random syllables of his sentences.

"They make you fight me?" I ask.

He shakes his head and looks up with emerald green eyes. "I volunteered long ago, young lady. I fought many prisoners to earn my chance to fight in the Hidden Ring. If *you* earn your mark, you win your right to be Tried. If *I* earn the mark, I win freedom to go back home and see me daughter, me wife. Or I could die on my way there. Either way, I'll be free."

I drop my backpack and pick up an old shield from the grim white circle. "I am your last battle, the only thing standing between you and your freedom." A primal fear grabs me. Like me, he fights for his family, and in his eyes, I see he is dangerous.

The man grabs a short sword and a spear. He wraps fabric on the spear's blade and lights it on fire. The witnesses stay outside the ring, singing in whispers that get louder and louder.

"Name's Alastair McRae. What's yers, lassie?"

"Thyra Ener."

"Well met, Thyra Ener." He puts his two fingers on his forehead, I silence a groan when I start to panic. Alastair slides his finger from crown to chin. The Cutting Sign.

My legs feel weak, my lungs feel absent of air. "Death or surrender?" I ask, stupidly. I know perfectly well what that gesture means.

"Death only, Miss Ener." He bows slightly.

"I have never killed before. I don't want to kill…" I mumble with a last-second realization.

He nods, and his eyes lower again. "Then you were born in the wrong country. Don't worry. It's easy, Miss Ener. Point that knife at me and hate away." He folds his hands as if in prayer. Little sparks fall from the flames on his spear. I cry in this deadly circle and before a heartless crowd, begging for time to go back.

There is no going back. There is no holding back. Cut, kill, destroy.

I do the Cutting Sign, take Fortitude's stance, and hit my shield with my knife.

We circle around the flames. I test the treacherous ground. The stones will roll and cut my ankles if I am not careful. The man walks surefooted. Shadows stretch behind him, long and animated, almost demonic.

Don't get distracted.

Alastair hits his torch-spear with his sword. Death opens its hungry maws, ready to devour life. It won't be mine. It can't be.

He cuts with his rusty weapon, and I parry with my knife. His bad steel vibrates as it slides down my blade. I feel it in my bones and shiver. Chips of steel and rust come off my opponent's sword whenever the weapons clash. I avoid the spear, which showers me with sparks if I block it.

His attacks follow an unfamiliar rhythm. Too quick. Too light. The flames on his spear distract me. I am supposed to be the quick one, anger's deliverer, but I don't want to kill this man. He has gentle eyes and a life to go back to. My enemy is desperate, much more desperate than I, and his attacks come at all times and from all angles.

I am not a warrior. I am a stupid girl who thought too much of herself. How could I save my family when I can't even save myself?

Stop holding back! It's all or nothing, all the time!

His steel bites my sides, my legs, my arms. He dictates the fight's rhythm. Death is near, just a handful of cuts away. My knife barely finds him. His jagged sword leaves wounds that burn. He is killing me, and I am not fighting back.

Who will save your father, then?

"Noooo!" I swing desperately and take a few steps back, creating space and gaining a few more seconds of life. I put the fire between us while I catch my breath.

Cut, kill, destroy.

The pain recedes. Fortitude takes over. I had forgotten my purpose, but now it's clear.

The crowd's chanting becomes a loud hum, a primitive song urging violence. My heart beats to this music. I stretch and reset to find the right stance. Light, quick, every motion like the wind.

Alastair stalks me, but I dance out of his range. He closes the distance when I let him, prepares to kill me, and attacks. He swings his spear, grazing my leg and burning my skin, but this time I hold. He stabs with his sword exactly as he did before, but this time I know it's coming.

I sting before he does. I let myself hate him, and my body does the rest. Mother had shown me how to finish an enemy in one strike, and I just do it. I slash his forearm open from wrist to elbow, his short sword flies from his grip. In the same motion, I strike his chest. Easy.

Blood spills from the cuts on his skin. They look like red smiles. He kneels abruptly, leaning on his flaming spear. "You're...so fast," he says.

"Sorry it had to be this way. You'll meet your daughter in the afterlife, many years from today," I say while I help him to the ground. The light leaves his eyes, but I am certain he heard me.

My enemy. My first kill. A weight crushes my mind, but the danger surrounding me gives me no time to grief. The witnesses grab me, drag me close to the fire, and hold me down with ice-cold hands.

"Let me go!" I try to fight them off, but their grip is steel.

The chanting increases to deafening levels, then a guard comes closer with a red-hot iron. Someone opens my mouth. I try to bite their fingers, but I can barely breathe, let alone hurt them. They stretch my lower lip until it feels like it's going to come off my face, then the guard applies the hot iron.

Pain expands through my entire skull. I cry and beg and kick and punch, but it's all futile. The smell of searing skin climbs up my nostrils until I pass out.

"Go! Go!" they yell and bring me back from the darkness. "You have your mark, go!"

The guard with the brand, Arin, holds my face. "Show this to an instructor to get your tattoo. You'll be ready for Trials. Tell no one else."

Bony fingers point Coldward. I take my backpack and knife and leave with a bleeding body and a wounded conscience. A man's blood stains my hands, but I must leave, or it will be my blood spilled on this desolate desert too.

My breathing slows. My mind spirals. I fall on my knees and rocks bite my shins. The wind is blowing again, or maybe it never stopped. I curl up against a boulder and wrap myself in the few layers of clothes I have. The eyes of the man I killed look at me. He is at peace, but my soul isn't. The price is high, but the stakes of failing are worse still. It could be Dad hanging on that post, getting his eyes picked by the crows.

"Why did you come here?"

I throw my knife at the sound. It cuts the air where a man's head was a heartbeat ago. I scramble to get on guard as the figure raises his two hands to pacify me.

"You followed me," I say, breathing fast.

Gunnav shrugs and looks Coldward. "We can return together. I know the path. I almost came back many times. I was not brave enough, but seeing you... Why did you come?"

"Why else? I needed a challenge."

"But you have time."

"I don't. No time, no options. I do what I must and pay the price." I start crying, trembling. It is too much. What has happened and hasn't happened yet is too much of a burden. The treason, the lying, the heartache, and the killing. Mother turned herself into stone, and I think I know the reason. "A soft heart does not survive this life."

"We must be as dead as the rocks beneath us." Gunnav turns away and starts a fire. He skins a rabbit and stakes it. Tendrils of delicious-smelling smoke make their way to me while I study his rough yet boyish face. He hands me a small bowl with warm water. "Thanks for finding me. I was lost."

The moon travels across the night sky in a slow arc. Just before it fades in the morning light, we reach the school gardens. Gunnav goes his own way before we enter the hall. Doesn't even say goodbye.

I reach the barracks and find them empty. Most students are in class. I slip into bed, thinking that those tools still need to be fixed. Kora-Elena starts biting my ankle, but I pass out from exhaustion anyway. This path I walk is lonely, full of death and suffering. Warriors like Mother and Klausen know this, and it's what they were trying to teach me.

Every person is a teacher, and every moment a lesson. Mother's saying makes more sense now.

Chapter Nineteen

Obituaries in the Land of Titans

Knight Descendant

Agnor

That same day, near an Antarian village

Yana looks about, facing each of us for a moment. The smell of leather, sweat, and dirt stirs as we help one another with our gear. We wear the heavy armor we stole from the

Korps and Guardias and cover it with our thick cloaks. Leather belts squeak as we tighten them. Steel plates click against one another and slide into place. "We choose the battlefield. The storm is finally gone. Now they come."

Walver loads bolts into one of his crossbow fans, making the spring inside it whine softly. *Tap, tap.* He hits the fan-like magazine against his helmet, then jams it into the weapon. He flicks the fuel bomb hanging at his side. "Be in your position by sun fall. If you see Pacificadores, neutralize them. If you see the knight, let him through." He stares at each of us to check we understand.

The Traitors exchange some last words of encouragement. Saxon takes his flask of *Fogo de Alma* from his pocket and raises it. "Let's finish this," he says. We bump our flasks and bottles with his and drink the sweet and spicy liquid. The fire spreads from my throat and belly to the rest of my body.

The door closes after the last Traitor, leaving Yana and me alone.

"If things go sideways, will you have my back?"

"Of course."

"And that Descendant is mine," she says, squeezing my arm. "You *must* leave that knight to me. Promise you will."

"I promise."

A smile forms on her lips. The beauty beneath the coldness comes out again.

We take the room upstairs because its windows allow us to see all around the house. We leave the family tied at the back of the room, between the bed and the wall. They kick and complain, but the bonds are too secure. "Sorry," I say. "Be quiet, and this will be over before long."

Have a life worth living, said Mother. Here I am, facing death, committing crimes, and putting innocents in harm's way.

"It's only a matter of time. They're coming." Yana stands by the window, looking out. Her mind seems elsewhere, her eyes focused in the middle distance. Her hand rests on her left hip. The lights are off, the curtains down, but enough light remains that I see her tremble. I sidle up to her, my boots scraping the rich carpet, and grab her shoulder.

"Where is your protection?" I whisper, panicking. I pat, searching for plates, and feel only her body.

A smile stretches her lips only half an inch. Her eyes remain distant. "*You* are my protection."

"You can't go like that," I say. I turn around to get her things, but she spins me with a firm hand.

"Agnor, stop. I need all my speed, all my strength, and all my stamina."

"But without armor -"

She puts a finger on my lips. "The Descendant will not touch me. Trust me." She looks up at me. I kiss her softly and hold her face.

Her expression becomes steel. She's got the eyes of the Vulture again. "I have not been myself lately. I know that. I lost my center and was not in touch with my Virtues, but not anymore. I lost more than half the Traitors. I failed you! *You*, specifically." She says, her voice almost breaking. "You asked me to help you find Fortitude, and all the time I was losing mine. You said I should be more, but I am less than when we left the Edge."

My chest fills up with pain, like shards of glass piercing from within. "I am with you, Yana."

"But *they* aren't," she says, looking outside. "The Traitors will leave if I don't show them it's worth staying. Even Walver's trust is flaking."

I squeeze her hand. "I can't let you die."

"All I want is to be the one to finish the knight."

I return to the window and check on the other Traitors. I spot Walver, Nefri, and Saxon, about fifty yards from the house. "Everything is still quiet."

"This happens tonight," she says. "They're coming. They're coming."

A bird takes flight noisily from Yana's side of the house. She nods and squeezes her weapon tighter. "They are here," she says. She spares a second to look at me, then resumes her watch.

Another bird takes flight.

"Whose bird was that?" she asks.

"Walver's. Looks like he took care of two Pacificadores. Do you see anything?"

"One Titan in Arsen's area, treading through the snow. She'll take care of it."

Another bird takes flight, and another one right after. "This is it, Agnor. The biggest fight of my life." She pushes her face against the glass and scans around the house.

"Saxon hasn't released his yet." I squint and try to find him again. "I think he moved. He must have seen the Descendant."

The wind grows soft, the night sky clears. The big crescent moon pushes its light through the windows, making the room look like an ink illustration.

"It's here," whispers Yana. She brings a finger to her lips. She closes the curtains. The darkness is almost palpable. We get close to the tied Titans. They push with their legs to slide deeper into their corner, but their backs are already against the wall.

Something creaks in the house. I sense a presence approaching, invisible to us. Silent.

Yana aims her repeating-crossbow at the door. I level Nefri's steam-musket, putting the buttstock against my shoulder. Its smooth wood frame rubs my cheek. The fancy iron sights line up, covering the door. Yana left one single candle burning outside the room so we could see shadows if someone approached. Its dim light dances on the walls.

Until it's snuffed.

Heavy steps approach, softened by the carpet. My heart hammers in my chest.

A door opens. The hinges creak. Another door opens, closer this time. The knight checks every room on the way here.

"*Estan ahi, Gigantes?*" says a voice deep, smooth. A dark, dark shape steps into the door frame, blocking all light coming from the windows like an eclipse. The shadow seems to bend over to step in. Once inside, its helmeted head swivels on a heavily armored neck. The metal screeches softly.

"*Se mueren hoy.* You don't need to die as sinners. The true God, the one you forsake, is merciful if one repents. My God put you in my path for a reason, and as a follower, I must listen." This beast seems to take up most of the room. The knight holds a cannon and aims it around the room. The three hostages behind us are the only reason the knight hasn't blown up the room. The house, even.

"We aren't dying, Descendant," answers Yana, but not from my side, where I thought she was. The Colossus turns quickly and levels the weapon at the sound. Moonlight touches the monster. I spot the inside of an elbow and take my chance.

Phoom!

The steam-musket springs in my grip and sends a bullet whistling through the air. The explosion expands inside the room with absurd concussive force. The projectile hits the mark and bursts, but the knight doesn't even flinch. He shoots at Yana and blows a hole in the wall.

I cycle the bolt, aim, and shoot again; a chunk of armor flies off. The Descendant ignores the damage, if there is any, and searches for Yana. I reload and shoot until my weapon is dry, but the monster still stands.

Yana slides from behind the knight as if solidifying from liquid darkness. She strikes the head, neck, and elbow, then fades into a dark section of the room. The Descendant fires twice, and the whole house shakes. Yana takes the Colossal's back, looking like a child in comparison to this huge foe. She stabs the shoulder, and the enemy finally cries out. Bleeds.

Yana wraps herself around the cannon and twists it away from its hands. She falls, rolls on her back, aims, and shoots it from a seated position.

The recoil throws her back.

The shot smashes into its mark.

Crushing metal screams and the sound fills the room. The smell of smoke and burnt salts makes my eyes water. The Knight Descendant stumbles. It recovers its balance, rips off the damaged armor, exposing a thick, dark arm with tattoos inked in gold. Bright blood pours from a big shoulder injury. The Descendant produces a short sword from a sheath hidden along its thigh. It somehow unfolds into a long two-handed blade, as black as the armor except for the gray edge, hungry for Jattarian flesh.

"*Por que peleas, Jattariana?* Surrender now and avoid all the pain."

A click. The cannon Yana stole must be empty. The knight steps forward, slashing. Furniture gets cut in half and thrown. The knight swings again, hitting the wall and breaking through it. The roof will come down on us at any moment. Light stabs in like thick spears through the handful of holes in the brick walls, revealing the huge Descendant.

The knight and Yana continue to clash and break away; the knight misses each strike and Yana delivers no significant damage. Their breathing is loud, hers like a panting leopard, the knight's like an enraged bull. A glass bottle, empty by the sound of it, shatters against the knight's helmet.

Fogo do Alma. Yana downed the whole flask.

That burning feeling must have all her spent muscles spasming with new energy. "Die!" she bellows suddenly, then charges unrestrained. Her blows are deafening, like a hammer on an anvil.

Fortitude aligns her body with her purpose, drawing strength from every fiber of her being. Gratitude makes her flow like air around the Colossus' blade. The styles she has tried to teach me are patent in how she moves.

She finds her opening and springs. The attack is so powerful that her sword shatters. The knight strikes back, punching Yana across the room. She hits a bedpost and falls to the floor with a grunt. The Knight dashes at her.

I tackle the beast as it's about to stomp her head, and it's like hitting a stone pillar. We crush against the wall, go through it, fall onto the roof, and smash against the garden. Pieces of the house fall around us.

Yana lands by me and pulls me away just as the knight buries an elbow where I was only an instant before. It gets on its feet and jabs an armored fist at her, missing by a hair's width.

"We need to finish this," I say, retreating with Yana and favoring my right side. I give her my blade and go to take the Descendant's folding sword, lying on the ground just a few steps from me. It weighs at least twice what mine does.

Nefri and Wanda come from around the house, exhausted but ready to join. Walver and Arsen come a few seconds later. "We got this," I say, panting. "This beast can't defeat six of us."

The unarmed Descendant reaches behind its back and produces a flail that detaches from its armor. Each plate seems to also double as a weapon that the knight can access as needed. The flail's chain links the long handle to a metallic skull with inch-long spikes coming out of it.

"Attack!" I scream.

Nefri, Wanda, Walver, and Arsen surround the knight. Yana moves, staying always at the knight's back. The Traitors shoot their repeating crossbows, keeping the knight moving defensively. Yana and I stab and retreat in a coordinated attack. The knight keeps that terrible spiked skull flowing around him, unpredictable and deadly, and always minding the spots without plates.

The Traitors run out of bolts, so they go in with swords. The knight takes hits that chip its armor but never reach flesh. Walver takes a chance, but a burst of red comes from his midsection when the Descendant quickly parries and stabs. Walver falls, growling in pain, spilling blood as he rolls away.

Nefri and Wanda force the knight to face them. Arsen charges when the knight turns away from her. Her knees hit the ground hard, her headless body falls, spraying blood from a jagged wound. Her fingers twitch as if playing an invisible instrument.

I didn't even see the flail swing.

The Colossal throws the weapon at Nefri, picks up Arsen's sword, and dashes at Wanda. Yana darts in from behind the knight, who drops to its knees, pivots, and thrusts the sword into our leader. Yana twists away from the flash of metal, but the blade bites flesh.

She goes down screaming.

Glass shatters. Flames engulf the knight when the oil bomb bursts. Walver is on his knees, laughing and pointing a broken finger at the knight. "Roast, you monster!"

I step up and slash at the knight's naked wrist, then jump away as the sword slices the air in front of my face, scraping my helmet. Blood droplets fly from the sword as it swings by; streams of fire splash my chest.

The enemy retreats and puts the flames out with handfuls of snow. Smoke and steam rise from the distressed black plates of its suit.

"Follow my lead, Agnor. Wanda, you too," says Nefri. He signals us to step away.

Our foe looks around. "You cannot defeat me, Roamers." Its voice is not as steady as before. Scratches cover its armor. Its exposed arm drips blood. Its breathing is labored, shooting steam against the cold air.

Nefri breathes heavily, keeping a hand up. He flicks a finger, and I know he wants me to move to the right. Wanda follows another direction, and in a minute, we are moving as one. He coordinates our attacks, telling us to retreat or advance, generating openings we carefully exploit. Wanda strikes behind the knee and ducks under a swing. I hit its shoulder with a downward swing and block a savage elbow. Nefri smacks the hand holding the weapon and barely avoids a kick to

chest.

We patiently dismantle the Titan's guard, whose movements get more sluggish each passing second.

A plate around the neck comes loose after I land a hard blow. The knight counter-attacks and grazes my chest. Nefri then climbs on the knight's back and rips the helmet off. Long, brown hair flies free as the knight slams a fist on Nefri's side. He crashes into a bed of flowers, rolling in a tangle of his own limbs.

Wanda jumps in to distract the knight and gives Nefri time to get on his feet. I parry a devastating drive meant for Wanda, and the clash jolts my entire torso. The knight turns to see me. A beautiful rounded face with big brown eyes stares with unnatural fury. Her snarl shows perfectly white teeth stained with red. She tries to cut, but her stance is awkward and weak. I leap and strike like a scorpion, just as Yana showed me.

My bones crack and my muscles pull painfully with the otherworldly effort. Sharpened steel travels in a descending arc, aimed at her shoulder. The heavy sword slips between two armor plates and changes trajectory, slashing her throat.

"No," I grunt, pulling the blade out. Hot blood jets all over me. "I am sorry. Oh, no..."

Her eyebrows go up. Her sword falls from her fingers. She struggles for a few seconds, trying to stop the bleeding.

"I didn't mean to kill you," I say, holding her head.

"Forgive them, Father," she grunts. I put my hands over her wound, but she dies anyway. A warrior too big to fall, she remains on her knees after passing. Nefri and Wanda come, panting and blowing clouds of steam from their mouths.

"All these deaths are someone's fault," I say. "A holy warrior died defending her country, her people." I look up and hope for redemption. "We will pay a high price for this sin."

"You killed the knight," says Yana, rolling in the bed and kicking the blankets. I pour water over the gash on her side, and she winces. "You betrayed me."

"Shush. Don't move."

"You robbed me of my victory, Agnor." She tears up. Her pale face looks almost transparent.

"You don't know what you are saying."

Walver is on the other bed in the room. Wanda and Nefri hold him down and wrap him in blankets. "I'd let you die if we didn't need you," grunts Wanda, frowning.

"What do we do now?" asks Nefri when they are done. His hands are trembling. Mine are too. Cold, fear, strain.

"We get out of here." I leave the room and go to the next one.

Saxon wakes up when I touch his shoulder. "How are you doing?"

He looks down at the slash across his chest. His guitar is in pieces next to him. "Been better," he says weakly. "Where is Arsen?" he lifts his head with effort and looks around the room. "Is she with Wanda?"

I shake my head. "I am sorry."

He cries softly, his face screwed and red. Fresh blood spills from that terrible wound. "She was pregnant, Agnor." He grabs my jacket and pulls me down. "We were going to be a family."

"I am so sorry," I croak, feeling crushing sadness. Sorrow claws at me from within, tearing me apart.

"There is no living without her," he whispers, his chest rising in spasms. "You are a good man, Agnor," he says, fading. "Don't let them break you."

"Goodbye, friend."

He closes his eyes, red from crying. He falls asleep after a few minutes, his breathing gets shallow. His chest stops moving. He sighs one last time and leaves as well.

I walk outside and take in the Arctic air. It slips into my lungs like a million razors. "It's hard to see beauty in this, Emma."

The wind swirls around me, messing up my hair. All my tears freeze as they fall. My sobbing gets lost in the gusts of air.

"There's more out there. Things to see, people to protect, words to learn, songs to hear." Emma would push me to keep going.

"I know," I say after a while. I fell to my knees and grabbed bunches of ice and dirt. "It is just so hard to see past all I've lost."

The sun comes up, regardless of all the suffering.

CHAPTER TWENTY

TO NOT FIGHT

Armed

Thyra

The next day, in the school gymnasium

Klausen paces behind me. I lie face-up on a bench, my arms stretched out at my sides with forty-pound weights in each hand. The tension in my arms and chest is searing. He won't hear me complain. A scream builds up in my throat as I endure the most painful exercise known to mankind.

"You think you are in your last year, don't you?"

"I think nothing," I repeat for the hundredth time today. It's the only thing I'm allowed to say.

"You think you are ready to be Tried, right?"

"I think nothing!" If I bite any harder, my teeth will shatter.

"We know you don't think. You act before the right time. When will you learn? Is your life the price you must pay? Let's hope not. I'd hate to see my time wasted. Don't you think?"

"I think nothing! Agh!!!" The dumbbells slip from my fingers. I jump off the bench and run as fast as my tired legs can toward the edge of the gardens. A mile there, another mile back, and then I will hold those weights again. I better make it in less than fifteen minutes, or I won't see the day's end.

Kar and Oniv spar with a bunch of other students in a ring nearby. All of them have their teachers' seals of approval and enough challenges and victories to walk in unquestioned.

Erika is among those students. She stops her exercise to watch me go. Not an ounce of sweetness is left for me. One of her friends joins her, then a third. They throw nasty looks as I ran by them.

I should have stayed away from Oniv, as she asked. I shouldn't have allowed myself to be distracted by this stupid nonsense, but I got carried away like some idiotic little kid. Get it together! Don't you know what's at stake? Don't you know lives are on the line?

Sweat freezes on my skin and hair. Winter's chill stabs at me, eager to snatch the warmth of life from my flesh. This burning need to stay alive keeps it at bay. I will not let Nefri bring ruin to our family. The guilt from taking a life burdens me, as well, but I will shoulder that too. Alastair's haunting face will remind me of the price I had to pay.

When I return to Klausen, he has set up the two pieces of machinery I failed to fix on the bench. I put my hands on my knees and bend over as I try to breathe. I turn away from the tools in front of me, still unable to confront the memories of my father.

Puke shoots from my face and hits the grass, splashing my leather boots and the equipment around me. Once breakfast is gone, out comes the bile, burning my throat. After that, dry heaving until my mouth is dry. I am sweating and crying and shivering.

"That is some way to get it out of your system," says Klausen as he walks to me. He grabs me by the shoulders and pulls me up. He helps me sit on the bench and throws his jacket over my shoulders.

"Why did you go to the Hidden Ring, child?"

"I..." but I can't answer. "I think nothing."

He takes my lip and stretches it. The cauterized wound inside itches and hurts. He chuckles and pats my hair. My sides are getting long, they need to be shaved again.

"You'd better start thinking, Thyra." He sighs and looks up. After almost a minute, he speaks again. "What would your mother say? You could have died out there, and for what?"

"I have my reasons."

He shakes his head slowly.

"So you found the Hidden Ring?"

"I won. I killed my challenger, an Edgen named Alastair McRae." I start crying, sobbing loudly, and shaking uncontrollably. "I held nothing back, and I killed him!" The shudders are so violent my bones hurt. The tears flow until my eyes burn and itch. I spit more bile and wipe snot from my nose.

Emotions rush out of me like a tidal wave, and my instructor waits.

"Fix those tools, Thyra."

After lunch and an hour-long massage in the spa, I walk to one of the few classes I take. I kept just three in my schedule:

Leadership, Human Studies, and Advanced Tactics. The rest I tested out and were covered by Mother's extensive lessons.

Good.

This gives me time to focus on what I need: strength and fighting.

I can also avoid the students and their meaningless opinions. Only Trials matter.

I push the door open and enter the crowded classroom. I spot an empty chair near the wall and walk to it.

"Miss Ener, a moment," says the teacher. The rest of the class quiets. Two hundred heads turn toward me. "Stand there, if you will." The teacher points her long finger at a spot in front of the blackboard. She's drawn advanced war maneuvers schematics. I missed a few important lessons in my walk-about. They are already studying siege machines and combined attacks.

There's so much reading I must do to catch up. Maybe Klausen will give me the essentials.

"Explain yourself. What's more important than taking this class? Instructor Klausen wouldn't suggest skipping this course. Unless you already know everything there is to know?"

I am tempted to tell them, but I won't. I can't. The Hidden Ring must remain a legend. That's part of the deal.

"Sorry, Professor Bente. I shouldn't have missed your class." She knows my words are empty. Her blank face tells me so. We battle with our gaze, and she wins. I look down.

"Find your seat, Ener."

The students' eyes follow my progress, then snap to the front of the class when Bente slaps her hand on the table. "We are finishing the chapter on armored support today. Open your books to diagram two-hundred-and-seventeen."

When I put my books and papers on my desk, the girl sitting beside me stands up and goes elsewhere.

"I heard you went to the Hidden Ring," whispers another student, taking the now empty seat. Arvo. He is a seventeen-year-old boy with more muscles than I have seen in someone his age, and Oniv's favorite fighting partner.

"I wish. I got lost during an exercise."

The boy shakes his head. "Gunnav is back. That guy that went looking for the Ring last year. We thought he was dead, but oh, no. People saw you two coming back together. You went there, and you won. This means you have your first kill." He touches his forehead with his knuckles to show respect as the blood drains from my face. "You are something else, Ener. The rumors about you are true. I would like to fight you when you have some free time."

He tilts his head and gives me a charming smile.

"I am a First-Year. You'd crush me."

"I don't know. It could be fun. It's not official, just a spar. Lots of us are following your progress, *Little Stinger*."

"What did you call me?" I say much too loud.

"Shhh!" he says, and his face turns red.

"Arvo, Thyra. Step outside for five minutes and finish your conversation. If you are not done by then, consider yourselves expelled from this class," says the professor. Her spear-like arm points at the door.

"Sorry, ma'am. Won't happen again," he apologizes. Her arm remains pointing at the door.

"Freezing death." He stands up. I follow.

Once outside, Arvo leans against the wall and counts the seconds out loud. Instructors and trainers walk by and stare. Arvo stops counting when he gets to ninety-nine seconds. "So? A friendly fight to test our styles? They say your strength is Fortitude, but that you get in and out of Solitude and Certitude stances with ease." He smiles again, but there's a twist in the way his eyes gleam. "Please. I won't take no for an answer!"

I shake my head. We are too close to Trials to be fooling around in unofficial fights. I have my challenge, and I am still undefeated. If I make it through Trials, I will be a Golden Blade. What a way to start my military career! I would be promoted to First Diamond right after boot camp. There is no better way to earn redemption for my family. "Sorry, I can't."

"Very well," says Arvo. "Thyra Ener, I challenge you."

"You can't," I say, panicking. "I am a first-year! The customs say that -"

"I don't care about customs," he says, cutting me off. "Challenging First- Years is frowned upon, but I'll survive." He grins. "One hundred, one hundred and one, one hundred and..."

Two months.

That's all I have until Trials.

"Thyra, pay attention!"

"Sorry, Instructor Klausen!" I shift my gaze to him. The grunts of the hundred students exercising in the gym suddenly get louder.

He snorts angrily. "It's the last time I take a student so young, I swear."

Oniv and Kar find this hilarious, but they silence their laughter to avoid his attention.

"These principles are vital to win a war, children. Deception, timing, strategy. You can defeat your enemy without fighting if you manipulate what they think about you. Appear big when you are small, close when you are distant, threatening when you are harmless, and wounded when you are strong.

You'll find that the result of a battle is decided before the first arrow flies."

He drones on, but I struggle to grasp what he is saying. Arvo has challenged me. I remain undefeated only because I am young and a First Year. If he challenges, I will eventually lose my claim.

"Thyra! Run five miles!"

Oniv and Kar's laughter bursts out of them.

I leave the gymnasium running at a good pace. Maybe the cold air will give me clarity. I must find balance. I sleep less than six hours a night, and all my classes and exercises overlap. My body, heart, and mind are at war with each other, and I can't ask anyone for help.

As I run, I get the feeling the answer is dangling in front of me. To fight or not to fight? Do I accept that challenge? What would Klausen do? Mother? Father's face invades my thoughts. My guilt comes and goes like waves.

Those freezing tools. I still have to fix them.

Maybe that's it. One less thing on my mind.

Instead of finishing my miles, I run across campus to the dormitories. I get to my bed quickly and open my footlocker. Kora-Elena bites my knee and scratches while screeching angrily. "Stop, you lizard!"

Kora lets go and hisses. She hates it when I call her lizard. She slaps me with her spiky tail and cuts a bit of my skin.

"Ouch!"

She coils on the opposite end of the bed. She is still upset that I left her alone for days. I would be upset, too, if I was chained up for so long. "Sorry," I offer.

She looks away.

I sit cross-legged on my thin mattress and wipe the sweat falling from my forehead with my wrist. "I have things to do, Kora. I hope you'll forgive me." I reach for one of the tools, an old mineral grinder used to carve small holes in mine walls. My stomach tightens. I push through the guilt. There is nothing left to vomit anyway. "Let's do this," I say finally and make up my mind. I memorize how the mineral grinder looks before I disassemble it. I have seen many like it and in worse condition before, but it's part of my process.

My hand starts as insecurely until I touch the cold, dirty metal. Then, it finds a course. The parts are stuck with old oil, caked mud, and a nice layer of rust. My body knows how to deal with this, and my mind now has time to think. Of Dad.

The corners of my eyes burn as I cry and find a calm spot in my mind's storm. I shouldn't have run away, hurt him that way, and ignored his feelings. Nefri shouldn't have put us in this position either, but that shouldn't be an excuse. He was the circumstance, I was the reaction. I will have to make things better with Dad. Soon.

And Arvo's challenge. He's surely told everyone by now, making it official. I have to fight him or decline.

What do I do?

The safest choice would be to decline and surrender my title of Undefeated. At least then I would still have my chance to graduate this year. If I accept and fight him, I'll certainly be defeated. Arvo is one of the most talented wrestlers in school, extremely proficient with blades, and an expert with ranged weaponry. He has trained extensively in the styles of Fortitude and Certitude. I have trained in all styles to some degree, but skill and speed can only take me so far. I have only battled Mother and a few others thanks to her strict rules against training outside our home. If I miraculously defeat him, I'll likely get injured and diminish my chances of performing well during Trials. There is just not enough time to properly heal before then.

But Golden Blades get immediate promotions to First Diamond. If I won I would break so many records: Youngest Tried, youngest Officer, youngest Golden Blade. Everything in one day, if I could just make it to Trials undefeated.

But it's impossible.

Dust and metal bits fall on my lap and on the bed sheets as the grinder gears give and start working.

If only I could win without risking a debilitating injury. Win without fighting. "Ha! That's ridiculous, Kora-Elena. How can you win without fighting?"

My alligator seems unimpressed.

The tool's hand crack easily slides out from the body now, exposing its insides. The metallic burr is pretty smooth, but there's no fixing that. I grab a corner of my bed sheet and clean the sockets and teeth.

Wouldn't that be ideal? Trick *him* into withdrawing? But why would he do that?

Because he has much more to lose than you.

He doesn't. He'd fight for his Undefeated claim, while I'd fight for my family's lives.

Does he know that? Does anyone know that?

The grinder assembles perfectly. The bedsheet is a mess of stains. My cold hands have small cuts all over, but the tool works properly. I grab the second machine and get to work on it immediately. It looks like a small straightener for steel wire.

Arvo does have lots to lose. He is seventeen, a Last Year, and *must* go through Trials this year, or he will be loaded in the Dark Runner as an Appeasement Offer.

The tool's inner rod slides out after I push and pull to loosen the mud inside.

That's the answer. He doesn't have to be afraid of losing but of being so injured that he *could* fail the Trials.

But how?

Deception. Make yourself big when you are small.

Clearly, that's the only way. I knew this strategy is useful in war but never considered it for something petty like this.

He called you Little Stinger.

He is close with Oniv, then. Kar knows him too, and he would be willing to help me. He always is. I only wish Oniv was the one giving me attention.

Focus!

Deception is misinformation. Arvo must somehow learn the wrong things about me, in circumstances that will facilitate his decision to surrender.

"Kar, I need your help."

I grab him by the arm and pull him out of his match.

"I was about to win that one!" he complains, but half-heartedly. He has that look again; the one that tells me I'll get whatever I ask for.

"Sorry. This is so important!"

He nods and follows. His opponent is panting, bleeding, and happy to put a stop to the fight. Kar truly was going to win that match.

"I need you to do me a huge favor."

"Anything. What is it?"

I smirk and know I must look devilish.

"I *need* to trick the entire school. I want you to spread a rumor that I sparred Oniv, and he wasn't able to fight properly for months afterwards because of how much I hurt him."

"Why?"

"Does it matter?" I reply curtly, then remember I need his favor.

"Most have seen him fight. They will know it's a lie, or he would deny it. It's pointless."

"Isn't that how rumors work? A lie that changes and grows, especially if it comes from you. It's the only way to avoid a fight." Saying those words makes me realize how big a favor I am asking. He would be spreading lies about his best friend to help someone he met a few months ago.

"Oh, this is about Arvo! He did say he was fighting you. I thought he was joking." His face goes pale.

Things have progressed so fast in the last few hours. "Not a joke, but we are too close to the Trials to be playing these games."

"So you were listening to Klausen's lesson!"

"Huh?"

"About deception. Tricking the enemy?" His voice gets smaller.

"Oh, yes. Last week. Sure!"

"It was this morning," he mumbles.

"Please! Just say something here and there. That should be enough. Don't overdo it."

"I'll do this for you," he says solemnly.

"I see your Virtue. You are a good friend."

"Friend," he repeats. He seems to taste the word and dislike the flavor.

"This should be fun," I say. "Lying to the whole school." I kiss his cheek and run to my next class.

"I won't disappoint you!" he says as I leave.

By the next day, people are asking me what I did to Oniv at the beginning of the year to hurt him so badly he could never move right for months. Denying the rumors only seems to feed fuel to the fire.

"Why is everyone asking if I am well enough to do the Trials?" Oniv holds the door of the empty classroom open for me to enter.

"Oh, I don't know. Some rumor," I say. His pretty face goes through a range of emotions. Kar stands behind him and shoots me a quick smirk when I look at him. Maybe he overdid it after all.

Oniv's helmet is lopsided, and I reach to fix it. He grabs my hand in a reflexive movement. The pressure of his fingers on mine eases until it's just a gentle touch.

"Sorry."

"I'd never hurt you." I blush so hard my face feels on fire. His hand still holds mine, but he lets go after a moment.

Klausen enters the classroom with a handful of scrolls under his arm. "Crash course on mobile maneuvers and modern weaponry before sparring. We only have thirty-five minutes, so let's make them count. Thyra, draw three armored units in a basic formation while I prepare this."

"Yes, sir," I say and leap toward the blackboard. I take a piece of chalk and start working.

A day later, Arvo and I cross paths. He stands in the middle of the corridor, still as a statue. I walk to him, nervous and afraid but trying not to show it. He eyes me the way I would look at a rabid dog.

Kar has definitely overdone it. The rumors reached levels of insanity. The collective creativity took this story to heights I didn't predict. I like the version where I bite his kneecap off best. Oniv often leaves his legs exposed, and a quick look at them would prove it's a lie. Maybe people don't care.

"No later than next week, Arvo. We are too close to Trials as it is." His friends around him react when he doesn't. Nervous laughter, giggling, people covering their mouths and looking around. I can only hope the general excitement in school plays in my favor. "Arvo?"

I might be imagining it, but a shiny film of sweat develops on his forehead.

"Agreed. You have the choice of weapons. Practice swords?" he says with a thick voice. He clears his throat with a cough.

"No. Battle gear. Spears or swords, it's up to you," I say, shrugging. "Let me know when you decide." I walk by him and pat his arm twice. "As early as possible. We are *very* close to Trials, and I'd like to have time to recover."

"You are doing Trials *this* year?" He frowns.

"Maybe. If I am not too hurt after our fight. Otherwise, I'll have to wait till next year."

I walk away and people in the wide corridor behind me grow loud. My anxiety threatens to break through my skin, but I hold my pace.

CHAPTER TWENTY-ONE

LAST A MOMENT

Thyra

A day later, at the School's entrance

The white marble block at the school's entrance shines fiercely this clear morning.

I close and open my hand as I walk to the Spear of the Tried. Will the time I spent exercising make a difference? None of my clothes fit anymore and even the marble block seems smaller.

The ice on the spearhead reflects the morning sun, and sticks softly to my skin when I run my fingers along its frigid blade. One of the few sunny days of this winter, the timing couldn't be better.

"Hi, Thyra."

Dad's voice travels easily through the garden. I run to him and wrap my arms around his neck. I stay there for as long as he lets me. He grabs my shoulders with his big hands and makes some space between us. His eyes are watery.

"You have grown so much, my baby," he says, and I could touch the love in his words. His beard and hair are longer, mangy, and threaded with much more gray than the last time I saw him. His skin is thinner, not padding his bones as it did before. I cry freely in his arms, which aren't as thick as I remembered.

"Dad, what happened to you?"

"Nothing, nothing. I am just glad you are well." He touches my cheek with a trembling thumb. I push his hand against my face and close my eyes.

"I missed you, Daddy." His jacket smells like engine oils and iron. New stains decorate it, so he is still working, at least.

"How's school? Are they treating you well?"

I chuckle. "That's not what they are here to do."

"Class stops for Trials, correct? We should do something for summer break." I pull away from his touch. I forgot he doesn't know.

"No," he says, answering his own question. Maybe he read it on my face.

"I'm doing the Trials this year, Dad. I'm ready."

"How could you possibly be ready, Thyra? It takes most people years! You are only thirteen years old!" He tears up again, big drops sink into his graying beard.

"I will be fourteen soon. I have your strength and Mother's training, Dad. Klausen, Mother's old instructor, is teaching me too."

"Why are you doing this, Thyra? I don't understand." He shakes his bony face. "I thought you liked working in the shop with me. I thought you wanted to be an engineer."

"I do want that, but this is something I must do. For our honor and Jattaria."

"You sound like Lagas. You are so much like her, *wissen sie?*"

My hair stands on end. I hate that he said that, and I love it too. "I am sorry, Dad. It has to be this way."

He bites his lip until it bleeds. "I'll support your decisions, my dear girl. What else could I do?"

I nod and hold his two hands in mine. One of his nails is broken and black. "Let's spend some time together, Dad. I can show you the gardens and school, the places where I train. I'll even show you my new moves!" I punch his gut, much smaller than months ago.

"That sounds fun," he says, poorly blocking my blows. He doesn't know the first thing about fighting.

"I know an empty teacher's room you can sleep in tonight," I whisper, squinting. I snicker and raise my eyebrows. It's still fun to be mischievous, especially if Dad gets something out of it.

So I show him to his room for the night and leave the absurd amount of suitcases he brought with him there. "You are only staying until tomorrow, *wissen sie?*"

"*Ja, ja.* I know. I just want to be ready," he says suspiciously.

We leave the room and walk around campus, sitting at benches under trees and next to old statues. I show him my perfected moves in an isolated corner of the gardens, and tell him about everything that's happened so far. Except for Alastair and the Hidden Ring.

Maybe he senses there's something dark inside me, but does not ask about it.

The sun starts to set and a chilly breeze picks up. "We better turn in," he says, shaking. He is such a wimp. We finish the day eating toast and hot milk in his room. I tuck him in bed as he did me a million times. "Heart, heart, heart," I say before closing the door.

"Let's go to Solitude and have lunch," I say the next morning. I fold my schedule and put it out of my mind. My teachers can deal with my absence in any way they want. "I'd love to have a meal with flavor for a change."

"Absolutely, my girl."

We walk slowly toward the gates with all his bags. A wagon waits for us. The driver helps us with the bags and then we leave. "Where to?" he asks.

"The Shicksal Inn, please," says Dad. "That's where your mom and I would eat when I came to visit her." He smiles dreamily and shrugs a little bit. His hand touches the side of his leg, where he keeps his purse. The fabric and leather muffle the ring of a few coins. He frowns, but it dissipates when he sees me. "I am so thankful I got to see you, Thyra. Thanks for asking me to come."

I hug his arm and lean against him. "I wanted to see you every day I was away."

The wagon pulls out of the driveway, slowly leaving the school behind.

The Inn's waitress makes her way to our table. Her chubby hands collect the used silverware, then I notice that most of the used utensils are on my side. As Dad talks about the changes in the factory, I realize he barely ate. He only ordered bread and butter while I ate most of the chicken. A leg and two toasts wait uneaten in front of me. "We are not done yet," I say, stopping her with a gesture. She nods and leaves. I smear big chunks of heavy cream and jam on the bread slices and push them to him. He devours them without pausing his story. He is breaking my heart. Why isn't he taking care of himself?

"Dad," I interrupt and put my hand on his. "Tell me! What's happening at home?"

"Nothing happens at home, baby. It's a bit messy, I have to admit. It's just me and my tools, and they don't care if I don't put them away." He pulls his sleeves as if embarrassed by them. "What matters is that you are well and that you're taken care of."

"Why are you so thin? Why aren't you eating?"

"I, well -" He avoids my eyes.

"What is it?"

"I am just being careful, that's all."

"How?"

"Don't worry about that, Thyra."

"Dad!"

"I am just making sure you are getting the best training. That's it! It's nothing to worry about."

"Klausen."

"I -" he hesitates. "Yes," he admits finally. "I asked if he could take you as a student. Your mother reached out, too. She is very proud you are in school, but she is just as concerned about you as I am."

"You send me letters every week and have come to see me twice. She hasn't come or written once. How proud and worried can she possibly be?" I say with all the resentment I harbor for the woman.

"She is at the Edgeslag, Thyra. She can't leave, and you know that."

"You don't need to pay for my instruction, Dad. That's the School's purpose."

But he shakes his head. "Private instruction. He only takes one student a year, and he already made an exception for his grandkid's best friend. Your mother said it's expensive but worth it. I listen to her."

"Dad," I whisper desperately.

"*Nein, nein.* Few things have less value than money."

It's dark when he brings me back to the school entrance. We walk in silence, me holding his arm, him holding one of his bags. It's one of the old ones he kept in the shop back home.

"Are you going to tell me what's in the case?" I bug him.

"Oh! Ha! Your tools and your mother's First Circle gear. I fitted her suit of armor so it's more your size." He hands me the suitcase, which is as heavy as I imagined.

We stand in silence in front of the Hall entrance.

"*Jeg elsker deg, rakas.*"

"I love you too, Dad."

"Be careful." He grabs my hand a little tighter than usual. "Please, be careful."

"I swear."

He holds on a bit more, then let's go.

"You be careful too. And eat more."

Once again, I walk away. It should be getting easier by now.

Arvo waits for me in the Hall.

"Are you ready?" he asks. His friends are around him. My gambit failed.

"I am ready," I say as convincingly as I can.

"Good, cause they are waiting for us. Follow me."

Oniv and Kar are in his crowd. Kar smiles a shy grin. Oniv's face is empty, emotionless. He has figured out my move, most likely. Did he tell Arvo? Is he loyal to me?

Why would he? He barely knows me, and my feelings only go one way. He loves Erika and her stupid brown hair that shines like molten chocolate. I'm only a foolish kid in his eyes. It's time to stop dreaming.

A cold, ugly sensation settles in the base of my guts. Kar beckons covertly, and I give him a few seconds of attention. He nods almost imperceptibly and smirks.

Will my plan work?

I hate to depend on someone else. And why is Kar even helping me? Unless he isn't helping me but setting me up.

Arvo walks beside me, carrying his gear in his arms while I carry the heavy bag Dad brought. We approach the biggest gymnasium, the one with fewer rings and more bleachers. Two Last-Year girls I have seen in my lessons open the doors for us. One of them looks at me and touches her knuckles to her forehead.

Do I have supporters?

The gym is full. Half the school must be here. The kid from Battle Maneuvers class that kept bothering me to teach him the swift scorpion, the popular girl who seems to have a trail of students following her at all times. Dozens of eyes focus on me while a few loud students run around collecting bets.

Teachers, instructors, aides, and proctors stand around the ring. I heard fights like this one are important events in school, but I didn't think they would be this big.

Maybe two Undefeated fighting is a rarity.

I drop my bag and open it.

"Zeefja," I call, making sure Arvo hears. "Write me down for a bet."

People's eyes me, but I make myself ignore them. I am burning inside, but I must appear icy. Everything all depends on small details like this.

"What do you want to put down?"

"Everything I have," I say, gesturing to the contents of the bag. Dad handmade my mother's equipment. Even rich kids like those around me know armor like that is expensive. The bright gymnasium lights make the black plates and shiny leather gleam.

Bets must be heavy against me. Zeefja's face pales and confirms my thoughts. He scratches his chin, then tugs at one of the many braids hanging from his head.

"Let's say a thousand marks," I offer and help him assign a value to my belongings. The gear's value is much higher than that, but it doesn't matter.

"I can't cover a bet that big, Thyra," he says with doubt. I took a quick look at Zeefja's notes when I walked past him.

"You can cover it."

He looks at the instructors around us. They nod. "Freezing death. *Varfor inte?*"

"Exactly, why not?" I turn before he can answer and see my fear creep in.

The armor finally settles after several adjustments. I grab my mother's sword and shield. The blade splits my skin when I try the tip. A little drop of blood. I face my opponent and run my finger from scalp to chin, ensuring it goes over my left eye.

The Cutting Sign.

The audience reacts immediately. Some with anger, some with laughter. It doesn't matter. The stakes couldn't be higher. This is now a fight to the death. Hits and scores do not matter. Even the proctors shake their heads. I see it all with my peripheral vision, but my eyes don't leave Argo's for a moment.

"Freezing death, Thyra, we are just supposed to fight."

"Then let's fight."

He looks at the instructors, but they shrug. He is the challenger, after all. We step into the ring. He brings up a practice blade that has been recently sharpened. He doesn't even own a real weapon, but it will cut. I stuff all my fear deep inside, where such a feeling belongs. I channel Fortitude, but also the other Virtues. I might need them all today.

The tip of his sword seems to vibrate as he stares me down. He takes a side step.

I remain in place. I couldn't tighten the hold on my sword anymore. Tendons and muscles threaten to snap, heart and veins threaten to burst, but I am ice. I must be.

I follow him only with my gaze. His weapon trembles as he approaches.

Now I move. "Come on, Arvo. I have class in thirty minutes." I slide my left foot forward and bend my knees. I bring my shield up and my sword back in a scorpion stance. On guard, ready to sting. The Swift Scorpion is meant as a finishing maneuver, used only when opponents have been weakened already, or for when enemies are below one's skill. Assuming this stance when we haven't even touched steel is an insult, but I try not to make it look so. I want to appear casual when I am tense, strong when I am weak, and indestructible when I am one strike away from crumbling.

The lights are blinding. The audience falls silent.

His shield shakes, he takes another step, and I tighten my stance. My stinger is ready; the lower edge of my shield is aimed at his knees, the upper one up to my nose. I scratch the ground with the sharpened tip of my weapon. The metal rings as it scratches the worn surface. *Grishhh.*

His sword drops. His shield too.

He takes his helmet off and throws it at my feet. He steps out of the ring, forfeiting the fight and his title as Undefeated. The crowd opens up as he exits, but everyone remains quiet. Arvo pushes the doors open and lets them close behind him.

Something hits my shoulder. I launch my attack. I stop it an inch from Oniv's face. I never dropped my stance. His beautiful features melt away the ice I'd built up inside. I drop my sword and shield, get rid of my helmet, grab the back of his neck, and bring him close to me. He is tall, strong, handsome, and powerful, yet I control him without much effort. At least for this moment.

I find his lips with mine and let myself burst with joy.

Till Valhalla.

Hands grab me, pull me back, lift me up, separating me from him.

The gymnasium is a storm of cheers, screams, and applause. I am thrown into the air and caught by unknown students as the school breaks into an absurd celebration. Many of them lost hundreds of marks just now, but it doesn't seem to matter. They are all with me.

I let them carry me, I flow with the celebration until I land in front of Kar.

"Hey, you did it," he says with half a smile and shining eyes.

"Oh, yes!"

"I did as you asked. I helped you, *ja?*"

"*Ja!* I owe you!"

"You don't." He looks down and scratches his neck. "I really care about you. I am glad it went well."

"Thanks, Kar. You are a great friend."

"Friend," he repeats again, rejecting the term almost.

"A *great* friend!" I stand on my toes, lean forward, and kiss his cheek. "Even if you don't think so, I owe you."

He touches the spot I kissed. His face turns bright red. I smile and leave him there while hoping to find someone else. A fresh and ticklish excitement flutters in my belly.

On my way back to Oniv, I run into Erika. Still like a statue, she glares at me. There is hate all over that perfect face. "Was that you staying away from him, Ener?"

I step back.

"Here, Thyra! Drink this!" Some student I vaguely recognize pushes a small cup into my hands. I follow the student and down the contents, which burn going down my throat. I cough into my arm as my nose and eyes water. Better than facing Erika.

"Ugh! That's awful," I complain, but the aftertaste comes and it's not so bad. Sweetness and warmth. "Give me another one," I order and let alcohol wash away the guilt.

The top of my footlocker swings closed. I secure it with my lock and prepare to go to bed. It's late, almost morning already. Trying to get some sleep is almost not worth the effort. I must be up in a couple of hours, and the party we had still rings loudly in my ears.

"Kora," I call and reach blindly into the dark. I slam my hand against my helmet. "Ouch! *Jagar sa dum!*" I rub my fingers and decide Kora-Elena will have to sleep alone. I am not going to spend hours searching. Sleep. Always rest when possible. Klausen has said that more times than I care to remember.

"Good choice," says a raspy voice from the door.

My hand shoots to grip my practice sword as I jolt up.

"Instructor!" I say with my heart in my throat. "What are you doing here?" He enters the barracks, and the darkness seems to swallow him. Kids snore, passed out on their beds, or maybe on a random bunk they found empty. The smell of contraband alcohol emanates from a hundred bodies.

"Just checking on my student."

"You didn't go," I say.

"I can't show favoritism."

I try to read his face, but it is too dark to see anything other than the whites of his eyes. "Are you saying I am your favorite?"

"I thought you weren't paying attention to my classes," he says, ignoring my question.

"I would have paid more attention if I knew how expensive they were." I exaggerate the accusation in my voice.

"You would have refused to take them. Your mother refused to let me give you free lessons. It runs in your family. Stupidity, stubbornness. Greatness too."

"I made enough money tonight to pay for the lessons." I kick the bag under my bed. It contains my new fortune. Being an underdog pays four to one. It's good business.

"Your father will have his money back, Thyra. I never intended to keep it."

"We pay for what we get, instructor. I shall send what's left of my earnings to my father after the Trials. Would you see to that?"

"And there's that stupid stubbornness. Wait, train, grow, and live."

"I can't. Will you send him my earnings when I'm gone?"

He sighs. "Yes, I will." He starts to go but stops. He turns only his head, so I see his profile. The light coming from the door draws his old face perfectly. He looks like a black-and-white illustration. "It was wise to use Kar's help. Cold, but wise. You could win the Trials, but do you know what you are giving up by going to war so young? You haven't lived yet."

"I die, we rise. Right?"

He wants to say more. The muscles in his jaw work under his skin, but his shoulders drop, and he leaves.

I slip out of my student uniform and crawl under my covers. It's cold, always cold. The covers are thin. I throw my clothes on top to add layers.

The sounds of the party still going on die away with the minutes. My thoughts unravel, my fears and doubts escape the hole I threw them in, and the day's tension breaks me once more.

I'll put myself together again. I have to.

CHAPTER TWENTY-TWO

GIANTS OF THE COLD

Tools of the trade

Agnor

Later that day, on a road near the border

We go toward the Raging Sea, traveling along Antares' border with Sargena. A chilling breeze blows from up ahead. The sky promises another flash storm. This weather will kill another horse. The road seems new and cuts through a dense forest. The green foliage thrives and blossoms despite the cold. The branches bend low under the massive weight of snow and ice. Telegraph lines run along the road, likely carrying news about the dead Knight Descendant and the Roamers who defeated it.

The display we left behind will be remembered forever.

We laid the knight, absent her armor, in front of that manor. We tied up the Pacificadores who came with her and put them with the other prisoners in the house. Walver cut their hair and keeps it in his backpack. Sometimes I see him knitting strands of it into a long, scarf-like abomination.

I massage my leg, sore after that fall from the second floor. Wanda sprained her ankle and maybe even broke a rib. Nefri's eye looks better, he might not lose it after all. Yana sleeps curled around the Knight's black helmet. She hasn't spoken since we left the manor. Walver, on the other hand, wanders about and speaks even while he sleeps. Nefri stuffs a piece of cloth in his mouth when the ramblings get too loud.

I know the feeling. We make a camp and build a fire under an *ombu*, a massive tree with thick roots that come from the ground. We pitch the tents between the roots, making the roof and floor thick and thermic. The two surviving horses have their own tent, bigger than ours. The poor beasts follow us blindly, trusting we'll keep them safe.

"Walver is delirious," says Nefri after we watch him wander away again. "If he screams tonight, I'll kill him." He sits on one of the roots by the tent.

"Or," says Wanda, looking left and right. "We could do what we said and cash his reward."

"Bounty hunters," says Nefri so softly. He nudges me.

"Maybe," I say, thinking. "They know more than one robbed those houses and killed the Descendant. They've seen us."

"We look just like any other Giant," says Wanda. "Walver, on the other hand, leaves an impression."

"We have to act quick, though." he whispers, looking over his shoulder. The ever-present wind blows through crystal-lized branches and leaves, whistling through the woods. A few birds, the few that can survive this cold, sing as they fly by. Yana remains in the wagon, asleep under five or six heavy blankets. Walver still does his rounds.

My guts churn. "It's what we must do."

"When?" asks Nefri.

"I don't know. You two decide."

Wanda pokes my shoulder. "Agnor, your word goes. We need you more than you need us."

"She is right, *du vet?*" says Nefri.

Walver returns. His disgusting scarf flaps in the cold breeze. He rummages through the hundreds of pounds of food we brought and brings some to the fire. He sits on his backpack, starts mixing ingredients in a pan over the fire, and sits back as they sizzle. He takes his knife and carves runes on the tree's roots. He does this every time we stop.

"The sooner, the better," insists Wanda.

"Agnor?" asks Nefri.

"Now," I say, swallowing dread and bile. "I'll do it." My intestines fill with slate. I just sentenced Walver to death. Is this what Yana felt every time she had to make a call like this?

"It's the right call," adds Wanda. "We will figure out where to deliver him after." She reaches into her backpack and takes one of the many jars of sweets we stole. The lid pops when she opens it, and the smell of sugar and fruit slips into my nostrils. She smears some on slices of bread and hands it to us.

Nefri eats his in one bite.

Walver drools and twitches by the fire. His fate is sealed. This is undoubtedly a necessary death. "I am supposed to follow," I mutter, answering my own questions.

Wanda shakes her head. "That's the programming speaking. Jattaria jams Servitude down our throats to make us obedient. You have proven yourself a leader time and time again. Better than her," she says, looking pointedly at Yana.

"Get rid of all that stuff they put in your head," says Nefri, then he sniffs the air. "I will miss his cooking." He looks down.

I take Saxon's repeating crossbow and check the fan. There are only two bolts left. Wanda's must have three or four bolts. I swallow hard, pull the lever to load the arms, and a bolt slides into the bed. The arrowhead reflects the sky above, sharp and eager to fly and kill.

But the leaves behind us rustle. The grass crunches softly. Icy twigs snap. Nefri exhales a defeated sigh and lets his head hang. We stand up. Wanda grabs her sword. Yana slowly rises too. Walver keeps cooking, smiling like an idiot. "At last," he says.

"We've been looking for you." The unknown voice is raspy and aggressive, like a hiss from a snake.

"Here we are," I say, forcing confidence on my voice.

"We heard some things about you. Things that couldn't be true."

"They are," says Nefri. "About time you showed up. We want to join you."

"Maybe we don't want you," says another voice behind a tree. The vegetation and the darkness hide our stalkers.

"Is that why you tracked us down?" says Yana with disdain. "To not let us in?"

Silence. No one but the breeze speaks, and even it seems cautious.

"We heard you killed a Knight and a squad of Pacificadores," says yet another voice. "Some say you killed Sargenian Guardias and took their armor. Others say you are runaway Regler Korps."

"Is any of that true?" asks a fourth.

"All of it. Except we are not Korps. We just wear their armor," I say.

"I'd like to see all that stolen gear if you don't mind." The request doesn't sound like one.

With a wave of my arm, I allow them. A mere gesture because they will, regardless. Seven Giants step out of the darkening shadows. Their ragged clothes and ghostly features glow in the weak light.

"I am Vathra, Jattaravkalt envoy and leader of this family," says a woman who resembles a viper: big mouth, dry skin, squinty eyes. Her clothes are baggy and brown except for a bright green headband. Only Vathra wears something colorful. "The runes you left for us said you wanted to join and how to find you. Wise to use the old language to contact us."

So that's what Walver was doing. He was leaving a trail for them to find us. Others move around us, out of sight, but still making sounds when they walk or move a branch out of the way. It's impossible to count or place them. One climbs on top of our carriage. He searches through our things, disappears among the bundles, and re-emerges with a black bucket. He looks at it with disbelief. "A Descendant's helmet. These rats really did it. Where are the weapons and armor?"

"We only took this," I say, but that's a lie. Nefri and I buried the Knight's armaments and suit close to the manor, near Arsen's and Saxon's graves, where no one will find them. It's our insurance.

"Freezing death. How?" asks Vathra. Her eyes don't leave the monstrous helmet. More Roamers come out until they number about fifteen. Giants hardened by years of absolute hell and hunger.

"With this." They go on guard when my sword flashes out of my sheath.

These Roamers are jumpy, ready to kill us. We won't walk away from them.

Vathra clears her throat and looks around. "As tempted as I am to accept you, I am not the one to decide. The Kalt Sun is. We'll take you to her." She stares at Yana. "Can that one follow? The weak go to the wolves. Do you know what wolves do to weaklings like her? They eat them alive. The whole pack feasts while the victims scream."

Yana straightens. Beat up and weak, she is still ten times the soldier any of these criminals could ever be.

"That's Yana Hensin," I say. "She fought that Descendant alone."

Yana's eyes are steady, but they glimmer the slightest bit.

"She fought it without armor and survived a direct blow. I think you'll want her."

"Is that true? Are you *the* Yana? Even here, we've heard of the Terror of the Fifth."

"They call me the Vulture," she answers.

I shiver. "She comes with us," I declare. Our plans to be on our own dissolve just like that. Nefri and Wanda mask whatever they are feeling

"Let it be," concedes Vathra as if finishing a prayer.

After four days of traveling, we ride deep into a settlement near low mountains. A hundred giants in various levels of emaciation come to watch us march. These devils are malnourished. Their worn clothes hang loose on even more worn bodies. Lips curl in angry snarls.

Our horses jerk from one side of the road to the other as Jattaravkalt Giants come from nowhere and startle them, but their pace remains steady.

"This isn't what I pictured," says Yana in a whisper only audible to me. "These can't be the Jattaravkalt. Look at them, starving like street dogs."

"Maybe we can change it," I say, inspired. The misery in these people moves me. "You could take over, protect them from whatever brought them this low. Maybe that's what we are meant to do."

Her scarred face lightens with a tired smile. She means something to me, and whatever that is, I will protect it. "You really believe in me, don't you?" Her eyes are downcast, her back slouched. "I don't deserve it." The words spill out like shattered crystals. "I am sorry about what I said before."

"Forgiven." I would say more, but even whispers could be heard in the dead quiet around us.

The path through the settlement leads to a meadow before the mouth of a cave. The sun is at its highest, shining with blinding splendor. I shield my eyes against the brightness.

Vathra crosses a few steps into the meadow and clears her throat. "We request an audience, Kalt Sun!"

A large armchair sits at the cave's entrance, surrounded by dozens of bones, including a handful of skulls. Two men exit the cave, walk by the chair, and approach us. Their steps crack some of the old bones. Behind them, a huge white-furred beast follows.

"An Austral Bear," says Nefri with a shaky voice.

The two guards, who look much healthier than the rest of the Jattaravkalt, chain the bear to the throne and keep coming. They have decent armor and colorful clothes that must be worth a fortune. The two men walk holding hands, very close to each other, giggling and whispering who knows what.

Vathra and our escort kneel. Walver throws himself to the ground and bows his head as well. The bear smells the air, aims its head at Walver, and charges. It slashes with a huge paw while roaring a bone-rattling bellow in his face. The chain yanks the beast back. The claws swing inches away from Walver, who didn't move from his spot one bit.

"Easy, Luli!" yells one of the guards. "Go back to the chair! Go!" he says and pokes the monster with the blunt end of his spear.

Vathra seems embarrassed when she speaks. "Begel, Sigman. We found them. We are ready to see the Kalt Sun. They have been stripped of armor and weapons." Her voice sounds much less reptilian than before.

One of the two guards grunts and goes into the cave; the other one studies us. "They don't look like much," he says loudly. "Nathrel, are you out there?"

Leaves and branches ruffle. The foliage parts, and a male Giant with long shiny blonde hair steps into the circle. "Interesting game, Vathra." The beautiful man comes closer, sniffs the air, and studies us with calculating eyes. He takes a sword out and pats us one by one with it, checking for hidden weapons. Yana squeezes my arm and separates from me to stand on her own. Nathrel checks her and then me. "It's safe for her to come," he says.

One guard hums in response and returns to the cave. Steps echo from inside. The bear turns toward the sound and groans.

"Who have you brought to me, Vathra?" says a voice with a strange accent. Not Jattarian.

A few Giants from our escort invite us to kneel by hitting the back of our legs and touching their blades to our backs.

"The Traitors, Kalt Sun." Vathra sinks into the ground as low as her body will let her.

A shape comes from the shadows. A tall woman in colorful drapes steps out slowly. Silver armor with golden details shines from under her rich cape. An enormous sword hangs from her hip, hitting her thick leg with every step. She squints and looks about as she walks into the cleared area before the cave. She pats the bear and feeds it some treats. *"Mi Luli hermosa. Te portas bien?"* The Kalt Sun scratches the bear's chin while it chews on a bone.

The sentinels stay beside her, repeating crossbows ready.

"The Traitors! What a pleasure!" The Kalt Sun grins. Her voice is dense like oil. Her brown eyes stop on me, and her smile seems to quiver. The air stirs in the meadow, bringing a scent of honey and apples. That's what she smells like.

Yana takes a step forward. "You are a -"

"Titan," interrupts the Kalt Sun. "Yes, indeed. Born in Magnitude. A few bad decisions got my citizenship revoked and now I find myself leading these valiant Giants in a quest for greatness." Her round face and thick body do not indicate much questing on her part. "You have quite a reputation." She brings a finger to her lips. "There are telegraphed news of savages who defeated Pacificadores, Sargenian Lanzas, and even a Descendant! But some of it must be exaggeration. After all, you do not look like you could put up much of a fight."

"They have a knight's helmet, my lady," whispers Vathra. "They were wearing some Sargenian clothes and armor too."

"Rise, child," she says to Vathra. "You've done well. Now, bring me that armor."

One of them scurries up with the black helmet, kneels before her, and offers it with outstretched arms. The Kalt Sun reaches out to take it, then hesitates. Her fingers fold slightly, then she grabs the helmet and turns it in her chubby hands, studying it with reverence. Her eyebrows rise and fall, her breathing changes. She touches the head of the man who brought it to her.

"This will bring the Roamer gangs together." The Kalt Sun's greed leaks from her expression like a drool from a mongrel. She consults with Begel and Sigman, who nod in agreement. "Thousands of wandering Giants in Antares will unite under my rule. Vathra, you may go. You and yours will feast tonight!"

The escort that brought us leaves quickly. The Kalt Sun wipes the hand that touched her subject on one of the guard's clothes. "I served under a Descendant once. I truly thought they couldn't be killed."

"She died like any other enemy," I say.

The Kalt Sun takes a step back and puts a hand on her chest dramatically. "Oh, heavens!" She snarls in contempt. "You were lucky. Nothing else could kill a Colossal's heir." She flicks her hand at me. "But what matters is I'll finally have the rest of your filthy compatriots under my foot. I'll control every gang of Roamers in Antares." She looks into the helmet's visor. "The Jattaravkalt defeated a Knight Descendant, we will tell those wandering scumbags. They will come like roaches. They will kneel to me."

She cares so little about us, she spills her whole tale.

But her two guards exchange an uncomfortable look. The foundations of this little kingdom has cracks; pressure on the right spot could make it shatter. If *I* saw it, Yana, Nefri, and Wanda saw it too. Walver still kneels and looks down, but even he can't be that stupid.

Yana *could* take over.

The Kalt Sun steps past Walver, closer to us. She must have fifty pounds on me, and stands six inches taller, but I see no scars on her dark skin.

She signals for us to stand up and we do. The Kalt Sun grabs Wanda's chin. "So pretty. And you," she says, looking at Nefri. "Oh, my! He is as beautiful as you, Nathrel!"

The pale Giant leans into Nefri's face, touches his long, black hair, and sniffs his neck. "Beautiful, indeed."

"I appreciate the interest," says Nefri, looking into Nathrel's eyes. "But I am spoken for. I must regretfully decline."

The Kalt Sun laughs. She walks past Yana without looking at her. "Mixed blood," she says when she stands before me.

"I am."

"I'll keep you." She smiles and squints. "Good product."

Hate builds in my throat, burning like bile. "We'd love to serve you." I bow. The Traitors follow my lead. Not doing so likely means a swift death.

"Welcome to the Jattaravkalt. You are Traitors no more."

Chapter Twenty-Three

Against the World

Trials

Thyra

**At the school's arena, minutes before starting the first
stage of the Trials**

A heavy mist thickens the air, humidity sticks to my skin,
and the smell of almost a thousand students builds up in my

skull. Leather, sweat, hormones, piss. I would puke if I weren't so tightly wound. The midday sun cuts through the fog and makes it unbearably bright. I can only see my team near me and a handful of other applicants.

I shift three-hundred pounds of combined weight from one leg to the other. The sand crunches pleasantly under the rubber soles of my new leather boots. They won't look new after the first stage of the Trial.

The audience is around us, above us, and beyond the mist. They sit and listen to the master of ceremonies scream and stir everyone's emotions. The excitement feels as palpable as the humidity. The announcer presents each student who qualified for Trials listing their scores, challenges, and performance in classes.

When they call me, they don't even mention Dad. I am Thyra Ener, youngest Selected and Trial applicant ever, daughter of the famous Lagas Ener, soldier, instructor, and Master of Virtue. But it was Dad who made sure I stayed alive. It was him who showed me his beautiful way of seeing the world.

Toughen up. There are no flowers in the Kjedes.

"Our applicants are ready for their week-long journey through the mountains. Their young hearts pump with pride and passion to prove they are worthy to join the Jattarian Army." Cheers roar from around me, deafening, confusing, and maddening the rage inside. "In moments, we will release them into this deadly stage where their opponent is the world. Everything they learned during their time at Solitude's School of War will be tested to the extreme in the coming days, and it starts...now!"

The gates open, and we charge. The audience cheers.

Hours later, as the sun sets in the jagged horizon, the team gathers around a small fire. Me, Oniv, Kar, Erika, Arvo, and Sassi, a small Last-Year from Kar's and Oniv's endurance class.

Oniv shakes his head. "Kar, we cannot risk skipping posts. We need to get the items ourselves to score." He combs his hair with muddy fingers. The fire illuminates his beautiful figure and I must look away. It hurts too much; I haven't dared talk to him since I kissed him.

What was I thinking?

"Yes, Kar," says Erika, annoyed. "We are unarmed and will be at a disadvantage if the other teams come wielding the items, you know? Swords, spears, shields, who knows? You paid attention during yesterday's briefing, *ja*? We score by collecting the items the aides have for us at the posts."

She slides an inch closer to Oniv and grabs his hand. He holds her for a moment, then stands up and paces around the fire. Erika looks at him with obvious pain, but it all turns to ice and murder when our eyes meet.

I deserve it.

Kar looks around the fire. Five tired faces stare back at him. "An ambush is a perfectly good strategy," he says for the fourth time tonight. "It will keep us from being exhausted and exposed, which would compensate for the lack of weapons. Everyone has to come back to school after the circuit, so let's wait for them here. Staying safe and rested would give us the upper hand."

"It's too risky, Kar," says Oniv. We should go through the posts and get our gear so we can earn points for collecting the items. What do the rest of you think?"

Unfair question. Everyone will follow Oniv, who has the respect and love of everyone around him. Everyone he asked to be on his team joined him without hesitation.

"I am with you, Oniv," I respond.

Sassi hums his answer. "With Oniv."

Arvo, who faced his loss of the Undefeated title much better than I would have, nods toward Oniv from his dark corner. Erika takes longer to answer, maybe because she is skewering me with her gray eyes. "I'm always with you, Oniv." She pulls his arm and kisses his cheek.

He smiles softly. "Sorry. It's a great plan, but too risky." Oniv slips from Erika's hold again and grabs Kar's shoulder. "Please, never stop sharing your ideas. I'll always listen to your advice, *min bror.*"

"You can count on me, Oniv."

"I see your Virtue." He grabs Kar's neck and brings him closer. They touch foreheads.

Oniv turns to face us. "We rest and leave early tomorrow. We should be at the first post by noon. I'll take first watch."

More than a dozen other teams arrive at the old mining post at the same time we do. We are soaking wet from the freezing fog, but so are the other teams. We walk down the path leading to the small settlement at the mine's entrance and a group of five students joins us.

"Hey, Zevel. How was your night?" asks Oniv when the leader of the other team catches up to him. Everyone is friendly so far since there is no point in fighting at a post with items for all teams.

"This sucks. We should have done more expeditions to get used to it. Our instructors only made us go three times."

"We went three times last month alone, man," says Kar. "Now I understand why Klausen was so insistent on it."

"You had the Outsider, didn't you?" asks Arvo.

"Gunnav? Yes," answers Zevel. I hurry to get closer to them. I haven't seen him since I returned from the Hidden Ring.

"How is he?" I ask.

"I don't know. He ditched us as soon as the gates opened. Bad choice on my part. I thought he'd be familiar with the land after living here for months. Wait, you are Ener."

"Yes. So?"

"Shouldn't you wait a few years to do the Trials?"

"*Nein*. I like my chances." I slow down and let them get ahead.

"She is crazy," he says in a low voice.

I search the skyline for Gunnav's skinny shape but find only rocks, bushes, and leafless trees. We won't see him until he wants us to. I'm not surprised he is trying to do this alone. Teams are optional, after all.

As we near the little village, the sound of people gets louder. We line up and wait for the aides to give us our first item. "One per student and move quickly," repeats one of them.

"Move along," says an aide handing out shields. They guard the entrance to the mine where they store them. I peek at their cache, which is almost empty by the time we get ours.

"Are we one of the last teams to show up?" asks Oniv with a frown while he slides the shield on his right forearm. He noticed too.

"No. Half the students haven't shown up yet. Now move!"

"Maybe we skip the second post and go straight to the third," proposes Kar when we are far from the post. This time his words carry more weight. We now know there won't be enough items for every team.

"We have an advantage, but we must hurry. The ones who came earlier might not have noticed, but everyone else will," says Oniv. "Take the third item, ambush a team coming from the second post to take their things, then finish."

Kar nods with a satisfied smile. I go near him and bump his arm. "Well done." He turns red.

"Thanks, Thyra."

"Can you trace the best path on the map?" asks Oniv.

Kar goes to him. He keeps the paper from flapping in the strong wind and tries to trace a line. "Stick to this side of the mountains to get the most sunlight when we travel." They discuss supplies and calculate how long it will take to get there, but I give them only half my attention.

"When will you have enough, you freezing little twitch? You have to mess with everyone?" The icy voice makes it pointless to turn. It's Erika and all her hate.

"I am not messing with anyone," I respond quietly, but I know I am. Mother's lessons never had a chance with my heart's stupidity.

"You kissed Oniv in front of everyone, knowing he was with me. I cared about you, I tried to help, and all I asked was for you to stay away from him."

"I'm sorry," I reply, really feeling it. "That was terribly wrong of me."

"You are a base and desperate creature, Thyra Ener. *I'm* sorry for you."

"I am not base and desperate," I snap.

"Why are you teasing Kar, then? He is smitten, and all you do is hurt him."

"Nonsense. And *I* am teasing everyone? What about Mikael and all those other boys you fool around with?"

She turns crimson. "Don't change the subject. You can't play stupid with me, Thyra. Kar is in love with you, just like you are in love with Oniv," she hisses, poking me hard on the shoulder. My hand flies to her neck, squeezing. Her expression shifts from anger to pain, but she swiftly breaks my hold and locks my wrist with an efficient Suggested Stillness grip. "Oh, you don't see it! You really *are* stupid." She pushes the back of my trapped hand with her two thumbs to make me fold, but I don't bend when others want me to.

I bend when it serves me.

I resist for half a second, then give in to throw her off balance and elbow her jaw. Mother would have crushed her nose and windpipe using one of Certitude's forms. "Kar is my friend; that's why he cares." But now I doubt it. I look at Kar, feeling the weight of this new realization. Is he suffering the same way I suffered? Am I really causing all this pain to the ones near me?

Yes.

"Lie to yourself all you want, Thyra," she says, rubbing where I hit her. "We all know what you are. You should have died in the Hidden Ring."

"The Ring is a myth."

"Will you ever stop lying?" She exhales loudly and closes her eyes. "You are an idiotic child from a low Secondary Land family…"

My knuckles stop her babbling. Her teeth crack. She falls back. She gets up, hands bunched into fists, ready to fight. She spits out a tooth.

I read her quickly, measuring my chances. She is a head taller, thirty pounds heavier, and an expert at hand-to-hand combat. "You insulted my family's honor. Those are fighting words," I hiss.

She dips her finger into the blood dripping from her lips, I touch the blood on my knuckles. We do the Cutting Sign at the same time. A scarlet line splits her gorgeous face from crown to chin.

"Stop!" orders Oniv.

"It's too late now," I say. We claimed each other's lives when we ran our fingers over our faces. She won't surrender, and I will freeze before I let her insult my family's honor.

"Fight when the journey is over or you are off the team." Under his steely gaze, we lower our hands. Erika and I nod once in a silent agreement with each other.

This isn't over.

Chapter Twenty-Four

HUNGER

Night at the Kjedes

Thyra

Three days later, miles into the Kjede mountains

Night falls quickly, but at least the fog is gone. Not being wet
while walking across this vicious terrain feels almost pleasant

in comparison. We maintain a fast pace even after dark. I stay at the back of our single line, following Kar. He turns now and then. Something bothers him.

After miles of this, I step closer and tap the rough fabric covering his back. The light armor made of tarp and wire makes him appear threatening, but the soft moonlight makes him look handsome and older.

He turns when he feels my hand on his shoulder.

"Thyra," he whispers. We walk side by side in silence. Then, finally, "What is it?"

Looking straight ahead, I say what I should have said days before. "I wasn't fair to you. I am sorry." The words bump into each other on their way out of my mouth. "I didn't treat you the way you deserved."

"Oh, don't worry about that. I'm your friend, like you said."

"But I wasn't a friend to you."

"Your heart was elsewhere."

Erika was right. I was hurting him.

"I know you love him," he whispers. "Everyone does. I hoped that if you saw me, you'd like me too. Maybe you'd see I could be there for you. Every time we were close, I imagined...well, I was just being foolish."

Secrets, killing, lies, manipulations. Doing these things is easy, but the consequences are so great. It's the heart-crushing price of not holding back. "I am the foolish one. I didn't know what I was doing. But why? How can you like me?"

"*Ich weis es nicht.* I just saw you. That's all it took." He speaks but can't even look me in the eye.

"That's all it took," I repeat. It's the same for everyone, then. Pain, pain, pain.

"Don't worry. I got to know you, spend some time together. Who knows? We might be sent away as Appeasement Offers on the Dark Runner. Maybe we die in the arena."

"We won't fail. It's not our destiny," I say.

"What if I am selected as your match? Or Oniv's? I wouldn't fight either of you. If I did, you'd defeat me anyway."

"That won't happen, Kar."

But it could happen and we all know it.

Oniv lifts a hand to stop our march sometime after midnight. We make a quick camp and a small fire. Oniv approaches while I arrange my makeshift bed. Erika watches from afar, like a dark-haired war goddess. Her eyes are cold silver.

"Don't mind her," says Oniv. "She promised she wouldn't do anything."

"I am not afraid," I tell him.

"You should be. You have no sword, and she is incredible at hand-to-hand combat."

"Noted," I say, blushing so hard my body heat pushes the cold away. I recall the brutal lessons with Mom. How to read attacks, take kicks and punches, twist joints to break them, and slip away from an enemy's grip. Certitude's wrestling and hand-to-hand combat training was torture, but Mother loved it.

Get this close to someone, and you've already killed them.

"I heard you talking to Kar."

"Oh."

"You were brave, and I knew I was being a coward. I should have talked to you earlier, but I couldn't. This feeling grows every day. I wanted it to fade away, but I only made things worse."

"How?" I try not to melt under his stare.

"I suspected you liked me. Well, I liked you too."

"You did?" It's everything I wanted to hear him say, but this dread makes it ugly. "Why?"

"You are brilliant, talented, and so beautiful. Anger fuels you, but it looks like art when you let it out. Watching you was painful and wonderful too."

Each word stabs my heart in the most delightful way. "Erika is your girlfriend. She asked me to leave you alone, and I should have."

"You couldn't. We were in Klausen's class. And Erika isn't my girlfriend."

"You are not together?" I am confused and hopeful.

"We are. She is my wife."

"Your wife?" I choke on the words. Hope becomes a vacuum. My insides collapse and implode.

"We met last year and married secretly a few weeks after, just before school started. My friends warned me, they said I didn't see who she really was, but I was stupid and in love. She changed overnight," He looks up and seems to read a hidden message in the sky. "I can't remember what I loved about her. She had been cheating on me for months, then you come out of nowhere like a summer storm. Things kept getting worse with her and you were so great." He touches his chest. "I *tried* to hate you, but how could I? It's like I had waited to see you all my life, and then there you were."

I close my mouth and peel my sight from his face to look at Erika, her hands in fists at her sides. Of course he married her. She is a vision from Valhalla. "Why did you marry in secret?"

"Old blood feud. Her dad defeated my uncle during the Trials decades ago, and he was sent as an Appeasement Offer. My family claims her dad used an illegal weapon. Even Grandpa Klausen dislikes her."

"I am so sorry," I say and pray the ground opens and swallows me whole. I look into his eyes, warmer than the sun.

"I belong to her. Maybe one day she will be as she was when I fell in love."

"I don't know what to say, Oniv."

He shakes his head, then chuckles. "Spreading those rumors was clever. That fight was not a good idea."

"Mostly for me," I admit.

"You could have recovered and done the Trials next year. Some said you went to the Hidden Ring. Those were rumors too, right?"

I shake my head and pull my lower lip down. He sees the mark. "I killed someone to get this."

A different type of silence falls around him, one that consumes the sounds of nature and chatter. "How -"

The face of the Edgen I killed creeps from the depths of my memory. "Fortitude makes the impossible quite easy," I say, feeling the weight of each word. "What else could I do?"

"Wait. Train. Get stronger."

"Waiting isn't an option." I look away.

"Arvo challenged you despite the unwritten restrictions. You didn't need to go to the Hidden Ring to get your challenge."

"Arvo challenged me *because* I went to the Ring. And because he was greedy."

"You are one to talk! You chase all this glory, doing the Trials, and you aren't even fourteen."

"You don't think I'll make it?"

"You'll get your ink." His eyes search for Erika, who still watches us with cold hatred. "You'll be the next Golden Blade, become an officer, and go further than anyone else in history. But why? What are you after?"

"Honor. It's all there is for me, so I'll take as much as I can and die burning."

"What are you, Thyra Ener?" He studies me with a gentle frown.

"A sister, a daughter, a Jattarian soldier."

He nods pensively.

"Come get your rations," calls Arvo. He takes Oniv's bowl and throws some of the stew and a biscuit in it. I try to give Arvo my bowl, but Erika slaps it out of my hand and shoves me.

"Secondary trash goes to the back of the line, Ener," she says with venom. Tendons in my neck twitch, but I wronged her. Breathing deeply, I step back.

By the way she looks, she didn't expect this reaction. She smirks. "I am challenging you, Thyra. Here and now."

I look at Oniv, who watches with his mouth open. "Thyra, don't do it, please," he begs.

But I won't surrender my claim to Undefeated. Nefri's sin made sure of it. I arm myself with pride and anger. "I am sorry for what I did to the two of you, but I can't decline the challenge."

"Of course you can!" But he knows. He turns to his wife. "Erika, you have to withdraw!" He tries to speak to her, but she fulminates him with her stare. "She has apologized. You must get over this!"

"Impossible. We settle this now. I choose hand-to-hand combat. *Skynda!*" She unbuckles her chest piece and lets it fall. The pads on her arms come off, too, and she makes fists with her hands.

I leave my light armor on and get my helmet too. "You challenged me, Erika. It's my choice of weapons, and I choose shields," I say. The smirk on her face disappears.

"You can't."

"I absolutely can. Shields." I retrieve it from my bundle.

She stands with her hands now open, watching as I come back to her. "A shield is not a weapon," she argues weakly.

"Anything is a weapon if you swing it hard enough." I stand in position, waiting for her to get ready. Her breathing is quick, shallow. Her fingers tap her legs rapidly.

"Please, Erika," begs Oniv, coming to her.

"Shut up, husband. You are as useless as Father warned me you'd be. Bloodstains are hard to remove, apparently. Step aside."

She puts her armor back on and gets her shield, and then we step into the improvised arena with its uneven footing and treacherous terrain. The others step away and watch in silence as Erika assumes a fighting stance that does not match the type of combat we are about to engage in. She lowers her head until only her eyes peer over the edge of the shield. Her shoulders are up. She leaps forward and unleashes patternless attacks.

Her strikes leverage her superior height and weight and even when I block them, they rock me. But I have Fortitude and no desire to rein in my anger. The unreliable ground makes it hard to evade her, so I am forced to absorb some of her punches. Yet, I endure. She is a storm of jabs, uppercuts, elbows, knuckles, and knees. She is everywhere, then nowhere.

A rock slips under my back foot, making me lose balance. She buries her heel in my sternum with a front kick that sends me flying backward. I twist in the air and land on the shield instead of the rocks, avoiding awful cuts from the jagged ground. I stand up before she is on me, and we engage again.

My eye bleeds, my shoulder pulsates, and she keeps on pounding. She attacks with anger. That's mistake number one. She spends too much energy, which is mistake number two. She pulls her shield back to hit again, making her third and final mistake.

Fortitude demands I withstand her fury and wait for the right moment. The moment comes. She opens her guard and I slam my shield's edge under her jaw. She stiffens as if she had been electrocuted, goes slack, and falls to the ground.

Erika pushes herself up to her feet instinctively. I swing the shield once more, smashing it into her ribs. She exhales all air at once and spits blood on me, but doesn't go down. She roars and throws a wild haymaker that I block with ease.

Bones crack against my shield's wood.

She shrieks but tries once more. She punches the side of my helmet. I see stars. I slam my elbow into her nose and knee her hip. Now she falls and stays down. Twitching, crying, defeated.

"I am sorry. I should have stayed away, as you told me to. Forget the Cutting Sign. I will not kill you."

She spits blood at my feet.

Hours later, close to dawn, we wander in the moonless night. Erika refused to follow and went her own way despite Oniv's begging. We followed Kar's path. According to the map, we arrived at the third post, but we see no entrance.

The group spreads out and searches.

"*Da*," whispers Kar some fifteen minutes later. "It's beneath us! It's a hatch, look!" He pulls at the heavy cover. The rusty hinges creak.

"There might be others nearby," says Arvo. "Shields up in case there's a trap."

We carefully climb down the ladder into a mine. The last one in closes the hatch, but I can't tell who it was in the weak torchlight. We follow the mine almost blindly, advancing in a wedge formation, keeping front and sides protected. In the narrow, low-ceiling path, a claustrophobic fear creeps in, choking my throat. The humid air smells of rot and toxic spores floating in the air. My fingers are twitchy. The person in front of me, Arvo, trembles as well.

"What a place to make a post," whispers the unknown person taking up the rear. It sounds like Sassi, not Arvo. A few yards into the old excavation, we slow our pace even more. My senses are hyper-alert. My brain registers every sound as a threat. The tension in my exhausted body rises one heartbeat at a time. My muscles clench so tightly my bones might shatter.

Crack!

Stars and lightning explode in my vision. It all fades to a darker shade of black.

CHAPTER TWENTY-FIVE

DEPTH

Ambush

Thyra

A day later, in the mines

A soft, amber light comes through my eyelids. I close my hand and my fingertips scratch wet stone. The moist air smells of rot and stagnant waters.

"Thyra!"

With sound comes pain. Sharp and overwhelming.

Oniv shakes me back to consciousness. A fire illuminates the inside of the mine. We are in a huge natural chamber that has been turned into a storage room. The team sits around a fire, watching me with big eyes. They simultaneously exhale when I try to talk, even though no real words come out.

"Just rest," commands Oniv. He stops my attempt to get up with a hand on my arm.

"Glad you are well, Stinger," says Arvo. Kar and Sassi nod. Behind them, tied up against the carved wall, is a team of four.

"Where's the rest of their team?" I ask.

"Taken out. One with a snake bite, one with a broken leg," replies Kar without looking up. He uses two rocks to grind coals and old bits of wood into a fine powder, which he stores in a big bucket. A fox roasts over the flames, releasing an irresistible aroma.

"Maybe. Maybe they are out there, waiting," I reply, looking around and checking the many dark corners of this enormous space. Dusty tools and mining equipment crowd the place, stored on wooden shelves or hanging from the ceiling. "What happened to me?"

A new voice answers from the shadows. "They ambushed you." A chunk of shadow becomes Gunnav. "I had been watching them when you showed up."

"He jumped in right after they attacked. If not for him, it would be us tied and gagged."

"You seem fine. I will grab my items and leave." Gunnav grabs his shield, axe, and crossbow, and turns back to the shadows. "I will see you in the Arena," he says when he is out of sight.

"That guy makes me shiver," says Kar from the little fire. "But we have our items. Axes and halberds. Gunnav said the post we skipped has crossbows."

I try to grab one of the weapons, but pain shoots from my fingertips all the way to my neck. My head injury and the fight with Erika have left me in a pretty sorry state. I pat my body softly, searching for other wounds. A bandage squeezes my head, probably trying to keep my brains in place. I let it be.

"What's the plan?" I ask.

"We get these guys to help, and we wait." Kar takes a tentative bite of the fox. He smiles and looks around the fire. "It's cooked!"

"Is it tasty?" asks Sassi.

"It's cooked." Kar's smile is less pronounced. He takes another bite. "Mostly cooked," he corrects himself with a mouthful of pink meat.

"Why would they help?"

"We'll give them the items we don't need," says Arvo, and takes a smoking piece of meat. He stuffs it into his mouth and grimaces. "It's hot! It's hot!"

"But they are tied," I point out.

"We know," says Sassi, rolling his eyes. "We tied them 'cause we can't just trust everyone. They understand. Right, guys?" He kicks one of our prisoners' feet. They nod unenthusiastically. "They will be more like human shields anyway. They don't need their hands."

The prisoners nod.

"Understood. We wait," I agree.

And we wait.

And wait.

And finally, another team comes.

They approach with caution, just like we did when we entered the mines. We left Kar and two of the prisoners chatting loudly by the fire as bait. The smell of smoke and food and the little amber light reflecting on the cold surfaces will hopefully make the oncoming team eager and careless.

So far, the trap seems to work. Arvo and one of the prisoners hide with me behind a large rock by the entrance to that storage chamber.

I count five enemies. Six. No, seven. That's one too many.

"Erika," whispers Arvo and elbows me softly. I spot her walking at the back. She's defected to our competition. Oniv surely recognizes her too. Will he be able to go through with the plan?

The enemy team walks into the room we prepared for them. The fire throws the tiniest amount of light. For now.

Oniv gives the signal: two loud bangs with his shield. Kar throws the coal and wood powder into the fire. The little flame becomes a blinding flash of light, at least for our enemies - we have our eyes covered. When the brilliance fades, we charge.

Arvo, the prisoner, and I clash against one side of the opposing team, while Oniv and the rest crush them from the other. They fire their crossbows. Bolts fly by our heads, bounce off of our shields, and hit cold stones behind us. Our blunt axes drop on their helmets, hack at their legs, and reduce them to a mess of crying kids.

Only Erika, who dropped to her knees with her hands up, remains uninjured.

"Stop! We surrender!" they yell.

Erika stares at Oniv. Kar approaches with a torch. Its weak light reveals new bruises on her still gorgeous face. They weren't gentle with her. I put more pressure on the neck of the guy I immobilized.

Oniv kneels by her and offers her his hand.

She looks away. "We are done, Oniv. It's not like I kept my vows anyway. Go to that kid if you want." She takes her ring from a pocket and throws it on the ground. "We owe each other nothing." She leaves.

I forget about the Trials, my brother, my family name, and look at Oniv with new hope. He stares after Erika, then at each one of his teammates, then me. The two of us together is a possibility now. It won't be easy, and it won't be soon, still my heart swells with hope.

Before the morning clears, we are on our way back to school. Another day and a half of walking with fifty pounds of gear on our backs, but the weight of the world couldn't stop me from feeling light. Having Oniv next to me helps me ignore the pain and exhaustion. We don't say much but sneak little smiles as we carve our way through this inhospitable land. The ground bites at our feet, hungry for our flesh, but we keep going.

It's only when we see Solitude's skyline grow from the horizon that he reaches out and offers his hand. I hesitate a moment but then accept it.

He walks closer, just an inch or two, but the difference means everything to me. For the remaining miles, I rejoice in his proximity, his smell, and the heat coming from his body.

When it's too dark to continue, we settle away from the path under our covers. We have fires to attract other teams and only our coats and body heat to keep us warm. In my case, I have Oniv's warmth too. He pulls me close and makes me lean against him.

"Maybe one day we could be together," he says. I was almost asleep, but not anymore. "I do like you, Thyra, but she has been breaking my heart for a year. It will take time to forget I loved her."

"*Maybe* is enough for me," I answer.

CHAPTER TWENTY-SIX

TRAITORS' NARRATIVE

Jattaravkalt

Agnor

A week later, in Antares

Yana limps forward, holding a hand to her side and grunting with each step. Wanda, Nefri, and I follow, matching her slow pace through the slums. The tents and huts where the Jattaravkalt people live are even worse than those of Wasters, the lowest scum in Jattaria. There are fires, here and there, where groups of sorry-looking Giants gather to pick the roasted scraps from some carcass or another for breakfast. They eat rats, cats, and pigeons here.

"Freezing death," I say, surprised for the hundredth time by the squalor. The smell of trash and filth must be part of the ground by now. The stench invades my senses like fingers jammed up my nose. Day after day, as I starve in the mud and do whatever tasks the Kalt Sun gives us, I imagine freeing these people from this misery. What a story that would be. Exactly the type of tale Emma likes.

Two broad spear blades flash before us when we enter the throne's circle, barring our way. "Too close, " says Begel. Him and Sigman stand like thick towers. They take our weapons before allowing us another breath.

Nathrel is wrapped around the Kalt Sun, laughing as he throws bits of meat to Luli, the enormous bear. The pet lies without moving much, smelling the food but not eating

"She has not been feeling well, my love. Better give her some space," says the Kalt Sun with a look of concern.

Nathrel steps away from his queen, taking out his two daggers, and testing their edges while he looks at us. He has killed at least three Giants since we arrived, punishment for absurd offenses like asking for more food or taking too long to return from a mission. He walks around Walver, who kneels a few steps from the makeshift throne.

"Let them be, Begel. They are unarmed now, and she wants to talk," says the Kalt Sun from a safe distance. The spears still block us.

Yana speaks up. "My people and I wanted to -"

"Not your people, dear Vulture," interrupts the Kalt Sun, wagging a finger. "They are mine," she rests her hand on her chest slowly. "Proceed."

"We are ready to serve you, Kalt Sun."

"Oh! That fills me with joy! You have asked many times already, but I was not sure you were ready. Walver has not been shy about suggesting the best way to put your skills to use. Today I am tempted to take his advice."

Walver looks up when his name is mentioned. He is skin and bones, just like the rest of us.

That's how the Kalt Sun rules. A firm hand and crushing hunger. She walks to her chair and rummages in a woven basket filled with pastries, cheeses, and cold meats. She picks a cured leg and some bread and cuts slices with a silver knife. My mouth waters.

She arranges the slices in bite-sized servings and walks to Yana. "Sigman, Begel. Have something to eat. You two look starved." She puts food in their mouths in a manner so intimate I am forced to look away. The two royal guards, as she calls them, receive their gifts without taking their eyes off us. My deprived stomach growls loudly. A smile takes shape on the Kalt Sun's soft caramel face.

"Maybe they are ready, my lady," says Begel. "They seem *desperate* enough."

Because we only ate half the rations they gave us. We stored the rest, waiting for the time to strike.

The Kalt Sun eats the rest of the bread. "There's a spice delivery coming to a village nearby," she says with a full mouth. "What do you say, Vulture? Is your family interested?"

Yana nods. "Yes, my lady. We'd be honored."

"Don't come back without it, children." She sends us away with a wave of her hand. "Begel, outfit them. Walver, my dear, get up from the ground. You're going with. I'll tell you what I expect and where to wait for this shipment."

He does as requested, and the bear roars menacingly now that Walver is within her reach. Begel pushes us toward our tent and away from the Kalt Sun.

"Make sure you get what she wants, Vulture," says Begel. "She is not kind to those who disappoint her." It doesn't sound like a threat but a fair warning. He lowers his weapon and stops shoving us.

"She isn't kind to anyone," says Wanda, who has tried to get close to the two guards during these last weeks. "And why does Nathrel follow me everywhere I go?"

"He must be infatuated," says Begel, looking at the trees. "He gets like that with newcomers. It's better if you avoid him, Wanda. He kills for the smallest reason. Sometimes he even feeds trespassers to Luli. All those bones around the throne are people she ate." He looks over his shoulder. "I hate that beast."

Wanda hates it too. She has been tossing bits of food with crushed glass around the throne. The bear will turn out dead soon.

Nefri stops and faces the royal guard, who today is covered with a bright green and blue tunic over his suit. "How can you put up with this, man?" he asks Begel.

"Antares is a brutal place and takes brutal measures to survive." He puts the spear on the ground and looks up. He has a salt-and-pepper beard he keeps neatly trimmed. Now he scratches his chin, making a sound like sandpaper against wood. "I tried bounty-hunting before this, but more often than not, Titans wouldn't pay for the Roamer heads I brought. But they pay the Kalt Sun. That's why everyone ends up here. She keeps us. She has for a decade." He stops at a strongly reinforced iron chest at the end of the settlement. It looks heavy and has several hack marks around the strong hinges and lock. There have been mutiny attempts, apparently.

"The Jattaravkalt is the safest option." He takes a key from a pocket in his heavy tunic, kneels, and opens the huge lock. "The Kalt Sun is a Titan and trades for us. Without her, we die. Plain and simple."

"Forgive us," says Yana. "We just wish we weren't starved." Her eyes gleam when Begel opens the chest.

"Take those crossbows and some bolts. Grab those axes too. Here are some rations. Make them last a few days." He hands Nefri a leather bag with what I guess is old bread, dried fruit, and questionable meat.

A quick look at the gear leaves us disheartened. The crossbow and bolts are in terrible condition, and the axe heads are rusty and blunt. If we tried to assault Begel now, he'd kill us all without scratching his battle armor.

"I pray we don't need them, or we are done for," I complain.

"No Descendants around here, Agnor. This is an easy assignment. A test. You'll be fine, *du vet?*"

He escorts us to the dirty tarp riddled with holes we use for a tent and leaves without a word. The rations we saved and the two good short swords we salvaged are under the tent, buried.

"That bear won't last," says Wanda.

"Let's hope so," grunts Yana. "Get everything and muster Fortitude. The goal is clear."

"Fortitude was never my Virtue," says Wanda.

Nefri laughs. "I'll pray to our Colossal ancestors. Perhaps they have some to spare."

"Should we tell Walver we are making a move on the Kalt Sun?" I mumble.

Yana shakes her head. "No. I am not sure where his head is at." She paces around the tent without the limp she has been pretending to have. She has recovered from that nasty cut, thanks in part to Uma's handbook and all the plants it guided us to find.

Nefri digs up the stored food from under the tent and hands it over. We eat some and my malnourished body awakens with the carbs, proteins, and sugars.

Walver joins us after a few minutes. "We should leave at once," he croaks, avoiding our gaze.

The sun hangs high above our heads. The spot we picked has a little clearing in the middle of the high trees. A few miles from the village, it offers a great vantage point overlooking a big stretch of the road. We have seen almost no travelers and certainly no spice shipment.

Wanda perches on a high branch keeping watch. At the base of that tree, the rest of us sit waiting. I pick up big pieces of ice and chuck them across the meadow. They burst against the trees.

Walver rubs his shaking hands. "They'll come at dusk," he says for the tenth time today. "We block the road and jam the wheels. We kill all of them if they make a move. Agnor, you got that?"

I grunt.

Yana shakes her head. "What's wrong with you, Walver? You know better than this."

"It's what the Kalt Sun wants. Yana and Agnor, you'll wait across the road," he says and points to a jacaranda tree. "Nefri and Wanda can wait here. I will be about fifty yards away, blocking their retreat. With all these trees by the road, they won't see us come. It should be easy."

We nod, and Walver skips away with his disturbing scarf of hair flapping behind him. He leaps over vines and vanishes from sight.

"He has lost his mind, Yana," says Nefri. "Even you think we can't trust him."

She looks toward Walver. "I can't abandon him. He has saved my life more times than I can count."

Wanda lands among us like a lynx. She straightens and stares Yana down. "Then we can't trust you."

I shake my head and put my hands up. "Let's not discuss this now. The Kalt Sun comes first."

"This *is* the time to discuss it, Agnor," says Wanda. "When we kill her, we must act as one or they'll eat us alive."

"We will need a strong hand *and* an experienced leader." I touch Yana's shoulder. "Wanda, you will plan our every move. Nefri, you will do that thing where you manipulate everyone to control the families and their leaders. People seem to like you, for some reason."

"It's the way I smell." He sniffs his armpit. "Scratch that," he says, wincing.

Wanda slaps him on the back of the head. "What about you, Agnor?"

"I will be the contact with the Titans."

Yana shakes her head. "I know I failed you before, but I won't fail you again."

Nefri sighs loudly. "My heart is always in the wrong place, but let's hope yours isn't, Agnor. If you trust her, I trust her too." He pats my shoulder. "Yana, keep Walver under control or we will put him down."

Yana and Nefri shake hands.

Wanda steps closer to Yana and looks up at her defiantly. "And you can no longer be the Vulture. Agreed?"

Yana nods. "The Vulture dies with the Kalt Sun."

CHAPTER TWENTY-SEVEN

NECESSARY KILLINGS

Predators

Agnor

Days later, near an Antarian village

The Vulture leads me to our spot behind the blue-leaf jacaranda at the side of the road. Its lavender winter flowers are about

to blossom. The scent of the leaves and resin intensifies in the sun.

Through the leaves and thin hanging branches, I spy Nefri and Wanda across the paved street. She has once more climbed on top of her tree. He seems to sleep against the thick trunk.

Walver must be waiting down the avenue.

"How do things stay alive here?" whispers Yana. She takes one of the blossoms and smells it. She puts her pink tongue out and softly places the flower on it.

"A mystery. They harvest grapes in the winter and have crops that grow in ice."

We sit under the tree. She says she forgave me, but something still lingers. I miss her. I miss feeling like *I* could protect *her*; that I could protect anything.

"I can't kill him, Agnor," she says. "It's what they want, and I understand it, but I just can't."

"Then control him or send him away." The leaves whisper, the branches murmur. "Who cares what you owe him?"

"I do. I am not heartless."

"You are like the Descendant. I didn't know there was a woman inside until the plates came off."

She chuckles. "A shell to keep me safe. It's not all I am."

"I know that now."

"I was like you, Agnor. You kill and lose enough people, and those things that make you beautiful begin to fade. Except you lost so much, but you don't fade." She turns to me with eyes that seem centuries old. "Maybe that's why I like you."

"I like you too."

She scoffs. "You don't like me, Agnor. You are using me the same way I use everyone."

"I do like you," I repeat. This time, it is easier to say. It rings like truth. "It's unlike other times I've loved, but I recognize the feeling." I put a closed hand over my sternum, where that sensation feels lodged.

"Love, huh? You are so Virtuous." She touches my face. "Only that allows you to speak this way. I gave up on things of the heart long ago."

"It doesn't change how I feel." I offer her my hand. She takes it after some consideration. The icy touch of her skin sends pleasant shivers down my back. She sighs slowly. Inch by inch, she makes the space between us disappear. She lets me put my arm around her and together we watch the road.

The day fades with us still close together, and I study each detail of her profile, each mark on her skin. Even this morning, I was envious of Nefri and Wanda. I held onto a ghost of my feelings for Emma.

I show my forearm to Yana. The tattoo of my rank still binds me to Jattaria. "You'll have to help me remove this."

She stares, confused. "Forget the past, and you'll forget the lessons." Yana looks away, nodding softly.

I kiss the back of her neck. She looks at me over her shoulder. Little bumps form on her white skin. The moment stretches as we get closer. Her face is cold, her lips so warm.

A crossbow's snap. Muffled grunts. A tortured scream.

Yana and I get to our feet, grab our weapons, and take off running toward the noises. We make a beeline to the small clearing where Wanda and Nefri were posted.

Wanda is screaming her voice raw. "I'll skin you alive, Walver! I'll rip your ribs out one by one!" She holds Nefri in her arms and puts her body between her husband and Walver.

"I know you would," he says, and he somehow seems sincere. "You'd kill me a thousand times."

"Freezing death, Walver!" screams Yana. "What are you doing!"

Nefri curls up and holds his torso with both hands, blood bubbling and dripping from his mouth.

Walver lifts an open hand and stops our advance, his crossbow aimed at Wanda. "I have to, Yana. The Kalt Sun wanted to kill you!"

I try to get close to my two friends and keep my crossbow trained on Walver.

"Stop!" he cries with a broken voice. "Don't move an inch." His face is deadly serious. "Yana," he says without taking his eyes off Wanda and Nefri. "There's no other way. She won't let us back without their heads. Trust me," he begs. "It's the price we must pay!" There is no doubt in his crazy stare.

"We have another way, Walver! Put your weapon down!" says Yana.

Walver squeezes the trigger. A rusty arrow pierces Wanda's chest. It buries above her left breast and a crimson stain grows from the wound. She doesn't even scream; she coughs blood and collapses on Nefri. Her fingers twitch. Her eyes close.

I shoot my crossbow, but the mechanisms fail. It comes undone in my hands.

"Wanda," grunts Nefri when he sees her die. He bellows through his agony, gets to his feet, and charges with his rusty axe. Walver shoots again, but Nefri dodges it. moving like Yana did when fighting the Descendant. He swings and forces Walver to retreat, then tackles him when he is off balance. Nefri lifts him by the waist and slams him to the ground, scattering his weapons. Nefri puts Walver in a chokehold and twists the man's torso with his legs, squeezing his midsection.

Walver elbows Nefri in the stomach, right where the arrow is lodged, and my friend lets go. Walver shrinks away and gains his feet. He prepares to strike, but I kick his ribs with all my weight. He flies sideways and lands face-first. He wheezes through his bruised neck but scurries with unnatural speed for the crossbow, grabbing it and readying another bolt before I get to him. He aims it at my chest. "Back off!"

I stop in my tracks.

"Nefri and Wanda were going to kill me, Yana," he says, breathing heavily. "I heard them conspiring!"

Nefri tries to stand but collapses. I walk to him and help him sit. His wound has already drenched his shirt and pants with blood. I tear a sleeve and wrap it around the bolt to keep it from cutting his insides even more. Another bolt grazes my arm and sinks into his left side, right where his heart is.

"No, no," I say as my friend's eyes lose focus and close. "I am so sorry, Nefri."

His body goes slack. His breathing fades. He's gone.

I carry Nefri and Wanda to a tree, covering them with my coat, stones, and flowers. "Goodbye," I say, hands folded, head down. I throw a bouquet of jacaranda flowers on the shallow grave I dug with the axe.

Tears freeze and fall as clear pearls as I send them off. I take the candy Nefri gave me, the one he got from his sister, and unwrap it. The paper crackles between my fingers, worn after months in my pocket. The marble-sized candy tastes like mint.

I let it dissolve as I cry for them. "I die, we rise." Soon, the candy is gone.

I imprint their faces in my memory, sure that I will never forget them. Their voices will echo forever within my mind. "You would have liked them, Emma. I will tell you all about them when I see you. But now. Now I need revenge."

I walk to where Walver waits. He lets his arms hang by his side. I punch the soft spot in his neck, and he crumples. I grab his collar, make him stand, and hammer him back into the dirt with my fist. I fall on him and beat his face without restraint until it turns into a mess of gore.

"Why won't you fight!" I scream while I crush his body one bone at a time.

"Because..." he grunts between punches. "She...loves you. I can't...kill you."

My anger recedes just an inch, enough to find pause.

"She loves you." He has a handful of teeth left. "And I love her. I would have killed you a dozen times. Oh! I would have killed you so slowly, but I could never hurt her."

I stand, kick his jaw, and his body stiffens and shakes. His mouth opens, but no sound comes out. His eyes roll to the back of his skull. I grab Nefri's axe ready to put an end to Walver's madness.

He regains control of his limbs and sits. "I had to keep Yana and you alive. Let me live and I'll follow you as I follow Yana."

My axe is high above my head, ready to cut him in half. A hand, firm yet gentle, touches my back. I want to break him, but it's me who breaks. It all flows down my face, burning, cutting, shredding everything I thought I was fighting for. Everything comes apart.

How could I ever find Fortitude if everything I care for dies? This has been a path of suffering and constant loss. "Someone has to pay," I yell between my teeth.

Walver stands up and backs away.

Yana takes the axe and the crossbow. "We had a plan, Walver. We were going to bring her down when we returned."

Walver shakes his head. "They'd kill us if Nefri and Wanda were still alive. I tried to warn you, but Nathrel was always watching. This is the best I could do, the only way to save you." He begs for her to understand. "I tried to see another way..." He touches his bleeding head, then looks up.

"Walver, come," I say. His unsteady eyes are on mine. Blood drips from his eyebrow. "You'll never kill again unless you have to."

"I swear it," he says.

"I swear," repeats Yana.

"Was there a transport coming at all?"

Walver shakes his head.

"Let's return, then," I order. "There are some killings we must do."

"They won't let us back without their heads," whispers Walver, crestfallen.

"You will not touch them."

"Shush…" says Yana, crouching. "Someone is coming."

Steps and a piercing scent of perfumes. A shape walks around us, just past the trees.

"It is done," says Walver. He goes down to one knee.

Nathrel steps out of the bushes, pushing the leaves aside with his sword. His white smile stretches and shines. "You actually did it, Walver. I can't believe Agnor didn't kill you. Shame about Wanda. That one will be missed."

I watch him move. His hair, long and blonde, flies behind him. It's not as light as Wanda's, but maybe…

Chapter Twenty-Eight

One Last Breath

Find Fortitude

Thyra

Early hours, in Solitude's school gardens

We should be sleeping, but there is still so much I don't know about him. We walk side by side through the marble statues of old and not-so-old heroes. Champions, Golden Blades, gladiators, and high officers. The sun will soon come out and the last stage of the Trials will commence. People have been arriving for days to witness this event as we fight for a place in the Army.

The grim and imminent future seems unimportant with him so close to me. I almost let myself forget what it is that I am doing here.

"Will you ever tell me?" His breath condenses as he speaks.

"Tell you what?" I stall and hug his arm tighter.

"What made you leave? You could have been an engineer or just waited until you were older. Why are you here?"

"I just have to be." He shakes his head, too aware of my deception. I let my head hang from my shoulders. Words only harm.

"I understand," he says and puts his hand over mine. "I had given up hope when I met you, Thyra. I am different now, thanks to you." He chuckles and caresses my elbow. Every time he touches me is so precious.

"I want nothing more than to be with you," I answer. "But you need to heal. Once we graduate, we will have all the time in the world." I am surprised by my own words and how bold I am. "As an officer, I will boss you around. Are you ready for that?"

He chuckles.

The sky lightens. The dark blue gives way to orange and red and celeste. The clouds swirl slowly like heavy cream as hordes of visiting Giants enter the school grounds. Several aides and instructors guide them toward the stadium on the other side of campus.

"We should go." He looks into the distance and breathes heavily.

I run a hand covered in scabs and wounds over my short hair. "So many friends will be lost today."

"They are not lost if their sacrifice is honored." He shakes his head, bites his lower lip. He takes my hand and our fingers lock softly. Dawn touches his face and traces cuts both old and new. A couple of days isn't enough to heal from all the punishment he took out in the mountains. I must look worse.

"Ready?" he whispers.

"*Skynda*."

"Finally!" says Kar as we walk down the stairs to the anteroom below the arena. He rushes to us and gives us our gear with trembling hands. His large frame is covered in black metal, and his innocent face looks out of place atop of all that scratched armor.

"We are here, brother," replies Oniv as he grabs Kar's forearm and pulls him into an embrace. "The day will be ours. Don't fear."

"*Aldraig*, brother." They touch foreheads.

Around us, hundreds of students nervously talk and prepare for the final test. Dozens did not make it to the end of the week. Some were severely injured, some succumbed to the desert and the mountains, and some were disqualified. Although the exact way they select the students isn't clear, it seems the more items one brings back, the better the chances of making it to the final stage and getting an easier match.

Oniv walks to me and ties the armor laces that are out of my reach. The leather strips squeal as they slide through the rings. He stops tightening them when I grunt.

"You don't want these to be loose," he says softly.

"No, I don't." I take a deep breath, ignoring the stench of urine, sweat, and old blood.

We hear the audience outside scream, desperate for action. Maybe they forget it's their own children fighting for their lives down here. Maybe the multitude of other blood-crazed fanatics makes them care less.

Nearly a hundred thousand feet stomp on the giant stadium bleachers. The structure trembles and appears alive with its own mad pulse. The Master of Ceremony makes sure the public stays wild and loud. Down here, all we can do is wait.

The announcer screams through crackling speakers. "Welcome to Solitude's School of War, Jattaria!" The masses respond with a roar. "The final stage of the Trials is about to begin! These young Giants will leave it all in the arena, fighting for honor and duty, and for the greatness of our nation! Our first match, ladies and gentleman, will be Jergen Ulsen against," he stretches the pause dramatically, the audience urges him to reveal the other student's name. "Veeria Har!" he says finally.

Veeria is an excellent specimen, if I remember well. Jergen I don't think I have met. If I did, I had already forgotten.

The public cheers and applauds. In the anteroom, we are silent. Two arms go up in different spots in the room. The students walk to each other, shake hands, "I die, we rise," they say. They go through the doors to the arena, and the crowd welcomes them. More names are screamed quickly, and students pair up and exit.

"Arvo Borg! Your opponent is Redi Seekat!"

Arvo gives us a nod and walks to his match. Later, Sassi is paired as well. I hear Erika called too, and Oniv's shoulders tense. Only a couple hundred students remain. We wait for our names to be called.

"Who do you think I'll get?" I ask him. He pulls me closer. I wish with my whole heart for this moment to last forever.

"Whoever you get, you will defeat. It's top students against lower ones."

"Gunnav Aran gets Kar Tursen!" The announcer's voice echoes.

"No," I whisper. The space between Oniv and me grows an inch. We seek through the crowd of students and find them. They walk to each other with their arms up, shake hands, and walk into the arena. Others are paired, but I stop listening. Two of the people that helped me get here will be fighting each other. Despite how awful it feels, I hope Gunnav falls.

The number of unmatched students dwindles. Something in my chest shrinks at the same rate. I feel imprisoned in my own body; I put myself here.

Erika, Arvo, Sassi, and every other student I know is paired, except for Oniv. I squeeze his arm.

Every new pairing makes the dreaded possibility that we'll be paired more likely. Ten left, then eight, six, four.

"Sanda Rein!" the announcer says. "Your match will be..." I hug Oniv and close my eyes. The other students come near us. They tremble in their gear. "Kaspian Yutz!"

I open my eyes and look at the boy in my arms. He looks down at me.

"Oniv Spehl, your match is Thyra Ener!" screams the master of ceremonies. "Now the games can begin!"

Oniv finds my hand and shakes it. We stand there, crying, close to each other. "I die, we rise," he says. We slowly walk to open the doors.

The blinding light from outside seems to swallow each pair of students as they walk out into the arena. The crowd in the stadium gives us a loud welcome.

"It's supposed to be random," says Oniv. Tall and beautiful, even in this horrible moment.

Kar stands nearby, a somber expression darkening his soft features. "It didn't feel random at all."

Gunnav stands with no one.

And I thought I was alone.

"I am sorry, Kar. Gunnav. Oniv." Words only harm; it's better to be silent.

More and more students step into the enormous combat zone where twenty fights happen at a time. The announcer calls out the victors as the matches end and summons the next students to fight. A steady flow of new contenders walks into the arena. Aides and referees take them to the designated rings made of colorful ropes on the sand. The fighters collect their blunt weapons before stepping in and starting their matches.

The defeated walk out with their heads hanging low. Sometimes a pair of aides drags them unconscious and broken. Only one has died so far. A young girl, though not as young as me. Not bad from a numbers perspective, at least. In the past, one or two deaths per event seemed acceptable and even encouraged. Killing brings the excitement up and keeps the pressure on the fighters.

This horror should make me feel something, but instead, I watch coldly. Why did it have to be Oniv?

Blood and broken equipment already cover the sand. Two hours into the Trial's final stage and the arena looks like a battlefield. Skilled students perform before thousands of eyes thirsty for violence. Only a handful stretch their time in the ring, drinking the momentary glory, dancing around their opponents, and playing with them until every drop of strength is drained. Not a bad event from the showmanship perspective either.

Heart or honor? An impossible decision. I look up and search for an answer in the clouds.

The sky, blue and endless like Oniv's eyes, unveils no secrets for me. The sun warms me almost as much as his presence, and I've stopped crying. There is nothing but a dark numbness that won't let me enjoy my last moments with him.

Erika and her opponent are called. Their fight starts quickly but each time Erika takes or delivers a hit, Oniv flinches. A thin layer of ice formed on his eyebrows and eyelashes. Sunlight breaks into rainbows passing through those tiny crystals.

Erika's fight continues. She outmatches her opponent in speed and skill, but seems to be running out of energy. Two referees follow them with their long poles ready to stop the encounter. They must keep the defeated students alive, because the Aftergods will take the injured as Appeasement Offers.

Erika prepares a complicated finishing move, but her opponent sweeps her base leg, rendering Erika's blows harmless. The other fighter recovers quickly and smashes his hammer down on her hip, knocking her off her feet. He readies another attack, but the referees stop him. "Siv Ahren, come with the victors!" says the announcer.

Erika stands defeated, using her spear for support. Blood flows down her leg. She steps out of the arena and into the defeated quarters, where she will be imprisoned until it's time for her to leave on the train we call the Dark Runner. Oniv swallows hard and watches her leave.

From the other end of the Arena comes Arvo with an uneasy grin and his fist up. His match lasted less than a minute, and now he climbs to the Victors Seats to join Sassi and the other cheering students.

"Oniv, Thyra." The announcer's words are loud yet far away, like a thunderous echo. The winter sun bakes me, its pale platinum light staining everything a bleak white.

Or maybe it all looks bleak because we are dying.

"Step into the arena!" says the announcer. Others continue fighting, but the audience quiets. "Ener is the only Undefeated this year, therefore the only candidate to Golden Blade, the highest honor given in School of War! This thirteen-year-old has already broken records as the youngest Giant to ever come this far. Daughter and sister to Jattarian soldiers, she adds glory to this new yet renowned family name. Will she take her accomplishments even further? Her mother, Lagas Ener, instructed our last Golden Blade. It has been almost five years since Yana Hensin's graduation and spectacular graduation fight. Our nation still cries the loss of that fallen hero, but perhaps we will see the birth of a new one. If Thyra wins today, she will be our newest Golden Blade. Is this the day?"

The audience screams. They barely know my name, yet they still send their passion all the way down to the bloody sands where I stand. The stadium trembles with the life it borrows from the fighters and the crowd.

"Oniv Spehl!" yells the announcer, and the stadium bursts in cheers and clapping. "Oniv already comes from a distinguished family! Everyone in the Spehl line has served for the Jattarian Army, earning accolades for our nation and their house. The bets put him as a crowd favorite," he says, as if talking to an old friend, and the audience responds loudly. "But there is something you don't know. The Ener and Spehl families have crossed paths many times before! Klausen Spehl is Oniv's grandfather, and he has instructed both him and Thyra this year, so it isn't the first time these two fight. Klausen Spehl was also Lagas Ener's mentor and distant uncle. So today, these two cousins will give us the match you've all been waiting for. The Favorite against the Undefeated!"

And now, the audience truly roars, but it doesn't cut through the noise in my head.

We are cousins?

I want to reach out and touch him, but I can't. It feels wrong in a new way. I stay still and honorable and hide it all behind a brave mask. I must put aside my confusion, my fear, and my anger.

"You will give it all at the ring, my students," says Klausen from behind us. He puts one hand on my armored shoulder and another on Oniv's. The sun's glare casts harsh shadows on one side of his face. "Any other path leads to death and dishonor. This is the time to be brave, my soldiers. My blood runs with yours, and I couldn't be prouder. Be Giants of Jattaria."

"He said we are relatives," I say. Speaking feels like vomiting ice.

"Is Thyra my cousin?"

"Far removed. Don't let this blow from destiny deter you, my warriors. Call for Fortitude and fight with every last ounce of strength. Leave it all on the arena's sand."

Fate and family have come between us. Instead of seeking Oniv's touch, I grip the rough surface of the spear I choose as a weapon. I slide my left arm through the leather straps of a shield and take my first step forward. I walk into the empty circle while the other matches continue. I am in a bubble where light, sounds, and time flow differently.

The one I love joins me in that bubble. The one who makes my heart skip and jump and race and stop. The one who makes me die inside and also makes me want to live forever.

I can't hurt him as I hurt Neros during selection three lifetimes ago. It's not like training, when there were no consequences. I can't send him off to die as I killed Alastair in the Hidden Ring a hundred years before today.

I stare hopelessly. I look around, above, and behind him. Somewhere there has to be an answer for me. Like a miracle, the answer appears. I spot my father. A little taller than the rest, a long mane of white and blonde hair, an old leather jacket, and a passive way of standing in the crowd. A timid hand goes up and waves. I greet him by raising my shield.

Freeze me.

My father's life and my family's honor. The weight of my armor multiplies, and my body barely stands it.

"I love you, Little Stinger. Fight me with everything you have. For honor, for Jattaria, for your family, and for me. You always hold back when you fight me, but you can't this time."

He puts his helmet on, closes the visor, and becomes something else.

"Gunnav! Kar!" calls the announcer when another fight ends. "Step forward and face off!"

We all step in willingly to feed the Jattarian war machine.

Why are we walking to our deaths this way? Is this why Nefri left?

Treacherous thoughts! We do this for Jattaria!

Honor, glory, and the future of our nation. The Aftergods demand their Appeasement Offers, and we obey under the threat of annihilation.

Oniv's body, for it's not him anymore, paces around the circle. Slowly at first, as if every step were a question. I cannot move. His pace and breathing increase with his agitation. His crying becomes a grunt. There is nothing else to do but fight, yet I still cannot move.

"I die, we rise," I say. I close my visor and try to be something else as well.

Two instructors stand outside the circle as referees. They signal the start of our match by lowering their heavy poles. Our fight begins at the same time that Kar and Gunnav begin theirs. Gunnav is elusive and quick, avoiding attacks and learning as much as he can from Kar's style.

Oniv moves on the opposite end of the circle, and I focus on him. We walk around the ring, our feet scuffing the coarse sand. Fresh blood cakes in the dirt. Many have already bled here today.

How long will we dance like this?

But this isn't dancing. Mother was clear about this.

He closes the distance and the sparring begins. Light blows that I return with equal or lesser force. He doesn't commit to his attacks, and I don't commit to my counters.

Then he lands a hard one, and it hurts. My ribs fold inward under the spear's dull blade. I instinctively push with my shield to create space, thrust with my spear, and hit him across the helmet from below. He retreats and puts his guard up. I withdraw my weapon and pull my shield close to my body.

"Are you hurt?" I ask.

"Be silent, applicant!" yells one of the referees. A huge woman who could pass for a Titan pushes me forward with her heavy staff. "Fight!"

And once again, we engage. We test each other, but after months of training, I know his style as well as my own. I focus and call for Fortitude, the base of all Virtues. I beg for the ancient strength of the Colossi to take a hold of me and free me from my tortured heart and mind.

Align my body with my purpose, ancestral blood. Make me a Jattarian or a child in love, but do not make me decide.

A flash of metal. I tap his spear with mine, and he stabs the sand instead of my leg. His stance gave the maneuver away, but quick like a viper, he attacks again. He goes for my core when I'm off balance. I twist, straining my muscles painfully, and avoid the hit. I whip my spear and slash at his head. I pull back just before the blunt edge pierces through his neck, but he still goes down to his knees.

Inside this cold steel and leather armor, I am weak and crying. The tears collect on the paddings under the metal plates and make my skin chafe. I lost sight of my father, but I sense his presence. His enormous fists must be tight, and his gentle face wet.

Oniv. Is he crying? I can only catch glimpses of his eyes through the slits of his helmet.

He comes at me again.

He tries to get my knees, goes after my elbows, then tries for my neck. He charges with his shield, but I slip under it and slam mine on his ankle. He screams and stabs with the spear, but I drop flat on the sand and roll away. He tries again and again, but I don't respond anymore. I hold my instincts and shrink into a defensive stance that resembles Servitude's Selfless Offer, but in reality, it's a broken heart giving up.

"Fight, Ener!" screams the referee behind me, poking me with her staff.

"I can't," I answer, my voice choking.

She pushes me forward, into the circle, and closer to Oniv. "Fight!" she screams again, but I don't engage. I move along the edge and hear her following. Oniv observes as he paces at the opposite end of the ring. I refuse to meet him. "Fight!" roars the referee, slamming her staff down on my shoulder.

Smack!

Pain bursts from my shoulder. Something inside me comes out of place. My guard falls. A dislocated arm can't hold a shield, so it slides off my forearm. I would scream, but what for?

Oniv's gaze seems to go through me. He trembles. An otherworldly battle cry explodes from inside his armor. He charges, cocks his spear arm, and throws the first wholehearted attack in this match. There is no love in how he moves, only murder, and it's aimed at my head. He is Death, and he is coming for me.

Primal instinct takes over, and my muscles perform by memory. I crouch to dodge his lunge, jump to compensate for the height difference, pull my spear arm, and kick back with my right leg to counterbalance a strike containing all my body's strength. The spear falls like lightning in the center of his visor.

The Swift Scorpion is devastating when performed this way, its purest form.

The sound of metal piercing metal is deafening, but I suppress my urge to flinch. I am used to it. Oniv's visor folds inward under the power of my attack. Blood bursts out of the helmet. He falls to his knees with my spear stuck on his headpiece.

"Oniv!" Two circles away, Kar stops his charge and screams. He drops his weapon instead of blocking, and Gunnav hits his helmet so hard it comes off his head. The referee stops the fight and declares Gunnav victorious, but Kar runs to us.

I stand and watch without believing my eyes. "What have I done?" I whisper. Behind me, a soft gurgling makes me turn.

Oniv's lunge didn't find me, but it found its true mark. The referee who struck me is on her knees with Oniv's weapon sticking out of her neck. He was aiming for her, not me. The referee's trembling fingers uselessly search for a way to stop the bleeding.

Kar comes into our circle. An aide tries to stop him and he easily pushes him away.

"The match is over! Thyra Ener is the victor!" calls the standing referee, lowering his staff between Oniv and me.

Kar kneels next to Oniv and takes his hand. "No, my brother! No!"

They take Kar away. He doesn't even resist. "I am with you until the end, Oniv!" he calls. Then, he disappears past the Gate of the Defeated.

"Unbelievable!" the announcer booms over the speakers. "Thyra Ener is our newest and youngest-ever Golden Blade!

Congratulations, young soldier! You have set a new record and brought our standards sky-high! Will we ever again see someone like you? Just thirteen years old and from the Secondary Lands! From a family only three generations old, and all this glory she brings them! What a way to finish! The Swift Scorpion has never stung so true! Your statue will forever stand in the gardens of this school!"

But instead of going to the podium, I kneel next to Oniv. I help him remove the spear, then the helmet. Half his face is covered in blood that pours from a deep gashes on his eye and nose. What was I thinking? How could I do this to him?

"I am so sorry," I cry, holding his beautiful face. His one remaining eye focuses on me. A weak smile forms on his lips. I kiss him again, for the second time ever, and taste the sweat and blood and suffering.

A pair of hands pulls me away. They make me stand and push me toward the podium. I almost pass out from this suffering, but the hands keep me standing, and the shoves keep me going.

"Show some dignity, Ener. You are a Golden Blade, for death's sake," hisses the surviving referee. Klausen stands by the stairs leading to the victors' seats. His eyes are shards of ice, his face inscrutable.

"Well fought, Ener," he whispers and steps toward me. I close my eyes and wait for a swift death, but it isn't swift.

Excruciating pain surges from my shoulder when something pops back in place. The suffering retreats to a soft, manageable throb. I open my teary eyes and see my instructor holding my wrist and elbow. "Don't let his sacrifice be in vain."

"I won't. *Ich verspreche es.*"

He squeezes my wrist until it hurts, and harder still. Then he is gone.

Two instructors grab Oniv by the arms and drag him to the dungeons. The barred gates close after he enters while I am lifted to sit on the victors' podium.

An officer with a needle takes my arm and tattoos a line to mark me as a Tried Jattarian. Another officer drapes a white cape around my shoulders, and a third one hands me a golden sword. I look into it as I would a mirror. In that half moment, I see pure anger and a new determination. The officer grabs the hand holding the sword and raises it. The audience explodes. If it weren't for the very real pain in every inch of my body, I would think this a nightmare.

"Applaud, Jattaria! Our newest Golden Blade!"

The applause is deafening. The screaming thunders and echoes along the stadium. The band, who performed our anthem before the events, now plays another national favorite: The March of the Giants. Thousands of Jattarian voices sing, I mouth along by memory.

And somewhere below the sands of the arena, Oniv sits locked in a cold cell.

CHAPTER TWENTY-NINE

OUT OF REACH

imprisoned

Thyra

A day later, in the school holding cells

The guard shakes his head, keeping one hand on the door
and the other on his belt, near his sword's grip. I search behind

me for Dad's eyes to give me strength. He squeezes my shoulder with his enormous hand.

"I am the Golden Blade!" I say to the guard.

"Ener?" He lifts his visor. His eyebrows go up a quarter of an inch. "You should have said that before." He straightens, pulls down the visor, and nods. "Make it quick, or I'll get in trouble regardless of how many times you didn't lose, Undefeated."

"I see your Virtue," I say, and we move past him.

We race down the spiral stairs until we reach the underground cells at the edge of campus. The air is dense and moldy. My knees buckle when I see Oniv, but Dad holds me.

"Thyra," says Oniv when he notices me. He stands and comes closer.

"I love you, Oniv. I'm sorry I did this to you." I touch his mangled face. His eye is covered with bloody bandages that should have been changed hours ago. The rusty cell bars leave barely enough space to let his arms through.

"It was clear to me when our names were matched. I knew I couldn't fight you. You are an unstoppable force, and I would have been a fool to stand in your way."

I shatter inside. His words are killing me, but I don't want to stop him.

"Now you are a Golden Blade and honors await. What you always wanted." He kisses the ends of my fingers with cracked lips.

"Why did it have to be you?" I whimper.

"It doesn't matter." He traces a finger along my injured arm.

"I'll die without you." I must not cry. I feel the eyes of every guard and prisoner upon me.

"I'll never forget you, Little Stinger."

"Love and death sometimes can feel the same," I whisper.

He locks his hands behind my neck and gently pulls me to his face. He kisses me goodbye.

"Enough, Ener." The guards approach.

"No," I beg, but they aren't listening.

Father steps between me and one of the guards. "How can you do this to them? They are just children!"

Their hands rest on their swords' pommels.

"Take this," says Oniv, handing me his red scarf. I grab it. I have nothing to give him in return. Except -

I reach into my pocket and grab the name tag my brother left. "This is the reason. This is why I came here and the reason why I couldn't wait or stop. It's because I had no other choice," I whisper. I push the name tag into his hand, just as Nefri did when he came to see me. "It's not much, but it's everything I have."

He takes it, frowns, then looks up at me.

"We must go, Thyra," says my father, his shoulders slumping. He pulls me softly, already comforting me with his endless love. I have no strength left to fight, so I leave the one person I would die for behind.

"Well done, Daughter," says a smooth voice I haven't heard in more than a year. I expected no one to come to talk to me in the barracks, but here she is, standing by my bed. Her dark uniform is spotless. Her medals ring each time she moves.

Kora-Elena peeks her black head from under my pillow. She flashes her teeth and retreats again.

"I am leaving for camp in an hour, Mother," I whisper in return. "I have no time for you." I eye my father, who stands by the entrance looking our way. He was supposed to keep watch. He shrugs. "I am surprised *you* found time in your busy schedule to come all this way," I say.

"It's an important family event, and I was working in Solitude." She picks at her shoulder, pretending to get rid of dust. "Quite a change in careers since the last time I saw you. Then you were wielding an old iron hammer. Now you have a golden blade."

"*Some* things change."

"Indeed." She walks to me and sits down on my bed. She crosses her legs and folds her scarred hands over her knee. Her back is straight, her eagle eyes study me. Something makes her lip curl. Disgust?

"Why are you here?" I ask.

"I came to see you, Thyra. You are my only child now, and you've left the path you were following. I thought you wanted a quiet life like your father's. What changed?"

"Nothing. I am well. As you see, your training and efforts to turn me into a killer worked."

"A killer already?" I would think she is teasing me, but she isn't one to joke.

I nod. Her seriousness becomes sad. She closes her eyes and shakes her head slowly. She touches my chin with her thumb. I know the gesture is a question, so I show her the scar inside my mouth.

"Why are *you* here?" she asks after taking a deep breath.

"I have to be," I respond too quickly. I turn away from her calculating scrutiny.

"You are here because of Nefri."

"Freezing death. So what?"

"Are you a soldier, yet?" She tilts her head two degrees and raises one eyebrow.

"No."

"Then why do you speak like one? This is not what your father and I taught you." She clicks her tongue. "Compensating for your brother's death was not your responsibility, your duty, or your burden."

"Dad said the same thing. You guys share a script?" I look up at her and feel so tiny. "You'll never understand. It's my choice, and it was the right one." I touch the golden sword they gave me. "Isn't this what you wanted, anyway? All you ever did was make me train and fight. No songs or stories to go to sleep. Just lessons upon lessons."

"And thanks to that, you are alive. You have brought honor to our house. You made our name a synonym with glory."

"Yes. I am good. You didn't need to come."

"I came because you are not well. How could you be? You lost your brother and sent someone dear as an Offer. I am old, but not so old I have forgotten what the Trials feel like." She couldn't be tearing up, because she has no emotions. It must be something else gleaming in the corner of her eye.

"Thanks, Mother," I say dryly. "I see your Virtue. Congratulations on your promotion, by the way."

She stands, straightens her Second Star uniform and walks quietly to the exit. She doesn't look back but leans into my father to kiss him. They whisper to each other, then she leaves. Dad watches her with longing eyes.

CHAPTER THIRTY

REWRITING THE JATTARAVKALT'S HISTORY

Aggression

Agnor

Days later, at the Jattaravkalt camp

Sharp pebbles stab my knees. Sigman and Begel pat us down and take back the weapons they gave us three days ago. Splinters and bent pieces of steel, really.

"Stay down. The Kalt Sun is coming," grunts Sigman. "She is in a bad mood, so you better be quick."

A handful of Jattaravkalt Giants gather near the throne's circle. They will witness this morning's judgement.

"Oh, my poor children. Sorry you had to go through that," says the Kalt Sun while toying with one of her many rings. Her shiny armor replicates the sun a dozen times. Her absurd white cape wraps around her shoulders. Golden threads gleam as she moves.

She walks to her enormous bear. Luli lifts her head weakly, growls, and goes back to sleep. A diet of glass will make anyone feel under the weather.

The Kalt Sun walks around her pet and approaches us. Her nose wrinkles. Walver, Yana, and I are covered in days' old blood. "It couldn't be an easy thing to do," she says, "but it was essential. Nathrel suggested we kill you all." She looks to the sky dramatically, spreading her arms. "I couldn't! I wanted you three to have a chance! Now you really belong to the Jattaravkalt."

Sigman and Begel level their spears with our heads. The weapons are sharp, like the small ones Walver has hidden.

"Did you bring their heads?" Asks the Kalt Sun.

"Yes, my lady." Walver stands up with a grunt and a wince, looks into his satchel, and takes the two trophies.

Blood-stained yellow hair escapes through his fingers. His other hand holds a dark-haired bundle.

"Nefri put up quite a fight. There isn't much left." He lifts his two offers and walks forward.

Begel and Sigman stop his advance as he bends the knee. The guards watch him and the gore in his hands with a frown. The Kalt Sun approaches to inspect the proof of death we collected. Her smile widens. Walver rolls the bloody bundles toward the Kalt Sun's feet. Begel and Sigman follow the heads with their gaze.

"That's not them!" growls the Kalt Sun, seeing Nathrel's head roll to a stop instead of Wanda's. For Nefri, I carved flesh out of Nathrel and dark hair from Walver's bag. Morbid, efficient.

Now Walver uncoils like a viper and stabs Sigman with the two daggers he took from Nathrel. Yana tackles Begel as he thrusts his spear at Walver. Walver dodges the attack, cuts Sigman behind the knee to immobilize him, and snatches his crossbow.

Yana and Begel roll on the ground. I leap forward and elbow him in the jaw as soon as there's an opening. His limp body rolls on the grass, spitting foam.

"No!" screams the Kalt Sun, retreating to her throne. "Begel, Sigman! Stand! Don't leave me! Nathrel!" she screams.

She unsheathes the huge sword hanging from her waist. She has probably never fought with that impractical weapon.

Yana points at the head on the ground. "It's his blood we are covered with. We'll wash it away with yours."

The Kalt Sun unhooks the bear's chain. *"Cometelos, Luli!"* The bear gets to her feet groggily, looking at the Kalt Sun with a droopy expression. "Get them!" repeats the Titan, pointing at us. The bear takes a hesitant step, then leaps forward with her maw open and drooling black spit. I rip Begel's crossbow from his shoulders. Yana and I shoot at the charging beast until the fans are empty of bolts.

Luli roars again and points her black nose at me. I back away and aim the spear at the monster. Her massive claws fling chunks of dirt as she runs at me. The bear looms over me, and I fall on my back, planting the spear on the ground as the bear bites where my head was.

The steel spearhead enters through the monster's mouth, splitting it in two. The weight of the animal smashes against me, crushing bones and muscles.

Luli breathes once, twice. Dies. I try to wiggle from beneath the bear as steaming blood spills into my face and chest. I breathe with effort, sucking the nauseating stench of gore through my mouth. Finally, I free myself, and look about.

Phoom!

The leaves and the air ripple. Yana is thrown to the ground, a burst of blood spraying from her leg. She rolls, screaming.

"Agnor! Help!" shouts Walver.

The Kalt Sun hides behind her throne, holding a steam musket. She aims it at me. I jump behind Luli's body - *Phoom!* My cheek burns. Bear flesh splatters all over me.

She prepares to shoot again when a thrown knife sticks to the musket's tank. *Pang!* Gas hisses from the perforation in an angry cloud. Walver hurls another knife, which finds the Kalt Sun's shoulder. "You dogs!" She screams, retreating into the cave.

She tries to shoot at Walver, but the steam musket spits a weak burst. The projectile bounces off Walver's forehead.

She dumps her gun and swings the heavy sword. Its weight throws her off balance. I crawl from behind the smoking carcass, get on my feet, and wobble forward. I summon Fortitude, praying for any god out there to listen. My goal is clear: Kill the Kalt Sun.

"Be more," says Emma from inside of me. *"Save these Giants. Be everything you are meant to be!"*

I rip the spear, slippery with blood, out of the bear's head and run at my enemy.

The Kalt Sun engages an unarmed Walver, who retreats to avoid her powerful blows. She tries to chop him in half, misses, and loses her grip. Walver slips, and she catches him by the neck.

Fortitude guides me. To save them all from this terror, I must reach inside, touch the Colossi part of me, and gain the strength I'll need to finish this tyrant.

The Kalt Sun pulls free the knife stuck in her arm and stabs Walver in the head just as I thrust the spear into her side. The sharp edge slides off her armor. I try again, lunging at her leg. She throws a slow jab and steps away, gasping.

"You've sat on that throne for too long," I say.

She deflects my cuts with her armored forearms, then attempts to tackle me but trips instead. I strike her shoulder, finally finding an opening. I push deeper, twisting the spear in the flesh, then jerk the blade out, ripping muscle.

"Aghhhh!" she roars, rolling away from me.

Swiveling on one leg, I swing at her head. The edge would decapitate her, so I hit her with the flat side instead. I want a spectacle. The Giants must see I can be brutal if I am to lead them. It's what I am meant to be. A protector. All my friends had to die for me to see it, but now I know.

I should have understood this before, when I protected Zeeri and her family, or kept Walver from killing those Regler Korps. I should have understood when I fought to keep the Traitors safe. It was only then that I felt whole. It's my purpose.

I step away from the Kalt Sun and look around. The Jattar-avkalt watches with wide eyes. Hungry faces that have seen too much suffering.

Walver stands up and brings a hand to his head. This guy won't die. He tentatively pulls the knife. "It only got under my skin," he says. He yanks it free and starts bleeding profusely.

"You should have kept it there," I say dryly, not really caring if he dies.

"*Ja.*" He puts the knife back in the wound and pats it gingerly with a maniacal smile.

"Go to Yana. I'll finish this," I command.

He nods.

"Stand up, Kalt Sun." My voice echoes off the rocky sides of the mountain and travels around the meadow. More than fifty starved Giants watch from the edge of the clearing. Many more must huddle out of sight, among the trees. I toss my spear to her and grab Yana's. A few Giants timidly step into the circle. Their starved bodies seem to gain strength as the Kalt Sun loses hers.

"Take this in, Jattarians!" I scream, pacing around the cleared area circling the throne. My tired bones scream for a pause, but Fortitude ignites. "She took your loyalty and stepped on it. She starved and abused you. She fed you to her beast. Not anymore! I am here to free you, to make you true Giants again!" I speak the words we prepared for Yana, yet they sound so right coming from me. "In Jattaria, the Highest must be defeated before it can pass its title to the new leader. So here I am! I am Agnor, and I challenge you, Kalt Sun! Stand and fight for everything you have!"

I square up with her as she picks up the spear. The old bones on the ground crack under her massive weight. She leans on the throne to gain her feet and faces me.

"A wounded lion is most dangerous," warns Walver.

She wears a hundred pounds of armor. I fight without protection. A single hit could kill me.

She steps forward, spear low. We lock weapons, trade a few blows, then step back. She tries again, combining high and low thrusts with quick jabs, but her style is basic and predictable compared to Yana's. I slip the spear past her guard and strike her hip, but the plates repel it. She swings again.

I pull away, but she cuts across my stomach. An inch closer and I would be picking my guts from the ground.

She swings, overextending. I step sideways and hit her with the butt end of my spear. Bones crack under her tan skin and her knees buckle. I stab at her chest, but the armor absorbs my attack.

"I did what I had to do, Giant," she says, cleaning her face with her blood-stained cape. "Nothing else would keep these savages under control. You can't kill me. You need me!"

I look around the circle, meeting the eyes of those spectating. "I will speak to the Antarians if necessary. Your star fades quickly. Everything you took will be returned to the Jattaravkalt."

She roars and rushes with her weapon aimed at my heart. I pummel her head but take her charge. My spine stretches and twists under tremendous force as we smash against the ground, weapons flying out of our hands. All the air in my lungs swooshes out.

She pins down with her massive knee and wraps her enormous hand around my neck. I block some of her powerful blows, but she is beating me to a pulp.

I time her next strike and thrust my hips up with every ounce of strength. She misses and punches the ground instead of my face. I slide from under her. She catches my ankle and pulls me closer. I smash my free heel into her already broken nose and slip from her hold. Once on my feet, I kick the side of her enormous skull. My leg cracks and goes numb on impact, but she falls and stays there.

She rolls to her back, wheezing and spitting teeth and blood. Her cheek is open, exposing bone. I grab the spear and thrust it into her sternum, driving it until it pierces through the armor. She screams and flails her arms and legs. The steel goes in slowly, breaking bones and tissue.

"For Nefri and Wanda. For Sil, Nova, and Uma. For Saxon and Arsen. For Siff, Ingrid, and Vinz. For every Jattarian who died hoping to find freedom!"

Hundreds of Giants stand witness. Their murmur becomes a clamor, and a hundred fists go up.

"We are the Jattaravkalt!" I yell.

"We are the Jattaravkalt!" they repeat. Their voices are wild, desperate, hungry, cracking under the stress of their screaming, but for once, they are truly free.

"Take what's yours!" I say, pointing at the cave. They walk, then run to the Kalt Sun's treasures.

Vathra moves more slowly. She is not hungry. She feasted some days ago, and her rounded belly shows it. "You will need to be as hard as she was." She snarls and spits on the dead Titan. "Fair, but hard. Or we will scatter and die."

"I'll be the leader you want."

Vathra shakes her head. "Be the leader we *need*. Terrify but give us hope. It has to be you. Not her," she says, looking at Yana. "Certainly not him." She eyes Walver with a snarl.

"I know," I say, realizing this is it. I put a hand on her shoulder. "Fetch me a healer," I grunt.

"Yes, Kalt Sun."

Walver kneels by Yana, who pushes her two hands against her left leg.

I get down and grab her face. "Yana," I whisper, looking into her glassy eyes.

"Don't move. I'll take care of you."

I lift her from the ground and bring her to one of the tents. I remove her shirt and inspect the wound. The bullet ripped a chunk of flesh, like what happened to me months ago. Blood keeps flooding. I pour water on the injury, then press clothes into it to stop the bleeding. She tries to speak but only babbles.

Vathra comes back with a man covered in grease and breadcrumbs. He swallows hard. "Leave us," he says without looking at me.

I obey and join Walver, who stands trembling with the knife still on his head.

"She will make it through," I say. "She is strong. Fortitude's with her."

"I didn't kill them," he says, his eyes fixated on the tent's entrance. "Begel and Sigman. I messed them up, but they'll live. I did as you asked."

I walk away from him, from the tent, from the Jattaravkalt. I find a meadow, get on my knees and look to the skies. "You bastard gods, keep her alive, or I won't rest until I kill you all."

Chapter Thirty-One

DIAMOND AND GOLD

Highest and Elite Knights

Thyra

Weeks later, in Solitude

Thousands of Tried Soldiers stand in formation behind me. We could be statues. Under this hail and rain and wind, maybe we will be. Two months ago, we graduated from school, and today, we graduate from basic training. The fire of those emotions is the only thing keeping us from freezing.

The Highest steps up to the podium. An impeccable Giant dressed in a black suit decorated with hundreds of shiny medals. The recruits and the audience of relatives and officials applaud as if on cue. The clapping dies down as the Highest lowers his hand. Six Elite Knights in their red uniforms stand guard at his sides, ready to put down anyone who dares break formation.

I stand alone in front of all the other graduates. The Elites scan the multitude, constantly evaluating threats to our leader's safety. The Highest dedicates a few moments to studying me. His gaze makes my heart race.

"What an honor to be gathered here. Don't let anything diminish the significance of this day. Jattaria receives the most precious gift of all: Our youth's loyalty. Welcome to the Army, soldiers.

"These last two months have been hard on you. You fought your friends, saw half your class lost to the demands of our gods, then trained without rest in boot camp. Finally, you are ready. More than three thousand soldiers from all over the country receive their First Circle tattoos today. Rarely have we had this many! We owe our gratitude to those who became Appeasement Offers. Their sacrifice must not be forgotten, must not be in vain. We see their Virtue."

His eyes sweep the crowd, which bursts into neat applause.

"And to have our recruits led by a Golden Blade! What a year for our nation! Thyra Ener, may her path lead her to glory and honor, and may her leadership and courage bring victory to Jattaria."

One more round of applause, meanwhile, officers and soldiers rearrange the podium to begin the last stage of the event.

"Recruits, prepare to receive your promotions."

The Highest steps back and a Second Star in a gray uniform takes his place. She opens a black book and clears her throat.

"Danz Klopp," she calls first. They go from lowest to highest scores and ranks. Today, I don't mind being last.

A tall and handsome recruit of about seventeen walks swiftly to the podium and climbs the stairs on the right side. He walks across the stage, shakes the Second Star's hand, and steps down as a First Circle. One of the many First Diamonds waiting by the stage takes Danz's forearm and starts to tattoo the rank symbol.

The Second Star keeps calling names for over an hour. I shift my body weight from one leg to the other, trying to move as little as possible.

I am so close. That ink must be worth it.

"Thyra Ener," says the high officer at last.

I walk the muddy field, trying my hardest not to shiver. My teeth rattle and my stomach growls. My pace must be steady. I climb the slick steps without slipping and receive my handshake.

"Congratulations, young Ener. You make us proud."

The Second Star nods, I nod back. I begin to walk away, but the high officer puts a hand on my arm and keeps me in place. The Highest steps forward, and the six Elites surround me. The Highest shakes my hand, but my senses don't fully register what's happening. The most famous person on the planet holds my cold hands. Piercing eyes stare into mine. His face is rugged and scarred. Each second I feel smaller and smaller. His black suit pushes light away, raindrops seem to avoid him. He is smaller than most Jattarians but emanates power. It's hard to breathe near him.

"Well done, First Diamond Ener," he says, then steps back. The Elites go back to their positions, and I am allowed to continue.

The officer waiting to tattoo my rank applies a flame to the needle and invites me to surrender my arm. I roll up my sleeve and offer my forearm. "The illustration will blur when you grow, so you might have to redo this later. Stay still, so I don't mess up," he orders.

"Yes, sir," I reply automatically.

"We are the same rank, Ener. No need to 'yes, sir' me."

"Sorry, sir," I reply. I shut my eyes and make a face when I realize.

"You'll get used to it. Now stay still so I can work."

I rest my arm on a table. He cleans and shaves my skin, readies his needle meticulously, and gets to work. He finishes the Circle, the decorations of the three Circle Ranks later, and lastly, the Diamond.

The constant stinging was a good distraction, but the moment it stops, I remember Oniv, Dad, Nefri, and Mother. I remember Klausen's face when he saw his grandchild dragged away.

"You are done, Ener," says the officer. "Before you go back," he stops me. He dips the needle in the glass one last time. The liquid is now as black as ink. Blood mixed with it too. "Have this." He hands me the cup.

I down the drink. Liquid fire crawls down my throat, burning with a sweet and spicy aftertaste. Steam shoots out of my eyes and toxic fumes exit through my nose - or at least it feels like that. I cough into my sleeve, as I have seen other recruits do.

"Now you are ready." The First Diamond pats my shoulder and pushes me toward the formation.

I find my spot and stand straight, facing the high officers and the Highest once more. The Jattarian flag plays with the wind, spraying heavy drops of water every time it whips.

"Welcome to the Army, Circles and Diamond. Will you give your lives for the Code of Virtues?"

"We give our lives!" we respond in a deafening roar.

"Will you give your lives to destroy the Takers?"

"We give our lives!" we cry with pride.

"Will you give your lives so Jattaria can rise?"

I bring my right hand to my chest to recite the rest of the Oath.

"Our lives for Jattaria! I die, we rise!"

"I am very proud of you, Thyra." Dad hugs me with his enormous arms. Kora-Elena rests on top of his head. A train's steam engine whistles loudly in the distance as it approaches the station. Not the Dark Runner. This one isn't black and ominous but red and promising. "That's your ride. In minutes you will be leaving us, *rakas*."

I sink into his leather jacket and take in the scent of him once more.

"I'll miss you, Dad. Promise you will take better care of yourself this time. And also watch after Kora-Elena."

"I promise. I'll miss you too, and I'll visit in a few months. Who knows? You might be Third Diamond by then!" He chuckles, and despite the hole in my chest, I laugh too.

He lets go of me and picks up my two suitcases. Heavy, bulky, full of precious gear he crafted for me. The Army provides us with gear, but nothing near Dad's quality.

We walk in silence, following the masses leaving school and going to the train station. That red train is bound Warm toward the Edge.

The closer the train gets, the more anxious I feel. Fear, guilt, anger. Instead of pride, I am haunted by what I had to do to get here.

I am a Golden Blade, a First Diamond. I touch my sword's pommel, yellow like the sun. I touch the lines of my tattoo, dark like the night.

"You'll do well."

"Thanks, Dad."

The cobblestone road leading us out of school comes to an end. A dozen or so students stand around the white marble block, taking turns lifting the Spear of the Tried. Some aim it at the sun for a minute.

Dad stops to watch. "Your mother couldn't do it when she graduated," he says. One of his massive hands shields his eyes from the morning sun.

"I'm not her."

"She sends you this. She is sorry she couldn't be here -"

"Ja, ja. Had to be somewhere else."

He hands me a leather sheath for my golden blade. It's decorated with the Jattarian Shield, my initials, and the family colors, green and white. I let the sword slip inside it and secure it around my waist. It fits perfectly. "Gorgeous." I resume our walk and pull Dad's wrist to get him going too. One of the soldiers trying his strength drops the spear as we walk past the block of marble. The noise makes a few heads turn.

The weapon stops just a yard from me. I pick it up with both hands and place it on the marble. It isn't as heavy as it was a year ago. It will feel lighter next year.

Chapter Thirty-Two

Induction of the New Kalt Sun

New Kingdom

Agnor

That same day, at the Jattaravkalt settlement

The Kalt Sun's chair remains empty.

I throw the fetid bearskin over my shoulders and prepare to exit the cave, my new home. One deep breath, then I step outside into the sun. The ground crunches under my boots. The armor I peeled from the Titan now protects me.

Feeling the sun's heat, I ready myself. The Kalt Sun's sword hangs from my hip and the Descendant's helmet nestles under my arm. The leaders and their families await at the edge of the circle. The chatter stops when they see me.

Yana turns to me with difficulty, using Walver for support. She nods, channeling encouragement with her gesture.

"People of the Jattaravkalt," I start, stabbing the huge sword into the dirt. A new story begins today, and I will shape it. "I am Agnor from Antares, a half-Titan, a Jattarian soldier, and the new Kalt Sun. Challenge me today if you don't agree and I won't kill you. But know that once I sit on that chair, it belongs to me." I give them time to think. "Are there any challengers?"

I look around at the white faces. There are twice as many people as I've ever seen before. No longer hungry, not abused, not forced to stay. Begel and Sigman hover at the back, still recovering. Not a single one of them could defeat me, not even Yana; and why would they? Only I can give them a better future.

I pace around the circle, looking deeply into the eyes of each Giant I pass. Let them absorb this new truth: The Jattaravkalt is mine not just to lead, but also to protect. This is my purpose and my source of Fortitude.

And the Giants around me stay still.

All of them but Walver, who steps forward unsteadily.

He stares at me, then drops to one knee. He bows his head.

A second Giant follows him, a third, then a handful. A dozen more. Everyone soon kneels before me. Yana is last.

I step closer. "You have been on your knees for too long, brothers and sisters. Jattaravkalt, rise!"

COMING SOON

Marcos F. Eguia
Code of Virtues Series
FortitudE
Code of Virtues Book 1
Marcos F. Eguia
SolitudE
Code of Virtues Book 2
Marcos F. Eguia
CertitudE
Code of Virtues Book 3
Marcos F. Eguia
MagnitudE
Code of Virtues Book 4
Marcos F. Eguia
RectitudE
Code of Virtues Book 5
Marcos F. Eguia
ServitudE
Code of Virtues Book 6
Marcos F. Eguia
GratitudE
Code of Virtues Book 7

Author's Note

Thanks, before anything else, to my wife Kelsey, who had to put up with the early versions of not just the story but me as a writer and storyteller. My first drafts lacked structure, commas, apostrophes, and who knows what else. Despite it all, she saw something worthy under the pile of manure I dumped on her lap and told me to keep writing.

My parents, Miriam and Jorge, were always supportive of my endeavors. When I was little, my father read and made up stories, and I emulated him. My siblings were witnesses and victims of my first attempts at storytelling, especially when they were adventurers in an RPG game I invented for them as a nerdy teen. Facu, Tomi, Mati, and Sole helped me in one of the most essential ways possible: They were guinea pigs for the most awful attempts of word-slinging and the inspiration for the most touching and complicated scenes in the series.

So, I was always interested in telling stories, but a few key people helped me push it past a simple hobby. Mariana helped me start the amateur graphic novel that would grow into this series. Melynda made sure I never stopped pursuing art in any and every form and gave me the laptop with which I wrote most of the books. Kyle found me writing once in May 2019. I remember this perfectly because his advice and encouragement at that time made me take this seriously.

A gang of degenerate misfits called the Writer Royale is the most significant source of my growth as a writer. We formed the group in 2019, and they allowed me to stay despite my obvious struggles with English and my thin grasp of the technicalities of writing. Thanks for your patience, Don, Donn, Niki, Tabby, Nigel, and Hannah. This project would never have been finished without your immense help.

I owe a great deal of gratitude to the Glass-Upshaw clan, especially Jess, who diligently edited every first draft of the Code of Virtues. Her passion for reading is borderline psychotic, definitely obsessive, and 100% contagious. I hope she never gets cured. Max and Holden assisted me with early reader feedback on Fortitude and with cover and concept art for the series.

Thanks to the ones who make this dream a reality: River City Siren Press is the safe harbor for this little boat I tossed in the ocean over a decade ago. Thanks to the timely intervention of writer and friend Don Mewha, they read my manuscript and took a chance on me. Thank you, thank you, thank you!

Thanks also to the many, many friends and readers who have gone through the book and given me feedback. Who would have thought writing took so much work, time, and effort? Some of the honorable mentions are: Delancey, with some on-point advice on the story and characters; Sarah and Sheena, who gave me precious insight to shape the minds and motivations of some of my characters; my close friend (brother, if I may), Rob Graystone, for his support and encouragement; Yamila, who lent me her knowledge in psychology and helped me get a deeper understanding of how certain different minds solve different situations; and Nico and Mati Eguia, who were with me during the most challenging time in my life and helped me cross a bridge that needed crossing. We traveled across the United Kingdom, wandering through fog and beaches and castles and ruins and lochs and islands and mountains and plains and ancient cities, talking nonsense and discussing my novel and so much philosophy. So much of what we talked about and lived during that trip made it into the series! That time is and will be one of my most precious memories and source of inspiration.

CHAPTER THIRTY-THREE

EXCERPT FROM SOLITUDE

Thyra

Four years later, in Jattaria, near the border with the Edge

All I wanted was to die on the battlefield, but now they drag me out of it as a broken thing. Even my thoughts are shattered.

"Let me die with honor," I beg the White Helmets saving my life.

We are not dying.

We all talk to ourselves, but is anyone else terrified by what their mind has to say?

I can't be the only one.

Maybe you are.

Raindrops rap on the dark tarp over our heads, drumming a pleasant, almost distracting tune.

Almost.

We travel farther away from the Edgen forest and farther into Jattaria on the back of a medical truck that lurches with every pothole we hit. At this point, I assume the driver is aiming for them.

The stench emanating from the wounded Giants sickens me. Most are passed out or doped up; some must be dead.

Death. You reek of it, too.

At least the smoke of the noisy steam engine covers some of the smell. Breathing through my sleeve, I force my thoughts elsewhere. Anywhere other than here. Even the past. I look to the sky as I try to remember how I got here in the first place. Strangely, I come up with nothing.

Another Giant sits across from me—a boy with blonde hair like mine. I am six-seven, about the same size as him - so he is small for a male Giant. He looks familiar. Guilt pangs. I should know him. I should recognize everyone in the truck, but my mind has lost its sharpness.

I feel around my skull and find no severe head injuries. What's wrong with me? Why can't I remember?

Just let it go. It's for the best.

"What's your name, soldier?" I ask.

He looks back at me and answers after a long pause. "First Circle Ziglit." His voice is as blank as his face. "I never thought a mission could go so bad."

"They are all bad." I look at my hands. The bloody tag in my palm reads *First Star Thyra Ener*. It came loose during transport, and it's almost unreadable. I held my traitor brother's tag similarly a lifetime ago. His actions lead me here. *That* I remember clearly. Nefri's treason set me on a path of violence seeking redemption for my family. It seems I ran out of time with lots of violence left to be done; I haven't earned redemption yet. My fingers tighten around the tag with an urge to keep it safe. I can't lose who I am before I finish what I started.

The blood-stained bandages wrapped on my left leg are a grim promise of what waits for me after this ride. My whole body is covered, actually. I don't know what's under the gauze, and I don't dare guess.

I cough with painful spasms when I inhale too much of the vehicle's exhaust. I start to question the intelligence of whichever idiot let the sick be exposed to the toxic fumes, but I stop my treacherous mind before the idea becomes a fully formed thought.

Suffering isn't an excuse to doubt the Jattarian system.

Look around. There are plenty of reasons to distrust it.

My dull mind turns to the rapidly passing landscape. Road signs tell me of our progress as we approach Fort Advan. All my senses, including my sense of time, deteriorate with the minutes. The meds I took earlier must be kicking in.

My eyelids grow heavy, and each blink seems to last ages. I am still on the truck, then one blink later, I am lying down in a bright operating room undergoing surgery.

"Can you save it?" asks someone behind a medical mask. A doctor shakes her head.

"No!" I scream and leap at them, trying to snatch their cutting tools. "How will I fight without it?"

They push me down and shoot something into my thigh. I blink again, and I am being rolled down a corridor. White ceramic tiles line walls and ceiling, and the echo of Giants in pain travels with me. The foot of the bed pushes a door open, and we enter a recovery room where hundreds suffer like me.

The sudden sting in my arm brings me back from hazy dreams. The world solidifies around a man in a Third Star uniform talking to another in a gray robe. Doctors in white come into the room, and the patients quiet. The bright over-head lights keep me from seeing their features. Cold fluids drip into my body. I feel the chill in my forearm as the liquid flows through my veins. I am awake but feel asleep. Things that I know should matter seem irrelevant.

"Sir, you are not supposed to be here," says one of the doctors in a worried whisper. "She is in recovery." He tries to grab the Third Star's arm, gesturing toward the door.

The Third Star gently pushes the doctor's hand away, ignoring him as one would ignore a fly. "Ener," he says, picking the file with my case from the folder at my bed's feet. "A young family," grunts the Third Star, speaking more to himself than to the other men. "I was there when she earned her Golden Blade. A shame we lost someone so promising, and at only sixteen years of age." He shakes his head softly, now looking at me. "What happened during your last mission, Ener?"

"I—"

Shh! I will answer this.

"I remember the training. Big machines, new ones. I don't recall the mission," says my inner voice using my lips.

The man in gray leans into the Third Star. "She has forgotten everything, sir. We've tested her several times already and got nothing. She barely knows her name. With time, she may improve."

But I know more than that. Plenty more! I'd tell them, but an invisible hand chokes me and keeps me quiet. *You will say nothing.*

The Third Star, who looks somewhat familiar, shakes his head again. "She's the only one with information about the Third Wall. We need the intel. We need to know what she knows," he says between his teeth.

"The Third Wall?" I ask in disbelief. "*I* was at the Third Wall? "Who are you?" I ask him.

He taps his chest, but I can't quite read the tag. One of the men around me whispers something in the Third Star's ear, and he straightens. "Is there a drug you can give her? Or a treatment to make her function again?" asks the Star. They talk about me as if I weren't here, or worse, as if I were nothing, no one. I'd scream, but everything is so numb. Even my rage is just a little tickle in the back of my mind.

The man in gray shakes his head. His smooth, cold voice makes me shiver. "We can wipe her mind clean but cannot bring her memories." He looks down at me with a twisted lip. His disgust matches the Star's expression. "Someone in this shape is hopeless," he says, looking me over head to toe. "It might be good to have a survivor," he whispers to the Third Star.

One of the doctors steps forward, trying to get between them and me. "Enough! You need to leave. She is lucky she's breathing, sir. She gave it all on the battlefield. With time, she will return to service and–"

"Return?" scoffs the star, shaking his head. "Send her home. We have no use for someone in this shape," he orders, almost throwing my file at the doctor.

"She could still serve, sir!" insists the medic, holding my file. "Even if it isn't on the battlefield, she can–"

"Nonsense. Someone with so little time in the Army is useless," he says, interrupting the medic. "Do as you are told and send her home. We've kept her here long enough."

The man in gray puts a hand up, silencing the coming question from one of the two medics. "The Army will check on her, and we'll ensure she gets her retirement."

The two medics shake their heads and seem to bite their tongues. Orders are orders; everyone knows this. My room empties, and my mind slips once more. I try to feel my face, but leather belts restrict my wrists.

When I wake up again, I am alone in a different room. My arm itches in a familiar way. I look at it, but my foggy mind can't focus. The lines take definition in my sight only after what feels like an hour, or perhaps a day. I rub the new tattoo with my thumb, but it won't fade.

I got promoted?

You got the black triangle. Retired.

I scratch it harder and harder, thinking maybe I can remove it. They won't care, and they won't know any better. As my skin comes off, the tattooed triangle starts to come off.

"Stop, Ener!" a blurry white-coated man yells, rushing into the room and fastening the belts. He bandages my bloody arm, cursing in the old tongue, then injects something into my drip.

"I can't serve if I am retired!" I scream, but my words get jammed up in my mouth. I swirl away from consciousness and not just because of the drugs. My mind's voice has a cold claw that pulls me under when my thoughts become too clear.

Don't fight me. I am your way out of this.

The climb starts. The train engine revs noisily, as if complaining, but ascends the inhospitable Kjede Mountains. The morning sun touches the peaks toward the Raging Sea, the Stor Plains spread toward the Sullen Sea, and the Svinnen forest stretches up Warm all the way to the Edge, bordering the Fifth Wall. Every second, I am farther away from Edgeslag, our war against the Edge.

The railway twists and turns as we progress, returning to the interior. We slow down near the end of the day and come to the first stop of my trip back home. The crackly speakers in my wagon come to life. "We've arrived at Solitude, Jattaria's capital. Have papers ready. This train leaves in three hours, bound Cold." I hear the announcer noisily hand his microphone.

I get my release from my bag. Not having those would mean a quick death at the rope's end. Maybe they'd spare me, given my condition.

Past the window glass, enormous buildings of stone and concrete reach up to the sun. The Colossi Knight of Solitude founded this city centuries ago and gave it its name. When the Colossi and Titans left, we took over. The original buildings still stand, larger and more beautiful than anything us Giants ever made.

None of that matters.

What matters is that the Edgens will build the Sixth Wall, and there will be nothing left of Jattaria. What matters is earning honor for my family. When they discover my brother's treason, our name will be stained. Hopefully, my medals will be enough to compensate for his sins and earn redemption. Maybe the books with Jattarian history will not condemn our name.

People gather at the windows facing the train station. One little child pushes his face against the glass, fascinated. "The Dark Runner," he whispers, excitedly stabbing his chubby finger into the window. I follow his gaze and spot the infamous black train. His little hand waves at the line of teenagers loading into one of the cars. "It has like a thousand wagons, Mommy!" he squeals excitedly.

"Be quiet, Bjark!" His mother scans the faces around while hers turns red.

The Dark Runner is headed to the Sullen Sea to deliver the Appeasement Offers. A cut of everything Jattaria makes, even her very children, will never be seen again. Our Gods demand it, and we obey. Not doing so summons their anger. Just the idea makes me shiver, imagining the smell of flesh burning and the cry of the reapers coming from above to punish those who violate the Code of Virtues' Directives.

Let's not think about that right now.

The soldier sitting next to me knocks on the dirty glass. "Those are the lucky ones, the ones defeated at the Trials. Wherever they go must be better than here."

I ignore his comment and wait for the train to leave. If I weren't so doped, I'd beat the dissidence out of this Waster in the making. The boiling rage inside me is neutralized by the narcotics running through my veins, like soft chains keeping me from even feeling emotions. I am a shell, almost comatose.

\#

The following morning, we approach the train's final station. Vai is the largest city in our region, sitting on gentle hills in the middle of the Secondary Lands. Here, we have industries and processing plants. Our cities are blocks and blocks of factories surrounded by suburbs and low-income apartments.

As we slow down, I watch thousands of workers change shifts. The blackened streets get swarmed with Giants coming in or out of work. The air is thick with the smoke from hundreds of chimneys and smells acrid and slightly toxic. Most people here will die with a bad cough before they are forty-five, but that's not a bad life. So many Giants die before they're twenty.

The engine stops, and they call for all passengers to alight. I leave the train on my own but with considerable effort, aware of every broken thing inside me. My shoulder seems to be full of glass, my hip put together with hot barbed wire, and my leg... well... I better get going. I hand my documents to one of the Regler Korps Officers on the platform, but she waves them away after a quick look at me. "Move along, soldier," she says from under her heavy black helmet. I picture the disgust on her features, witnessing failure in the flesh. I'd spit at my feet if I were someone else.

I do as ordered, slower than everyone else.

"First Star Encr. We are preparing your transport," says a young man who appeared out of nowhere. He has a First Circle tattoo on his forearm. Some low-rank sent to help me, I bet.

I lose balance, surprised by the sudden apparition, and drop my things all over the station floor. He helps me regain my footing and grabs my belongings.

"Sorry I startled you. I was calling, but I don't think you heard me. I will take you to your carriage."

"Thanks," I reply, out of breath. Moving is so much harder than I remember.

He helps me get on the old carriage and puts my things on the back. "You are almost home, First Star. Thanks for fighting for Jattaria," he says. The words felt mechanical, and it's understandable. Being discharged for injury is not an honorable way to leave. Heroes die. They leave it all on the battlefield.

The driver cracks the whip, and the horned beast pulls the vehicle away. We roll down the cracked concrete road. The many kitchens along the station spill the smells of roasted turkey, grilled vegetables, and spiced drinks. I should be starving but feel no need to eat.

I take the bottle of pills in my pocket and look at them. These meds steal the life out of life.

And you should be taking your next dose.

Two a day for the next month. I throw one of the tiny white pills in my mouth, chew it, and swallow the bitter stuff. We leave Vai, and my mind is spinning slowly, drifting into a comfortable haze.

Night approaches, and we are still on the road. We traveled through plains and countryside for hours. The streets become familiar as we get closer to the region's hillside. Houses here are single-story homes on half an acre or less. Most are painted white and have tile roofs, but one can find colorful ones here and there. Business owners who are doing well sometimes show their wealth that way.

Old cobblestones, smooth after decades of traffic, take me back home. The first warm feeling I've had in weeks grows from within. My village has not changed in the last few years, but have my parents? She retired a few months ago. Is she more loving now? Is Dad less patient? Is she less strict? Is he more organized?

I doubt it.

People their age don't change. Lagas is a strict mother and a decorated officer; Amberson is a loving father and renowned engineer from the Tertiary Lands. Maybe Kora-Elena is better behaved. That spoiled spike-back gator must be two yards long by now.

We pull up to my house, and my parents are waiting outside. I assume they were told we'd arrive at this time, and Jattarians are always punctual. *We even die on time*, like the old ballad says. The driver helps me down. Mother and Dad look at me, absorbing the shape their daughter is in. I read it all in their expressions.

They wrap me in their warm arms, and my crutches fall to the ground. That's fine. I don't need them if I lean on Dad's large frame and Mother's athletic body. I have been trying to ignore them since I left the hospital.

"You are with us now, *rakas*," says Dad in his low pleasant voice.

"Let's go in and have some of your birthday cake," says Mother.

"Birthday?" I ask, frowning.

"You turned seventeen yesterday," says Dad. His voice falters mid-sentence. We used to love birthdays, making colorful parties just for the two of us. That was four years ago when I was little.

They bring me in and sit me at the table. There is a plate with cake before me, but I can only focus on my lap. The left sleeve of my green pants is hemmed right below the knee. A ghost itch along my missing calf makes what's left of my leg tremble.

I look away, searching for a distraction to make the dizziness disappear. Through the window, a colorful scene develops. The cobblestone street stretches down the village. Daylight fades, and the sky turns from bright red to deep purple. The gaslights by the road flicker on one by one, giving the village a renewed charm—quiet and peaceful. I try to draw from that feeling and find balance.

You can't.

www.ingramcontent.com/pod-product-compliance
Lightning Source LLC
Chambersburg PA
CBHW061041310726
48969CB00004B/1042